THE LOST GIRL

the lost girl

Anne Ursu

Drawings by Erin McGuire

WALDEN POND PRESS

An Imprint of HarperCollins*Publishers*

Walden Pond Press is an imprint of HarperCollins Publishers.
Walden Pond Press and the skipping stone logo are trademarks
and registered trademarks of Walden Media, LLC.

The Lost Girl
Text copyright © 2019 by Anne Ursu
Illustrations copyright © 2019 by Erin McGuire
For information address HarperCollins Children's Books, a division of
HarperCollins Publishers, 195 Broadway, New York, NY 10007.
www.harpercollinschildrens.com
Library of Congress Control Number: 2018954201
ISBN 978-0-06-227509-7
Typography Sarah Nichole Kaufman
19 20 21 22 PC/LSCH 10 9 8 7 6 5 4
❖
First Edition

For Tina Dubois

CHAPTER ONE

Treasure Hunters

The two sisters were alike in every way, except for all the ways that they were different.

Iris and Lark Maguire were identical twins, and people who only looked at the surface of things could not tell them apart. Same long bushy black hair, same pale skin, same smattering of freckles around the cheeks, same bright hazel eyes and open face.

But Iris and Lark had no patience with people who only looked at the surface of things, when what lay beneath was the stuff that truly mattered.

Because the girls were identical, but not the same.

Iris was the one who always knew where she'd left her

shoes. Iris was the one who could tell you what the collective nouns were for different animals and that Minnesota was home to the world's largest ball of twine. Iris always knew when her library books were due.

Lark always knew when their parents had been arguing. Lark could tell you what the consequences for stealing were in different fairy tales, and that the best bad guys had interesting backstories. Lark always knew which books she wanted to check out from the library next.

No, they were not the same. But Iris always knew when Lark was feeling too anxious to speak in class, and Lark always knew when Iris's anger was getting the better of her. Iris always knew when Lark was too busy daydreaming to pay attention, and Lark always knew when Iris was too reliant on finding order when things were in chaos. Iris talked for Lark. Lark talked down Iris.

This is the way it was.

No, they were not the same. But yes, they were twin sisters, and for Iris and Lark that meant something, something far deeper than what lay at the surface. They each knew the monsters that haunted the shadowy parts of the other's mind, and they knew how to fight those monsters.

That was the remarkable part, if you asked Iris and Lark. Though no one ever did.

Instead strangers treated them like a spectacle. People

on the street stared at them openly, sometimes pointed and whispered, as if their surfaces were all that they were. As if the girls were just something to be seen and not actual human people and would not notice. The girls always noticed.

And when I saw them, I stared too.

I could not help it.

(Though they did not notice me.)

But not because they looked identical. I stared at them because I can see beneath the surface of things. I stared at them because I wanted to know their story. And maybe because, somehow, I sensed how it would end.

This is a story of a sign and a store. Of a key. Of crows and shiny things. Of magic. Of bad decisions made from good intentions. Of bad guys with bad intentions. Of collective nouns, fairy tales, and backstories.

But most of all this is a story of the two sisters, and what they did when the monsters really came.

I first noticed them on a hot August afternoon. In Minnesota, winter was just two months away, and soon the more sensitive birds would begin the long journey south. But today, summer reigned. The sun stretched its beams across the sky and discarded change glistened on the sidewalk. Here in the shop-lined streets of this Minneapolis neighborhood, people fled for the air-conditioned stores and the comfort of the library carrying sweating plastic cups from the local coffee house.

And the two sisters came out of the library, clutching glossy books to their chests.

Lark was wearing a bright pink T-shirt with Captain Marvel on it and one in a series of her wide collection of striped leggings, Iris a light blue tank top over white shorts. Both stopped on the top step, the air admonishing them for going outside in this heat.

"Ooof," said Lark.

"I told you to wear shorts," said Iris, twisting her long hair into a bun. The back of her neck felt like a science experiment gone very wrong.

"You're wearing shorts and you're still hot."

"Yeah, but I'm less hot than you."

Lark looked at her meaningfully. "How do you *know*?"

Iris's lips smooshed together. She didn't *know*, for sure. She couldn't tabulate the degree to which she felt hot and compare it to Lark's. All she knew was that the idea of putting on leggings today made her feel like a snake whose skin was on too tight.

But before she could respond Lark was onto something else.

"What time is it?" she asked, looking around.

"About three thirty." Even without a watch Iris generally knew what time it was, as Iris tended to look at the clock a lot, as she had done before they left the library. Everything felt better when you knew what time it was. Sixty seconds in a minute, sixty minutes in an hour. There was always order, if you knew where to look.

And Lark didn't need to look at the clock, because she had Iris.

"Do you think the mail's there yet?"

"It's usually there by four," Iris said with a shrug. They'd had this conversation several times already today, but sometimes—Iris knew—Lark needed to say certain things, and she needed to have certain things said back to her. There was no harm in that.

Iris had figured out that school placement letters were probably coming today—they always came on the Tuesday three weeks before school started. Iris tended to notice that kind of thing.

And it was the Tuesday three weeks before school started.

This was their last year at Barnhill Elementary. Next year would be sixth grade, and everything would change. They'd have homerooms and class schedules and already Iris was concerned. What if they had some different classes? That was the sort of thing adults did while you weren't paying attention.

But that was next year. This year's worry was at least a familiar one: Which teacher would they get? Ms. Shonubi was their first choice, of course, because she was angelic. And all the other options were terrible: the extremely tall, extremely grave-looking Mr. Miller; Mrs. Scott, who was rumored to tell girls to act *ladylike*, whatever that meant; and a new teacher, a replacement for Ms. Urban who had left the school and moved to Paris to become a concert pianist.

Lark was scared of Mr. Miller, who she said looked something like a haunted tree in person form. And Iris had once been told by a random woman in the grocery store that she should be more *ladylike* and had not liked it much. *Ladylike* sounded an awful lot like *Be nice* and *Be quiet* and *Smile more* and *Stop arguing* and *I thought girls were made of sugar and spice and everything nice*, which someone in a grocery store had said to her once too.

So they worried about their teacher. And of course they worried about who was in their class with them.

Or, more specifically, if Tommy Whedon was in their class.

Tommy Whedon had been Iris's archnemesis ever since he'd made fun of Lark during a class presentation last year, and Lark still couldn't be around him without flushing.

But if he was there, Iris would protect Lark, same as she always did.

Ladylike or not.

"I don't think I want to get home till after the mail comes," Lark said, shifting.

"Okay. What should we do?"

In a blink, Lark straightened and squeezed her arm. "Let's go see what that's all about!" she said, voice hushed, as if she'd come upon a great secret.

"What?" Iris looked around.

"That," Lark said, pointing across the street.

That was the sign.

I told you there would be a sign.

Specifically, a chalkboard easel, which right now read

**WE
ARE
HERE.**

The sign sat on the sidewalk outside the darkened storefront of a new shop that had not yet opened its doors to customers.

That much Lark knew.

I knew quite a bit more.

The sign had appeared on the sidewalk a few weeks before the shop would open, as it did every time.

It proclaimed We Are Here, every time.

And that was all. No indication of exactly who the *we* of the sign referred to, let alone what this shop was going to sell. *A weird way to advertise a new business,* passersby agreed.

But the message on the easel was not meant for them.

A week later, the shop's name had gone up above the front door—Treasure Hunters—and its slogan was etched on the window: We Can Find Anything.

They, too, were the same every time.

We are here. We are hunters. We can find anything.

So the store stood now, as the girls noticed it for the first time. Treasure Hunters. We Are Here.

Iris herself was not inclined to look for the story in things, but she knew Lark was, and she was always happy to go along, especially if it meant Lark was distracted from fretting about class assignments. So Lark pulled her across the street, chasing the threads of a story.

Still, Iris was curious. It wasn't often that there was a new store in their Minneapolis neighborhood. Since the Maguire family had moved there, every storefront lining Upton Avenue had remained the same except this one. And this one had changed quite a bit. In the girls' memory it had been home to stores that sold hardware, new age paraphernalia, kids' shoes, overly pungent coffee beans, and, most recently, less pungent flowers. But most of these stores went out of business in less than a year—especially the new age one, which lasted one week before the shop owner burned incense all around the building and left it as it stood, and the florist, because the flowers kept dying.

"Some locations are just cursed," their mother had said by

way of explanation, as if that explained anything at all, as if that wasn't like opening up a giant box bursting with questions and pretending they weren't all now flying loose and hungry in the air.

Their mother was certainly right—some locations are cursed—though the truth of this particular place was somewhat different.

But Iris and Lark could not know that, not yet.

"I don't think it's open yet," said Iris, as they approached. "It looks dark."

"I just want to see what's inside," said Lark. "We can peek in the window. And this way we won't have to talk to anyone."

Lark spent a lot of her life avoiding having to talk to people. She never understood the admonition not to talk to strangers—why would anyone want to in the first place? It was fine: Iris could talk for her.

"Anyway," Lark chattered on, "the name is cool, right? Treasure Hunters?"

Iris knew that a store in her Minneapolis neighborhood was not going to be selling actual found treasure, and that the new shop was certainly something boring like kitchen stuff or lamps or something else old people considered treasure, and she knew that Lark was perfectly aware of this fact as well—but she also knew that some part of her sister allowed herself to hope the store would be filled with the contents of some recently uncovered safe from the wreckage of the *Titanic*.

That was Lark for you.

"It's antiques," Lark said, peering in the window.

"Boring," said Iris, leaning against the wall and shading her eyes. The sun felt like it was actively trying to burn out her eyeballs.

"There might be something cool in there. Like something really important that got lost and no one recognized it and then it turns up in an antique shop in Minneapolis and everyone gets really excited, like, 'Can you believe this lost masterpiece was right here and no one knew?'"

Iris pushed herself off the wall and looked inside, squinting through the glare of the sun. The shop was basically all clutter—every surface was covered in various assortments of *stuff*: lamps and figurines and picture frames and candlesticks and vases and dishes. It made Iris want to go in and straighten.

"If there is something really important in here," she said, "I don't know how anyone would find it."

"Don't you think the sign is weird?" Lark added, ignoring her, as she often did when Iris was not focusing on the point. "'We Are Here'?"

Iris shrugged. She was not ready to comment on the relative weirdness of people who sold used chairs and old teapots and called them treasure.

"Why would someone even say that when they're obviously there?" Lark continued. "I mean, it's pretty clear. Like, I could walk around wearing a sign saying *I am here*, but I don't. Or"—she spun around and faced her sister—"I could walk around wearing a sign saying *I'm not here*. Now, that would be interesting."

Iris grinned. "I could be, like, where did Lark go? And people would try to say, well, she's right there, except you're wearing the sign that states very clearly that you're not."

Lark shook her head tragically. "So careless, Iris. Losing your sister like that. You should really keep better track of her."

Before Iris could respond, she was interrupted by the sound of tinkling bells, and the shop door swung open to reveal a man in a buttoned-up mustard-yellow cardigan and plaid bow tie.

Lark stiffened; he seemed to intend to talk to them. Iris touched her arm. *I'll take care of it.*

He was short and roundish, like a snowman that had melted slightly, with skin the color of mashed potatoes, and yellowish hair shellacked onto his skull. His face reminded Iris of a mole.

"May I help you ladies?" he said, and then stopped and gaped at them.

Iris sighed and exchanged a glance with her sister. *Here it comes.*

"You're twins!" he exclaimed.

Yes.

"You look exactly alike!"

Yes. If you weren't looking carefully. There were subtle differences, of course. Iris stood a little taller. Lark hugged herself a lot. Iris's hair was usually neater, relatively. Lark was always in brighter colors, and always wore her silver bracelet with the small moon charm on her left wrist.

"How remarkable! A matching set!"

It is not always possible to say the thing you want to say to your sister out loud, and so a few years earlier the girls had devised a code where they could tap messages to each other with their fingers. Now, as the mole-faced man in the mustard cardigan gaped at them, Iris folded one arm over the other and tapped out, *Should we tell him?*

I'm not here, Lark tapped back.

Iris clamped her mouth shut. Telling him there was nothing remarkable at all about identical twins if you knew anything about biology was *not nice* and the sort of thing that meant people told you to be more *ladylike.*

"Well," he said, "I'm delighted you remarkable girls are interested in my treasure. But I'm afraid we're not open yet, alas."

"That's okay," Iris said. "We were just curious what the store was." She had to do the talking, since Lark was not there.

"I hope your curiosity is satisfied, young lady! I sell treasure, and you're welcome to come back to peruse it when my store is open. Though we do recommend bringing your parents or guardians. Or"—he smiled wanly—"any other responsible adult who can keep children at a respectable distance from priceless antiques."

Iris straightened.

Ugh, Lark tapped.

"I don't understand what your sign means," Iris said, gesturing to the chalkboard easel. "Anybody can see that you are here. Even"—she smiled winningly—"a child."

Next to her, Lark coughed slightly. *Iris. Don't irritate the weird man.*

"Ah," said the man, a spark in his grayish eyes. "Do you young ladies believe in keeping your promises?"

Iris blinked. ". . . Yeah?"

A grin crept slowly across his mashed-potato face. "So do I." And then he winked, as if he had answered the question, as if he had answered it so well and cleverly that they would find him utterly delightful, that they would be charmed by his wink and perhaps even wink back at him, like people who understood each other do.

An elbow in Iris's side. Lark.

"We have to go home now!" said Iris brightly.

"Pleasure talking to you!" He leaned forward. "You girls take care of each other. A matching set is quite collectible, you know!" And he let out some chuffing sound, and Iris did everything in her power not to look at her sister and she knew her sister was doing everything in her power not to look at her, because the girls knew that you were absolutely not supposed to exchange *what a weirdo* glances with your sister while said weirdo was looking right at you, even if you very very much wanted to.

They did not look at each other while he disappeared back into the store, door chimes singing, or while they crossed the street back to the library, where their bikes were parked, or while they tucked their library books into their backpacks and unchained the bikes. But when they mounted the bikes, Iris's eyes caught Lark's. Lark's eyes went big, as if to take in the great magnitude of the weirdness they'd just experienced; then her mouth twitched, and the whole right side of her face squished together in a showy wink.

As they rode away, Iris let out the laugh she'd been suppressing, and Lark laughed too, and the sound seemed to release something into the air, like a flock of birds bursting up from the ground and filling the sky.

And so I followed.

CHAPTER TWO

Good Intentions

The Maguire house sat on a tree-lined street about twelve blocks from the library, and over the years Iris and Lark had learned the absolute best route to get back and forth, avoiding the crosswalk at Forty-Fourth Street where the drivers never actually stop, the post-apocalyptically cracked sidewalks of Washburn, and, for coming back home, the excessive incline of Forty-Sixth Street. On this August day the girls' bikes followed the same tracks home, lined as they were with years of Iris's and Lark's histories. The closer they got to their home the thicker the world was with their pasts, and by the time they parked their bikes in the garage their stories were scattered everywhere, ripe for the collecting.

Today they were coming home to a slightly changed household. Their father had just left for six months in England, where his company was sending him for reasons the girls did not entirely understand. It seemed to Iris far more efficient to ask people actually from England to work in England, but her dad said large companies rarely did things that made sense to rational people.

Things were going to change now, their parents had said, at least for a little while, but the girls were going into fifth grade in a couple of weeks and they could handle it. Their mom would be working later, which meant that she couldn't be there when they came home from school anymore, and she'd been littering the house with catalogs and website printouts for after-school activities for them, things with dubious names like Mad Scientists Club and We Heart Nature. Iris and Lark had been politely ignoring the whole thing. It seemed best for everyone involved.

But that wouldn't start until school began. For now, their mom was still home in the afternoons and when they walked in they could hear her on the second floor.

There was no time for small talk. Lark's eyes had grown wide and she was gazing at her sister. *Are you going to check the mail?*

Yes. Yes, she was.

"It's here," Iris called, as she peered out the front window.

From the kitchen, Lark made a noise that was something like choking and something like squeaking. The letters from Barnhill Elementary were right on top, one addressed to her, one to Lark.

Closing her eyes, Iris made a silent wish. *No Mr. Miller.* The haunted-tree man would be bad, because Lark was scared of him already.

And another:

No Mrs. Scott. She was no better, because she would make it hard for Iris to stand up for her sister.

And another:

No Ms. Urban replacement.

That was the worst possibility. That person would be completely unknown. There was little Iris hated more than the completely unknown, and while normally Lark built herself elaborate homes there, when she was nervous about something her imagination and the complete unknown didn't exactly mix well.

Wishes made, Iris went into the kitchen, where Lark was sitting at the kitchen table, fiddling with the moon charm on her bracelet.

This was their tradition. Each took her envelope, and they sat across from each other at the kitchen table, as they did every year. And as they did every year, Iris solemnly opened

hers first: kindergarten, Ms. Ruby; first grade, Ms. Gratton-Parker; second grade, Ms. Jonas; third grade, Ms. Roy; fourth grade, Mr. Anderson. Then Lark opened hers and affirmed that destiny. Iris always thought it was nice that they got two versions of the letter in case there was some kind of clerical error.

Iris spent a lot of her life making sure there were no clerical errors.

Now Iris opened her envelope carefully, so as not to rip the contents. She unfolded the letter and gasped with relief.

"Ms. Shonubi!" she proclaimed, beaming like the sun.

Angelic Ms. Shonubi. Soft-edged and warm-eyed and probably smelled like flowers, though Iris had never actually confirmed that.

Iris grinned at her sister, who looked like she'd been wearing something way too tight for months and had just removed it.

Eyes shining, Lark's hand fell away from her bracelet charm. As she did every year, she ripped open her envelope, ready to confirm, ready to put the future in boldface. She unfolded her sheet and her face froze.

"What?" Iris asked.

"Mr. Hunt," she whispered.

The girls stared at each other.

One moment. Two. Then:

"Mom!" Iris yelled.

It was a mistake, that was all. The girls had been in the same class for five years, because everyone understood that they needed to be together. Of course they needed to be together. Of course Iris needed Lark, and more pressingly, Lark needed Iris. Lark wasn't like other people, and she needed her sister to keep her from cracking.

Who had distracted her in third grade when Leila Mason hit her head on the monkey bars and blood poured down her face like someone had installed a blood faucet on her forehead? Iris. When Leo Sullivan had taken to pretending to be a zombie and jumping around corners at them shouting "BRAINS," who had told him she'd lock him in the haunted janitor's closet if he ever did it to Lark? Iris. This was the way things worked.

The girls sat on the couch in the living room, clutching their letters while their mom pulled up a chair, lips pressed together as if to crush something. Her laptop perched on the desk containing their dad's smiling face beaming in all the way from London.

"Okay," said their mom, speaking in soothing tones. "So, the school believes it is in your best interest to be in different classrooms next year."

"You knew?" Iris breathed.

". . . We discussed it," said their father.

"With the *school*. You can't discuss things with schools. Schools are buildings."

"We discussed it with Principal Peter," their mother said.

"And you told him it was a terrible idea," Iris proclaimed.

"The school believes that you two need to learn to adapt to being on your own. It's middle school next year, and you won't be together—"

"Says *who*?" said Iris.

"You've been together every year until now," said her father. "Don't you think it might be time to try something new?"

"No, we don't!"

"We just want you to try being apart," interjected their mom. "Just try it."

"Besides," their dad added in his best dad-joke voice, "shouldn't we give the teachers a break? Together, you guys are a lot."

The girls' jaws hung open. This was not the time for dad jokes. This was not the time for any kind of jokes. The fact that their father thought that it was the time for dad jokes just showed how little he comprehended the situation.

Lark was wide-eyed and white-faced and clearly immobilized by the absurdity of what had happened, so Iris pushed herself up and barreled forward. "No! We're not going to do it. We don't want to be independent. We don't want to try something new. We're just fine! Plus—"

Plus what? Plus what, Iris? Plus *something*. Their mom wouldn't interrupt if she just kept talking, and her dad— well, the volume wasn't that high on the laptop. If she just kept talking, maybe the right thing to say would come out eventually, and then her parents would call the school and make this okay and everyone could pretend like it didn't happen.

"Plus . . . Principal Peter didn't even ask us! You can't just make decisions about us without asking us! We're eleven! We're not little kids. He could have called us in and said, 'Lark! Iris! Do you think you guys need to learn to adapt to being on your own?' And we'd have said, 'No! No, no, that's a ridiculous idea! A terrible idea!'"

Next to her, Lark focused her attention on the bracelet on her wrist. Iris could feel her trembling.

"We don't even know who Mr. Hunt is!" Iris went on. Was she shouting? She might be shouting. "I've never heard of him. He's new! He could be a horrible teacher. Principal Peter could have gotten a head injury or something and started hiring terrible people and making other awful decisions, like putting us in different classes. Head injuries are really serious, you know!"

Her mom put her hand up. "Iris," she said. "That's enough. Principal Peter has not had a head injury."

"But—"

"It's my turn to talk, Iris. Not everything we do is going to make sense to you. We get that. But everyone has your best interests at heart. Your father and I especially."

"If you care about our best interests, why didn't you ask us?"

"We've heard you out—"

"No, you haven't! You pretended to listen! But you'd already made up your minds!" She snatched Lark's letter out of her sister's hand and held them both up.

Her mother's lips disappeared so all that was left was one tight hard line. Her father's head bobbed out of the laptop screen. Because he could just escape: he could move slightly to the right and no longer be present, no longer have to confront the reality of what he'd done.

A tornado of words and feelings was whirling around Iris's head, picking up everything in its path and tossing it around so Iris could barely see straight. She opened her mouth to let some of it escape—something, anything.

And then Lark spoke, her voice a whisper.

"Please don't do this."

The line collapsed. The lips reappeared, setting in a frown and then pressing together.

Their father's head reappeared, and he and their mother exchanged a glance that crossed a whole ocean.

Silence. Both girls moved to the edge of the couch as one. The tornado hummed in Iris's ears.

"I'm sorry," their mother said quietly. "This is the way things are going to be."

CHAPTER THREE

The Way Things Were

Here, another story for you:

Once upon a time there were two sisters, twins, who came into the world looking just the same. Some said it was luck, some said it was fate, but Iris knew the truth: they were caused by a hiccup in development, something that happens three times out of every thousand births. One egg splits into two. Two babies with identical DNA.

Presto.

Another hiccup: two babies are hard for one womb to hold, and though they still weren't due for ten weeks, the baby girls decided they'd be better off on the outside than in. Anyway, they had a whole world to discover.

So after they were born, three-pound Lark and three-and-a-half-pound Iris shared a room in the neonatal intensive-care unit, all tubes and tape and tissue-paper skin, while Lark learned to breathe on her own. This was a skill Iris already had—somehow she had learned something important and not taught it to her sister. It was a mistake she'd never make again.

When their parents told them the story of their early births, they said the girls had been placed side by side in the NICU; the doctors had said it was better for them, that twins in the NICU had better outcomes when they were together.

Iris had always taken this literally—yes, of course they were together in one strange little plastic box, she somehow already a little stronger and a little more able to be in the world than her sister. Yes, of course she kept her tiny preemie fingers curled around Lark's tinier ones, letting her sister feel the rise and fall of her chest. *You can do it, just like that: breathe, breathe.*

But no. When their dad put together that photo album and they saw the pictures for the first time, they discovered their parents had been characteristically imprecise in their language. They were in two plastic boxes, side by side. There were no tiny preemie hands reaching for each other, no breathing lessons, no assurances. "We meant you two were in the same private berth," their mother explained. "Right next to each other, side by side. You can't put preemies together in the same crib!"

Iris was skeptical. The doctors had said it: they had better outcomes when they were together.

Perhaps that was why it took Lark so long to learn to breathe, why Iris was ready to go home a month before Lark was. Apparently Iris spent that month pronouncing her displeasure to the world; her parents thought she was colicky, but as soon as her sister came home—six pounds, with working lungs—she was happy again.

"You were a whole different baby all of a sudden," their mom said with a smile.

"Thank goodness," their dad said, with a different kind of smile.

After that, the girls stayed together.

Their parents said they were talking before they could talk, chatting away in some strange babble that no one else could parse but that each of them seemed to understand perfectly. "I was afraid you'd never speak Other People words," their mom always told them every time she told the story. "You didn't seem to need to. You could understand each other; that was all that mattered."

Lark picked up Other People words first; Iris was slower to adapt and seemed suspicious of the entire concept.

"It didn't matter," their mother told them, every time. "Even when you spoke Other People words, you were still really only speaking to each other. Always in your own little world."

As they grew up, other children revolved in and out of their lives. There was a little girl next door with a sandbox in the shape of a frog and a mother who overflowed with laughter and grape juice; there were two girls in preschool who liked to pretend they were twins too—they were most certainly not, but Iris and Lark let them pretend, to be kind. There was Maria in kindergarten, who always wanted to do dance recitals, and Gracie in second grade, who bragged to everyone that she was closer to Lark than to Iris.

In the end it was not worth it. After the grape-juice girl, everyone else seemed to want something from them, whether it was to exploit their obvious appeal as backup dancers (a matching set), or to borrow their status as semi-celebrities (for everyone knew about the identical twins), or to be the one who finally broke them apart (for some people were just that way). As if that could happen.

Who is the grape-juice girl, and who is the one with the chisel behind her back? You cannot always tell. So Iris and Lark responded by floating away, orbiting around each other, a binary star.

None of that saved them from the adults, who stared at

them like everything was suddenly a little off, as if they might be dreaming, as if the ground had just tilted three degrees—and they made everything inside Iris tilt too. When that happens to you enough, you start walking around feeling like you are perpetually three degrees off from everyone else.

People asked them the strangest questions: Which one of you is the good one? Which one of you is the smart one? Who is faster, stronger, sweeter, who gets good grades, who is a good little girl? Who is (ha-ha-ha) prettier?

Which one of you is the girl and which is the copy?

In the end, the adults were just like the chisel girls—so fascinated by what made them different from each other, slicing off little bits of each girl and comparing them. As if dividing them was what made them interesting, what gave them meaning.

It wasn't.

The story always went one way, and the moral of the story was clear:

They had better outcomes when they were together.

CHAPTER FOUR

The Way Things Are Going to Be

After the ill-fated meeting with their mom and their dad's digital head the girls huddled in Lark's room, trying to figure out what in the world had just happened.

Iris and Lark always hung out there, though Iris's room was always clean and organized, and therefore navigating through it wasn't a health-and-safety hazard. Getting to Lark's bed meant traversing a jungle of Lark's things—library books, bits and pieces of her various collections, bookstore books, stuffed animals, drawings, half-finished Rainbow Loom puppets and knitted scarves, plastic boxes of various sizes designed to help her keep her room clean, leggings and T-shirts and socks, stuffed animals, scrap paper, pens and markers of various colors and functions, and half-completed projects and supplies for her life's work: the dollhouse.

When the girls were seven, their parents had given them a fancy old-fashioned dollhouse complete with a family of four—a father, a mother, a girl, and a genderless baby the girls named Baby Thing. The girls shared a room then, and when they moved to the new house the dollhouse went into Lark's room and Iris kept the salamander cage (and with it Slimey the salamander—may she rest in peace). And Lark started to renovate the dollhouse one room at a time because, as she put it, dolls shouldn't have to have old-people furniture.

Then one day Lark decided it would be nice if the doll family could go swimming, so she began to turn the baby's room into a beach, complete with glued-on sand and a gel ocean.

Now the house looked like the set for someone's very weird dreams. It consisted of a room wallpapered in watercolor sky with a flock of origami birds dangling from the ceiling; an armory with tinfoil swords and shields; a haunted guest bedroom with spiders and felt ghosts; a bear habitat; a disco room; and a stage with velvet curtains framing one solitary plastic chicken in soliloquy. The family of five (they'd added one identical girl doll because the best families have identical twins in them) sat in the former attic nursery roasting mini marshmallows over a campfire on the surface of the moon, Baby Thing parked at Doll Lark's feet.

It would have never occurred to Iris to put a campfire on the surface of the moon. It wasn't just that you can't actually have fire on the moon; she was not one of those stick-in-the-mud people who insisted that people's imaginations venture no further than the laws of science allowed. It was just that the atmosphere of her mind could never allow such ideas to spark in the first place.

Now Lark sat cross-legged on her bed, clutching her beanbag cat, Esmeralda. Iris could not sit. She felt like pacing, but pacing in Lark's room would be fraught with peril, so she leaned against the wall and imagined she was pacing, which helped a little.

"Mom and Dad knew," Lark breathed. "And they didn't do anything about it."

"They could have at least *told* us!"

"They could have told us, and they could have told Principal Peter that they didn't want us to be separated."

"I don't understand how he could do this to us. Like, is he trying to punish us?"

Lark looked up at her. "Principal Peter? Why would he do that?"

". . . I don't think he likes me."

"Well, you did march into his office and tell him Tommy Whedon was a menace."

It was true. She had. Someone had had to do it.

Lark had always been a little frightened of Principal Peter, ever since first grade when he'd teased her about drawing in class instead of listening to the teacher. Iris, however, was not scared of him. Iris was the one who could look him in the eye and tell him the things that were awry in his school if need be.

"Remember next time you're going to tell me before you do something like that?"

"Okay," Iris grumbled. This was a frequent conversation between the two of them. The problem was, if she told Lark she was going to do something like march into Principal Peter's office to hand him the anti-bullying policy and inform him he was not enforcing it, Lark would tell her not to do it, that it wouldn't help, and that it would just make Iris even madder, and then Iris wouldn't do it because she'd never disappoint Lark like that. So she didn't tell Lark, she just did it, and it didn't help, and it just made Iris even madder.

"Still," Lark said. "I don't think he's punishing us."

Iris gazed at her sister. "Are you sure?"

"Yeah," Lark said. "I don't think principals are supposed to do things like that. You're not actually supposed to take stuff out on kids. That's got to be in the manual."

Iris exhaled, then flopped down on the bed next to her sister. "Then why?"

Lark's face darkened. "You heard Mom. Because he

thinks it's *in our best interest*. I don't know why!" She sniffed. "But I don't understand why Mom and Dad didn't tell him he was wrong. I don't. They seem to *agree* with him!" Her voice cracked.

Iris twirled a strand of hair in her fingers. She didn't know what to say. How could anyone possibly think it *in their best interest* to be apart? What did that *mean*? The phrase didn't even make sense—that wasn't how any of those words were supposed to work.

"Maybe I should talk to them again."

"It's not going to matter," Lark said. "You heard them. They made up their minds."

"But . . ." But if she could just explain it. If she could find the right words, and the right way of saying those words, then maybe they'd listen.

Lark shook her head. "Iris, they're not going to listen. There's no point. They'll just get mad at you for arguing with them."

"I don't care if they're mad at me!"

"But I do! And you get mad that they aren't listening to you, and Dad starts using that voice and Mom looks sad and then they act really weird and plastic with me because they don't want to let on to me that they're annoyed at you because they want to show us that they think of us as individuals, even though I'd actually rather they just acted annoyed with me than weird and plastic, and meanwhile everyone in the house is mad at each other, and it doesn't help. When has it ever helped?"

"Well . . ."

Lark was right. The truth was, never. It never helped. Just like at school. Instead Iris got talking-tos about how they were so glad she was able to stand up for herself and her sister and they always wanted her to know she could talk to them about anything, but at the same time, Iris, we're your parents and sometimes enough is enough, sometimes you need to accept things and move on.

But that didn't mean it might not work *someday*.

"What if Mr. Hunt is mean?" Lark said, clutching Esmeralda to her. "What if he's one of those teachers who likes to call on students who don't like to raise their hands? What if we have to do a lot of presentations?"

Iris eyed her sister. Lark seemed focused on the bed, but Iris knew she wasn't really looking there: she had suddenly retreated into herself, into that corner of her brain that occupied itself with spinning stories about the future, all with terrible outcomes. It was one of Lark's gifts and curses: she saw the story in everything. Once upon a time there was a girl who was given a new teacher at school, but no one knew that the teacher was really an evil sorcerer. He looked into the girl's heart and saw there all of her fears, and then he made her fears come true.

"I don't even know who else is in the class!" Lark

exclaimed. "What if Tommy Whedon's in there? Who am I going to be partners with? What if there's an odd number of girls and no one wants to be partners with me? What if I say something weird and everyone laughs at me?"

Iris inhaled. What could she say? There was nothing to say, and Lark was stuck in that storytelling room in her brain, where even Iris's words weren't always enough to get her out.

A quiet knock on the door then. Iris sat straight up and Lark shot her a look, as their mom came in and perched herself against the wall, a plastic bag in her hands.

Iris could feel the words swelling in her chest: a cold *What is it?* And a hopeful *Did you change your mind?* And an angry *What were you thinking?* And a desperate *Did you hear what Lark just said?* She opened her mouth, not knowing which question would fly out, but her mom held up her hand. *Wait.*

Iris swallowed. Lark blinked rapidly.

"Girls," she said, eyes guarded. "Your father and I are sorry—"

"So you're calling Principal Peter?" Iris exclaimed.

Her mother's eyebrows went up.

Shhh, Lark tapped quickly.

"Let me finish," her mom said gently. "Iris. Lark," she continued, looking at each girl in turn. "Your father and I are very sorry you're upset."

Iris blew air out of her cheeks. There was nothing sorry about *I'm sorry you're upset*. *I'm sorry you're upset* didn't mean *I did something wrong and I'm going to fix it right now*. It meant *I did something right and your reaction is the problem*.

"But," she went on, eyes on Iris, "we want you to understand that we have every confidence that you girls will succeed and be happy and have great school years. Just like you always do." Now she smiled warmly at them. "I know it must seem scary, but it's going to be okay. You still have each other's backs, and we have your backs, always."

At this, Lark's hand flew to Iris's knee. Iris clamped her mouth shut.

"We just want you two to *try*. Give it a chance. We have faith in you. And maybe after a few months you guys can have more faith in yourselves. Now," she continued, straightening, "as we've discussed, we need to get you girls signed up for after-school programs this fall, and the deadline for some of them is Friday. Lark"—she reached into the bag and pulled out the printouts and pamphlets she'd been waving at them for the last couple of weeks—"there's an art program at Barnhill that I think you'd be interested in."

"Yeah, but Iris doesn't—"

"I know. You guys are going to do different programs, too."

"What?" Iris exclaimed.

"Just to try it. Just this fall. Lark, you love Ms. Messner. You love art, and this is a chance for you to really focus on it, and that will be so good for you! And Iris, you really love . . ."

Her mom stopped talking. Iris waited. Next to her, Lark cocked her head.

"Well, you might find something you love. This is a good chance for you to do that."

"Mom," Iris said, "I don't want to do any of that. I might as well take art. I don't mind it that much."

At that, Lark made a small noise. Even Esmeralda seemed to laugh.

"No," her mom said. "It doesn't make sense for you to do something you don't like. This is an opportunity to find something you do like." She looked back and forth between the girls. "You guys don't have to do everything together. It doesn't mean you're not still sisters."

"That's not it!" Iris said, a tremor at the edge of her words.

"My sweethearts. You're still each other's best friends, and you still can be there for each other. Nothing important is changing." She smiled at them, eyes full of love and mis-understanding. "All we're asking is that you *try* this. There's nothing to be afraid of."

CHAPTER FIVE

Meanwhile, Back at the Shop

Right after the shop opened, the chalkboard sign changed from We Are Here to, simply,

ARE YOU?

As it always did.

Are you?

This stopped passersby in their tracks.

Am I what?

Here, I think. The sign said We Are Here, before.

Well, of course I'm here! Where else would I be?

Others just gaped.

Are You? Are You?

Am I?

One man stared at the sign for a whole minute, and then shouted, "Yes! Yes I am!", and then ran home, quit his job, and started a cat rescue.

Are You?

Most people thought the sign was simply clever, clever enough to stop people in their tracks, clever enough to make some of them want to go check out the store behind the sign, to peruse the treasures within.

Good marketing! people said.

It wasn't, really. Getting potential customers into Treasure Hunters was just a happy accident. And it didn't always work—there are cities where people put their heads down and scurry away in the face of probing questions like *Are you?*

But, once again, the sign was not for them.

Still all the passersby were right, and I could have told them so. The sign meant both *Are you here?* and *Are you?*

Are you here? Are you still alive? Are you well? Are you paying attention?

Are you?

CHAPTER SIX

Missing Pieces

There was always a point where it was worthless to argue with their parents anymore. Lark always knew exactly where that point was, and Iris always argued well past it.

But now things were at the place where even Iris knew that arguing was fruitless. Lark was right: nothing they said was going to matter. Whatever had caused Principal Peter to enact this travesty, their parents were in all the way.

In fact, her parents had apparently decided that it was a wonderful idea, an inspiring idea, an idea so amazing it should have little baby ideas that could run around and ruin everything.

This is how it is with parents: they read some article by

an alleged parenting expert online or some psychologist says something on the radio or the principal gets a head injury, and they get inspired, and they start having their own ideas, and suddenly you're trying a new vegetable every night of the week, or going to bed at eight thirty no matter what, or having family weeding time every spring, which is supposed to instill a love of gardening in you but looks suspiciously like you doing the parts of gardening that your dad doesn't like.

Yes, Lark would do art camp at school with Ms. Messner, who adored her and who had once pronounced her milk-carton project *visionary*, and Lark could take the activity bus home afterward. And that would be fine—Lark would be fine. She loved art class, and it wouldn't even matter too much that Iris wasn't there because it wasn't like art required a lot of talking to people.

And Iris?

"Just pick something," her mom said the next morning before Lark had emerged from her room, spreading the fly-ers out in front of her. "What appeals to you?"

Nothing. Nothing appealed to her. "Why don't I just take the bus to the library after school? I can read and do home-work and stuff. You could leave my bike there on your way to work and I could just bike home."

Iris grinned. She hadn't even thought of the whole

transportation angle until she started talking, but it displayed just the kind of practical thinking that showed that she could be trusted to make her own decisions. Surely anyone who has thought things through so thoroughly can be trusted to be by herself at the library.

And indeed, her mother grinned at her, like Iris had had some great idea. And Iris felt some piece of dread break off and fall away. She didn't have to go to some silly class by herself with kids she didn't know. She could go to the library. She would be happy at the library! She loved the library!

"What a great idea! There's a wonderful program at the library that I think would be perfect for you. I wasn't sure how to make it work, but your plan is terrific."

"No, that's not—"

"You're going to love it. It's like . . . girl camp!"

"What?"

"It's called Camp Awesome. Here."

Iris glanced at the printout. Her mom was not characteristically good at details, and "girl camp" could have meant anything, including a camp only open to boys, but the printout showed that her mom was right. Camp Awesome was an after-school "enrichment club" at the library, for girls ages nine to twelve, where they would spend their time learning about a somewhat random assembly of topics, all of which would help girls "explore interests, gain confidence, and find their voices." And, presumably, keep them safely occupied for ninety minutes after school every day.

Iris sank in her seat. She didn't mind the idea of this, exactly: she herself was a collection of somewhat randomly assembled topics. But she did not understand why she needed enrichment at all. She was not white flour or garden soil. She was perfectly capable of sitting at the library reading through the kids nonfiction section—she could explore interests on her own. She was self-enriching.

"But I don't want to."

"Why not?"

"Because . . ." What? She had no good answer. She just didn't want to. Why was she supposed to have good answers for everything? Sometimes the not-wanting-to rose up inside you until it filled you up.

"I'm happy to sign you up for something else. There are classes at the park. . . ."

Iris looked down at the table. "Whatever. I'll do girl camp."

"Camp Awesome," her mother clarified, as if that made it better.

"Yeah. I'll do that. It's fine."

It wasn't fine. But there was clearly no point in saying that; her parents had made up their collective mind. Lark was right. This whole year was spiraling out of her control and school hadn't even started yet.

Really, she just didn't want to talk about it anymore. Her stomach was hurting, like something was gnawing on it from the inside.

Her mom gave her a small smile. "Okay. I'll sign you up right now."

Just then, Lark came padding down the stairs calling for them.

"I can't find my bracelet!" she said when she got into the kitchen, thrusting her empty wrist in front of them both. Her face was all twisted in worry.

"When did you last see it?" their mom said.

"When I went to bed! I took it off and put it by my lamp, like I always do."

"Could it have fallen on the floor?"

"I looked there! I looked everywhere." Lark threw her hands up in the air.

"I'll help," Iris said, standing.

"Me too," said her mom. "Don't worry, it will turn up."

This did not make Lark look any less worried, and Iris didn't blame her one bit. That was what her mom always said when things got lost: *It will turn up.* She said it like a fact, like sixteen plus sixteen is thirty-two and a group of owls is a parliament and blue whales are the largest animals. As if everything were absolutely sure, as if never in the history of the world had someone lost something and never found it again.

Iris had noticed, though, that when her parents lost something it was different: they got frantic and acted like the sum of sixteen and sixteen might just have changed overnight, as if yellow and blue now made pink, as if these sort of things could happen when you weren't paying attention.

"What if it doesn't?" Lark said.

"Oh, honey, it will. Things don't just disappear into thin air. It must be somewhere in your room—nothing could have taken it out of there, right?"

Her mom's voice sounded slightly strained, the way it always did when Lark's worries started running away with her. Like she didn't know whether to act like these worries were perfectly understandable or to demonstrate that they were completely irrational, and so she ended up doing neither.

The three of them went back upstairs and stepped into Lark's room. Of course, given the chaos there, if the bracelet had gotten on the floor they'd never be able to find it, and it might in fact have gotten stuck on something and be lost for all eternity. Still, they looked valiantly—around the nightstand, under the bed, in the covers.

Nothing.

Lark hovered, eyes wet, rubbing her wrist.

"Could you have maybe . . . taken it off in the bathroom or something?"

"No!"

"Maybe we should just check anyway? Iris, why don't you go look?"

"I didn't take it off in there!" Lark exclaimed.

Iris stopped, glancing back and forth between her sister and her mother. It was true that Lark might well have taken her bracelet off in the bathroom and just not remembered, because she was Lark and was far more interested in what she was thinking than what she was doing. It happened all the time.

Still, Lark clearly wasn't in the mood to hear that.

"Look," her mom said. "It can't be nowhere. And so when something isn't in the places you think it should be, it must be in the places you think it can't be. Right? So let's look in those places."

Lark's face screwed up as it did when she was thinking, and then she exhaled. "Okay," she said.

"Okay!" Iris said. She was used to finding Lark's things for her.

But the bracelet wasn't on the bathroom counter; it wasn't on the bathroom floor; it hadn't fallen into any of the drawers. It just wasn't there. So Iris went back to her sister's room, where Lark stood rubbing her wrist.

"It's not there. I'm sorry."

Lark's face fell. "How could I lose it?" she breathed. "How?"

"We'll find it, honey," their mom said again.

Iris didn't say anything. The bracelet was Lark's most treasured possession, and no amount of reassurance was going to help. Lark was already seeing the story play out: and then the girl lost everything she had, piece by piece.

Lark would not tell their mom that, of course. Because then their mom would try to tell her that now she was being irrational; stuff like that didn't happen. Lark already knew that. But she still worried.

She just needed to be able to say it out loud. Iris understood. And so later, when Lark rubbed her wrist and whispered to Iris that she was afraid this was a bad sign, Iris just nodded and listened and tried to ignore the feeling gnawing at her own chest.

CHAPTER SEVEN

Report Cards

Iris keeps her desk neat and orderly.

Lark is very imaginative, but needs to learn to pay attention.

Iris has a very assertive personality and sometimes the other children find her "bossy."

Lark sometimes forgets her daily assignments, and seems to have trouble staying organized.

Iris does not always act appropriately in disagreements with teachers or other students.

Lark excels in art!

One area for improvement for Iris is being a little nicer.

Lark is a dream student.

Iris has good fluency and intonation when she reads out loud.

Lark still struggles to participate in class.

Iris's presentation on presidential pets was outstanding.

Lark needs more confidence!

Since the incident with the brick of clay, Iris has been appreciably more successful managing her temper.

Lark did well catching up after her extended absence. We're glad she's okay.

Iris seemed to have a tough time this quarter, but it is understandable, given the circumstances. I'm sure she'll be herself again next quarter.

Sometimes it seems like Lark and her sister are in their own world and it can be difficult to reach them.

Sometimes it seems like Iris and her sister are in their own world and it can be impossible to reach them.

CHAPTER EIGHT

The First Day of School

On the night before the first day of school, Iris set out an outfit for the next day, as she did every year on the night before the first day of school, as is only sensible. There are so many unknowns you face when you wake up on the morning of the first day of school; at least you can know what you're wearing.

This year, though, she had to plan more strategically than ever, as she needed to make a statement to Principal Peter and anyone else who thought she'd accepted this separate-classrooms idea. After much consideration she opted for her gray T-shirt dress, with its decidedly unamused-looking owl gazing out from the bottom left, leggings, and cobalt-blue high-tops with magenta laces threaded through them. The dress said, *Like this owl, I am decidedly unamused,* and the combination of cobalt blue and magenta sent the clear message that she was attending school under protest. *I am here,* the shoes said. *I am so here, it hurts your eyes.*

But when she woke up in the morning and stared at her outfit, it all felt wrong, like it belonged to a different girl. So Iris put her clothes away and put on a black shirt and a black skirt over her black leggings, then her black boots, and finally tied her hair with an especially black hair tie.

There. The outfit said, *I am not here.*

"Girls!" her mom called from downstairs. "Breakfast is almost ready! I made eggs! Are you dressed?"

Iris was dressed, yes. But she'd heard nothing from Lark's room.

"Girls? If you come down now, you can chat with your dad before school!"

Iris walked to her sister's door and knocked.

This happened every year on the first day of school—not the video-chat part, of course, and Dad was usually making the eggs. But there were always eggs, and the expectation that the girls would be downstairs to eat the eggs, and there was always Iris who was ready for the eggs and Lark who was not.

Iris opened her sister's door. Lark exploded up from the bed, hair in chaos, blankets falling everywhere, Esmeralda going flying off the bed, as happened every year.

"I couldn't sleep," Lark whispered, rubbing her face.

This was why Iris planned her own outfits the night before. You can always sleep better the night before the first day of school if you plan your outfit.

"Breakfast is almost ready!"

Lark collapsed back in bed, covering her face, and groaned. "I'll be down in a minute."

It turned out that there was not time to chat with their dad. There was not even much time to eat, which was fine as the eggs were cold. The fact that this always happened didn't mean it irritated their mom any less.

In past years, as the girls tried to wolf down their cold eggs, they'd had to work to avoid catching each other's eyes, because if they did that, one of them would surely make a face to express how disgusting the eggs were, and then the other would surely start laughing, and cold scrambled eggs would come out of her mouth and fly everywhere, and that would irritate their parents even more.

But not this year. This year they sat across from each other—Iris's hair in a careful braid, Lark's in a hasty high ponytail—and didn't have to work to avoid each other's eyes. This year, the cold eggs weren't some kind of absurd exception, but rather a sign of things to come. Emotionally, it would be a whole year of cold scrambled eggs.

They finished their eggs in silence and stood up, and that's when their mom fully apprehended them. "Is that what you're wearing?"

The girls exchanged a glance. Which *you* did she mean? Iris was in her all black, while Lark was wearing a puffy black skirt, green-and-blue-and-pink leggings, green high-tops, and her bright yellow squid T-shirt. This was not protest, really—it was just Lark.

"Yes," Lark said, looking down at her outfit. "This is what I'm wearing."

"And this," Iris said, chin in the air, "is what I'm wearing."

"Isn't it a little much?" their mom asked, looking from one girl to another. She seemed to mean both of them. But both girls just shrugged and she said, "All right, but when the authorities come for me because I can't dress my daughters, I am going to deny knowing you."

Mr. Hunt's classroom was the first room in the fifth-grade wing. The girls stopped in front of it. Lark peeked in, and then looked back at Iris.

"You ready?" Iris said, though she knew the answer.

Lark's eyes were big. She shook her head, and then stared back into the classroom as if looking for booby traps, rubbing the place on her wrist where her bracelet used to be.

"Tommy Whedon's in there," Lark whispered.

Iris stiffened. "He wouldn't dare mess with you this year," she said.

Mr. Hunt was standing in front of the classroom eyeing his new charges, and as they lurked in the doorway, his head swiveled toward the girls. And so Iris beheld her sister's new teacher, who looked like he could be her older brother. (Was he even old enough to teach? Weren't there standards? Laws?) Mr. Hunt was young, small, with skin that eerily matched the hallway paint, and his head seemed attached to the rest of him oddly, as if someone had forgotten the neck and just done the best they could.

His eyes fell on Lark, and then on Iris behind her. Iris saw it, the little flicker of surprise that always passed over adults' eyes when they first saw the girls together. She stuck her chin up in the air.

"Does one of you belong in here?" the teacher asked.

Lark nodded, ever so slightly, and Mr. Hunt held an arm out toward the Larkless classroom and grinned. "What are you waiting for, Octopus Girl?"

Laughter from the classroom. Lark flushed, continents of embarrassment spreading across her cheeks.

Mr. Hunt's grin faded, and Iris opened her mouth, ready to lecture him on the inappropriateness of referring to students by the creatures on their T-shirts, ready to explain to him that that was not an octopus at all but a squid and what kind of a teacher was he that he couldn't tell the difference, ready to tell him that you should not just treat kids like they have hard outer shells when you don't know anything about them, ready to lecture the whole classroom on the bad form of laughing when a teacher makes a joke at the expense of another student, and what was to say he wouldn't start calling them all the names of various sea creatures soon—*like you, Tommy Whedon, you look like a blowfish*—and how would they like it then, when Ms. Shonubi peeked out of the classroom down the hall and asked in her soft voice, "Does one of you belong in here?"

And then Lark was gone, swallowed by her new class, by the laughing kids and Tommy-the-blowfish and the booby traps, though—Iris knew—her face was still flushed and her hands shaking just a little, the way they did whenever she was nervous. The way no one noticed but Iris.

And then it was her turn. Ms. Shonubi held out her arm and Iris walked into her new classroom.

Alone.

Every year she and Lark walked through together; every year the whole class turned as one to stare at them, the incredible identical twins. But now she was just Iris, alone— not startling, not a sideshow, not even worth taking note of. Iris on her own was wholly uninteresting.

She slid into the desk marked with her name, which was

placed in a square with Mira Vang, Jin Larson, and a new boy named Oliver in a blue button-down shirt, yellow plaid bow tie, and close-cropped afro.

Mira leaned over to her. "Iris! You're all emo now!"

"What does that mean?"

Mira waved her hands at Iris's black clothing. "That! Or maybe it's goth."

"What's the difference?" Jin asked.

"I don't know!" Mira said brightly. "Where's Lark? Did she move away?"

"Uh . . . no. She's in Mr. Hunt's class."

"Ohhhhhhhhhh. That's weird."

Iris could only nod. Yes. Yes it was weird.

"You're singular now!" Jin said.

"What?"

"You used to be a plural noun. Now you're singular." He smiled sagely.

"A person can't be plural," Oliver piped in.

"She can," Jin said, waving toward Iris. "She had a twin sister."

"I still have her!" Iris protested.

"Anyway," Jin said, "they're identical, and always together. Except now."

"Cool," Oliver breathed, turning to her. "What's it like to have a twin?"

"Uh . . . it's cool?" People asked Iris that all the time and she never had a good answer. It was like asking what it's like to have arms—you don't think anything of it until you wake up in the morning and they're not there anymore.

"How do you tell them apart?"

"Oh, that's easy," Mira said. "Lark is the one who has expressions on her face."

"What?" said Iris.

Oliver regarded her face and then nodded at Mira. "I see what you mean."

"Plus," Jin said, "Lark is always like this"—he waved his hands around in the air—"while Iris is more like . . ." He propped his elbow on the table and placed his chin in his hand, as if disgruntled.

"That's exactly right," Mira agreed.

Oliver turned to Iris. "Do you guys dress alike?"

"No," Iris said.

"Have you guys ever switched places?"

"No," Iris said.

"Do you have ESP?"

Iris sighed. It took everything in her power not to prop her chin in her hands. "No," she said. She'd given a report on twins last year just to fend off these kind of questions, but you can't give a report to the whole world.

Unfortunately.

"That's too bad," said Jin. "ESP could be super useful."

"Maybe you do have it and you don't know it yet!" said Oliver. "Sometimes powers appear when you are least expecting them."

Jin nodded as if he had just heard something very profound. "That's true! Try not expecting them and maybe they'll come!"

"ESP isn't even a real thing," Iris said.

"That's not true," Mira said, shaking her head earnestly. "My aunt is a pet psychic."

"That can't be real."

"It is too real! She has ESP with pets. Like if your cat starts yowling or peeing outside the litter box—"

"Ew," said Oliver.

"—then she can figure out whether it's in pain or depressed or seeing ghosts or whatever."

"There's no such thing as ghosts, either," said Iris.

Jin leaned into Mira, ignoring Iris. "When did her powers develop?"

Mira gasped. "When she was least expecting them!"

"See?" Oliver nodded meaningfully at Iris.

Iris shifted around in her chair, as if there were any possible position where she could be comfortable right now. She'd heard all these questions before, dozens of times. No, they had never switched places. No, they did not dress alike, not intentionally. No, they didn't have ESP.

It wasn't like that.

Still, when Iris was small and would wake up terrified from one of her nightmares, Lark would climb up from the bottom bunk and crawl into bed with her. Still, when some ugly arrow of the world pierced Lark's heart, Iris's hand went to her own chest and rubbed the sore spot.

People did not have words for these things, so they used the wrong words, too-bright lights that made the truths look stark and wrong.

As Ms. Shonubi called the class to order, Iris looked around the room, trying to find some comfortable place for her eyes to settle. If Lark had been there, she would have tapped something at her, something like *Help me* or *I wish my powers would develop now* or *I'll tell you the whole story later*. This was what it was to have a twin and a secret language—you were always connected to someone, and whatever was happening was not as interesting as your secret conversation about what was happening.

But now life only existed on one plane, just the surface world. The world where Iris and Lark were nothing but shells.

It was going to be a long year.

CHAPTER NINE

The Ogre

Neither after-school camp would start for another week, so today Iris waited for Lark outside Mr. Hunt's room. She did not peer into the door to see what was happening, because that would be creepy, but she very much wanted to.

Her own new classmates passed her, and in truth none of them seemed to care exactly what she was doing—which fit utterly with her new identity of Not Being Interesting. But Oliver and Jin waved as they passed, and Mira stopped in front of her, beaming.

"I figured it out!"

"What?"

"This!" Mira waved at Iris's outfit. "You're definitely emo."

"Oh. Thanks?"

"You're welcome! See you tomorrow!" She grinned and bounced off, her long black ponytail bobbing behind her.

Then Mr. Hunt's class came streaming out like over-excited salmon, and Iris took a census of her sister's new classmates. There were Mitali and Gina, who were nice enough; Gracie (now Grace), who Iris still hadn't forgiven; Ashkir, who'd been Iris's science-detectives partner in third grade and had impressed Iris with his organizational abilities; the two Naomis, who somehow apparently did not need to be separated. And Tommy Whedon, who Iris glared at, just in case.

And then Lark came out, clutching her bag in front of her. She looked pale, but undamaged. When she saw Iris, she made her eyes big and pressed her lips closed. *I have so much to tell you, but not here.* Iris grabbed her arm and they hurried down the hall.

"How was it for you?" Lark whispered as they walked along.

She'd been waiting to tell Lark about her day, because nothing really felt real until she told Lark about it. But when she tried to find something to say, the whole day just felt gray and mushy. Like there was nothing solid to hang on to.

"Mira Vang thinks I'm emo," she said finally.

"What does that mean?"

"I'm not sure," Iris said. "I have to look it up."

"Whatever it is, I'm sure she meant it nicely. It's Mira."

"I guess."

"What else?"

What else? She poked around in the mush in her brain. But there was nothing else there.

"I don't know. It was okay."

"So emo," Lark said.

"I guess so," Iris said.

The girls got on the bus and pressed in together, and this, at least, was familiar. In the mornings, one of their parents always drove them to school—their mom, now, as the trip would be rather difficult for their dad—and in the afternoons they took the bus home, sitting in the middle left for no good reason except that that was the way they'd always done it.

"So what about you?" Iris whispered when they were settled. "What happened?"

Lark's face twisted. She looked around the bus, then leaned into her sister.

"I am pretty sure," she said, voice intent, "that Mr. Hunt is an ogre."

Iris's eyes widened. This was not good.

When they were younger, Lark had made a big bestiary of monsters, complete with drawings and crucial information like the particular predilections of ogres.

To Lark, an ogre took great pride in his collection of children's hearts, and when the other ogres would come over for dinner (usually ogres serve yak to guests) he would show off his treasure, boasting about how he had the finest collection in the land. He'd take a jar off the shelf and tell the great and glorious story of the capture of the child the heart once belonged to. (Whether or not the story was actually great and glorious, or even true at all, only the ogre knew. After all, who was going to question him?)

"He seems kind of small for an ogre," Iris said.

"That's just his disguise. So no one suspects him. I mean, if you were an ogre and you really wanted access to some fresh children, wouldn't it make sense to pretend to be a mild-mannered fifth-grade teacher? He's probably actually eight feet tall and over five hundred years old."

"His name isn't very subtle, though. Hunt. Like, what he does to children."

"Ogres," Lark said darkly, "are not known for their subtlety."

"They also can't tell the difference between an octopus and a squid," Iris grumbled, nodding to her sister's shirt.

"It's obviously a squid!" Lark said. "Why would I have

a shirt with an octopus on it? Tommy and Jeff called me Octopus Girl all day, and I couldn't exactly be like, 'Duh, I'm Squid Girl.'" Lark flushed slightly. This was clearly not something she wanted to talk about.

"So, what exactly makes Mr. Hunt an ogre? Did something happen?"

"Not really. He's just an ogre. I can tell."

"Okay, good. I mean, not good that he's an ogre, but—"

"He made everyone stand up and introduce themselves and talk about their hobbies. I don't have any hobbies."

"What are you talking about? You have all the hobbies!" Lark was the one with hobbies, and Iris was the one who didn't have any hobbies, unless you counted being suspicious all the time.

"Not really. Not that people care about. Chloe rides horses and Elodie plays hockey and Adam does YouTube. I stood up and I could barely remember my name and everyone was looking at me and probably making fun of my shirt in their head. I finally said I played the piano."

Lark did not play the piano. The last time she'd even touched a piano was when she was six and they were at the airport and she started pressing the keys on the piano on the main concourse and some tall lady yelled at her.

"And then," she went on, "Caitlin Morris said she played the piano too and tried to come up and talk to me about it before gym so I ran to the bathroom and now I have to learn about the piano."

"If I'd been there I could have reminded you of your hobbies and then this never would have happened."

"Yeah," Lark grumbled. "I bet Mr. Hunt doesn't have any hobbies he can name either. You can't just *say* you collect kids' hearts."

"Probably not," Iris agreed, shifting in her seat. She could not seem to get comfortable today, anywhere. Maybe this was going to be the rest of her life—squishy uncomfortable seats and gray mushy days.

But Lark was okay. She'd survived the Octopus Girl incident, at least, and other than thinking her teacher was a mythological child-eating beast, she hadn't had a terrible day.

It was something, anyway.

Their mom wasn't there when they got home, but fifteen minutes after they walked in the door her computer pinged—their dad trying to Skype. The girls looked at each other. Iris shook her head, but Lark raised her eyebrows. *We have to answer.*

"My girls!" he beamed. "Now which one of you is which?"

"Dad . . ." Iris said. He always did this.

"Oh, yes. You're Iris. How was the first day?"

His eyes were so bright, his face so happy, like he just

knew they were going to say that it was really good, and being separated turned out to be a great idea, and they loved their teachers, and each of them had made six new friends.

"Lark thinks Mr. Hunt is an ogre," Iris said.

It was like someone turned off the light switch in his soul, and because they were on the computer and her dad sat way too close to the camera, they could see the minutiae of his emotions on his face—the way his eyes dimmed, the way his cheeks collapsed, the way his eyebrows transformed from perky arches to droopy caterpillars.

"I mean, not like a real ogre," Lark said. She'd gotten lots of talks on the difference between having a good imagination and creating problems for herself. "Just an ogre ogre."

"And why do you think that?" he asked.

"He made fun of her," Iris said. "In front of the whole class."

Their dad's eyelid twitched slightly. "Well, I'm sorry to hear that," he said after a moment. "If this happens again, we can dialogue with him about it."

"Dad!" Iris said.

"Huh?"

"That's not a verb. You can't dialogue with someone. You can talk to him, or have a dialogue. *That's* what you can do."

"Exactly." As he looked at her, his eyebrows knitted together, the caterpillars uniting in mutual concern. "Are you wearing all black?"

Iris shrugged. "Yeah."

"Have you gone goth all of a sudden? I've only been gone three weeks!"

Iris scowled. "No? I just felt like wearing this."

"Good. You're not allowed to go goth until you're at least twelve. How was your day?"

Gray and mushy. "Fine."

"Good," he said. "How's your mom doing?"

"Fine, I guess?"

"I miss her."

"Okay. Didn't you talk to her earlier?"

"Sure, but I miss her. And you guys too. It's lonely over here without my girls." The eyelid twitched again. "Anyway. Love to your mom. I hope tomorrow's even better than today."

"He seemed sad," Lark said, when they hung up.

"I guess."

"We should, like, make him a card or something."

Iris gave her a look. *Really? After what they did?*

"I know, I know," Lark said. "But . . . he still seemed sad."

This was why Lark was the nice one. "Okay," Iris said grudgingly. "So what do you want to do?"

Lark grinned. "I'll get my stuff."

When Lark came back downstairs, she had paper and a

box of markers and was holding a small green plastic figurine in her hands. "Look!" she said, placing it on the table.

Lark had innumerable figurines of various shapes, sizes, materials, and species, mostly from various dollar-store trips or Christmas presents from their assortment of aunts. This one was from some box of mythological monsters, purchased from the zoo if Iris remembered correctly. It was an inch high and had a round bald head on a thick body, with ears that stuck out straight on either side of its head, and it wore something like a large loincloth.

An ogre.

"Do you see the resemblance?"

"Not really?"

"Me neither. But I'm sure this is what Mr. Hunt looks like on the inside." She positioned the little figure on the table so it looked at Iris. "Hello, young lady," she said in an ogre voice. "Do you have any hobbies?"

"Ew," Iris said.

"Tell me about it," Lark said. She sat back and opened the big marker box while the ogre stared at Iris with its hollow gaze. She turned it so it was looking away.

"So," Iris said, pointing at the markers, "what do you want to do?"

"Well," she said, eyes brightening. "I thought we could make a little book for him? About England? You could come up with, like, facts about London or British history or something, and then I'll draw the pictures?"

Lark, being Lark, had come up with the perfect way for them to make something together. Iris could provide the hard facts, Lark the beautiful lies.

Iris considered. "I don't think I know anything about London outside of Harry Potter, which probably isn't historically accurate?"

"Go look stuff up, then. I'll work on the cover."

So Lark tilted her head and began to draw a double-decker bus, her tongue sticking out slightly as she worked. Iris got up to wander to the computer but felt the eyes of the plastic ogre on her. So she stuffed it in her pocket where it couldn't bother anyone.

Fifteen minutes later, she presented Lark with a list for her perusal, including:

• In the nineteenth century, people used to dump their sewage in the Thames, and once during the summer it started to smell so badly they had to close Parliament.

• If you put a postage stamp with the queen's picture upside down on a letter, that's treason.

• King Henry VIII wanted to get a divorce but couldn't under Catholic law so he invented a new religion.

• King Henry III had a pet polar bear.

• There's a legend that London will fall if ravens fly away from the Tower of London so now ravens are kept on the grounds at all times.

"I don't know if I want to draw the Thames full of sewage," Lark said, eyeing the list.

"You could just make stink lines coming from it."

Lark curled up her nose. "I guess."

People used to bathe in the Thames and drink from it, but Iris decided not to tell Lark that part. Lark was not a huge fan of any stories involving bodily functions, which had made it hard on her when they did a unit on the digestive system last year.

"I'm going to start with the polar bear. I don't think I can really illustrate the Henry the Eighth thing? I don't know how to draw someone inventing a new religion."

"He had eight wives, too."

"Oh, yeah! I can draw that. What else?"

The ravens. Lark loved the raven part, as Iris knew she would.

Ravens are the biggest birds in the crow family. The collective noun is either an *unkindness* of ravens or a *conspiracy* of ravens (which would sound bad, but their sister crows are collectively a *murder*). Like crows, ravens like to collect shiny things and hoard their treasure. Like crows, ravens are considered bad omens.

Because of the legend there are seven ravens in the Tower of London, and their wings are clipped so they cannot escape, though sometimes they do anyway—a raven couple once eloped into the nearby woods, and another time an elderly raven fled the Tower and began living in a pub.

And it was just when Iris was through telling Lark some of this that she saw a flash of black outside.

"What's wrong?" Lark asked.

Iris had no idea what had appeared on her face, but whatever it was, Lark had noticed. And of course she had. She might not notice a fire truck about to run her over, but she could catch any subtle shift in Iris's expressions. Which was obviously a big deal, since according to the kids in school she didn't actually make facial expressions.

"Oh, there was a big crow outside and it startled me."

Lark's eyes widened. "A crow! Is it still there?"

"No."

It was. It had settled on a telephone pole. It was staring at Iris as she spoke. Iris could see it, but Lark could not.

The *no* had just popped out of her mouth like a reflex, like when the doctor hits your knee with that little hammer and your leg bounces. And now it was there, this flat-out lie just hanging in the air, daring Iris to keep pretending it wasn't.

But she couldn't do anything about it now. It was a

mistake, that was all. A reasonable mistake. This wasn't a good time for Lark to get all weird about crows. She had enough to worry about.

"Do you think it's in the backyard?" Lark asked, eyes suddenly bright.

"It didn't go that way." Which was true. The bird, which seemed way too big to be a normal crow, was perched on the pole, and began nibbling at something underneath its wing.

"Bummer," Lark said, then looked back down at her project.

Iris glanced at the big crow, now a giant living representation of her ability to lie to her sister.

But Lark knew nothing. She was working happily, all thoughts of ogres and the school day clearly forgotten. Lark with her head in an art project was a girl with no worries at all.

So Iris put her head down to work on the text portion of the book too, trying to ignore the lie just above her. And when their mom finally got home, Iris was so absorbed in lettering the text that she almost forgot about the crow and the lie, about the ogre, about the school day, and almost forgot to be mad.

Almost.

That night, when Iris was getting ready for bed, she

found the plastic ogre in her pocket. It really did have weird eyes. She placed it on her nightstand, turning it around so it wouldn't watch her while she slept.

When she woke up the next morning, it was gone.

CHAPTER TEN

Meanwhile . . .

The Bell Museum and Planetarium in Saint Paul, Minnesota, began as a one-room natural-history museum founded to study the wildlife of the state. Over the decades it became known for its elaborate dioramas with stuffed animals placed in careful reconstructions of their natural habitats. More than a few local children were distressed to find, upon visiting the museum, that the figures in the dioramas were not stuffed animals as they understood them to be, but made of the corpses of actual animals, preserved through taxidermy.

(Lark Maguire was definitely one of those children.)

But the museum has some treasures very much not from Minnesota.

In 1890, an extremely rich Minneapolis man named Louis F. Menage sponsored a scientific expedition to the Philippines to benefit the Minnesota Academy of Natural Sciences, which was the sort of thing extremely rich people did back then. The man, a real-estate tycoon, funded the project with the understanding that his name would be associated with it, and that is a thing very rich people still do.

The scientists traveled around remote islands of the Philippines and Borneo for two years and came back with thousands of specimens—or, as other people call them, animals—which had never before been seen by American eyes. It was going to be the most glorious exhibition, a treasure trove for scientific discovery. New species of birds! Lizards! Orangutans! Wild hogs! Lemurs! A pig-tailed monkey! A stink badger!

Once the specimens were ready for display.

Which would just require some more time, and of course funding from the generous Mr. Menage.

But—funny story—it turned out that Menage's name was also attached to four million dollars' worth of fraud, and as the men were beginning their work, he fled to South America.

Some of the samples survived, though, and the Bell Museum has a few, including the Sulu Bleeding-heart, a species of bird that only exists on those islands and that no

Westerner has ever observed outside the Menage samples. Recent expeditions to those islands have shown no traces of it, and naturalists fear it is extinct.

I like to think it just got smart.

I also think that killing a rare bird and stuffing it so you can keep it forever is a strange way to appreciate it.

Nonetheless, the specimen of the Sulu Bleeding-heart is considered one of the Bell Museum's great treasures. And it was with tremendous excitement that a visiting ornithologist set out to view it.

But when she came to the window where the bird was supposed to be, instead of finding the stuffed corpse perversely displayed in something designed to represent its natural habitat before it was killed and taken out of it, she found an empty perch.

She spoke to a guard, and the guard called the curator, and the curator called the executive director. No, they would never loan out the specimens from the Menage expedition! No, no one should have removed the Sulu Bleeding-heart!

But the bird was not there. It was missing.

Someone had stolen it.

CHAPTER ELEVEN

Iris Dissents

No, Lark had not taken the ogre from Iris's nightstand, as Iris discovered when she called her sister into her room the next morning. She hadn't even known that Iris had pocketed it the previous afternoon, and in fact was somewhat confused as to why Iris had placed it on her bedside table in the first place, and Iris could not explain. "I just . . . felt like it?"

I just felt like it was a perfectly natural-sounding reason for Lark. But as to the question of where the thing had gone, she had no answer. It was just like her bracelet. It had disappeared.

"Gnomes?" Lark suggested.

"Oh, that'd be great." Iris had enough problems without fairy-tale creatures coming to life.

"Maybe the thing actually *is* Mr. Hunt. Maybe it had to go work on planning today's lessons."

"I don't really want that to be true, either."

"Did you look under your bed? Behind the nightstand?"

"Everywhere," Iris said. Something was very weird when it was Lark giving her advice on how to find things.

Lark was used to things getting lost—not important things, like the bracelet, but things from the clutter of random objects that populated her daily life. A plastic ogre getting up and walking away didn't bother her too much. Iris, however, was not used to it at all. If you paid attention, and you had places for things, and you put everything back in those places, they tended to be easily findable.

Or they were supposed to be.

"Hey, can I borrow a T-shirt?" Lark asked, motioning to Iris's closet.

"Sure. Did Mom forget to do laundry again?" Laundry had always been their dad's domain and their mom didn't seem to be adjusting well.

"No . . . I just don't want to wear any of mine."

"How come?"

She shrugged.

"Okay. Sure."

"I'm not going to wear, like, all black or something. I'm not going all goth-emo or anything, like some people."

"Okay." Iris, herself clad in black again, opened her closet door. "Whatever you want. I really like your squid shirt, though."

"Yeah, well . . . is this one okay?" She pulled out a dark blue T-shirt.

"I've got some striped leggings that go with that." Lark had many varieties of striped leggings, but few that would go with something as muted as dark blue. Not that matching was necessarily Lark's thing.

"No. I'll just wear some plain ones. Thanks."

Iris frowned. "Do you have plain leggings?"

"Yeah."

"Okay."

When they went downstairs to get breakfast, their mom was staring at an article in the newspaper as if the letters on the page had come to life and started doing a jig.

"What is it?" Iris asked.

"Oh! Sorry, I didn't hear you. It's just some thieves have been stealing stuff from local museums. It's bizarre."

"Maybe they have my bracelet," Lark grumbled.

Her mom looked them both up and down. "Is there any reason you both are dressing like you're going to a funeral?"

Iris raised her eyebrows. *Do you really want me to answer that?*

"Never mind. You guys get your breakfast, and we'll go in ten minutes."

Neither girl's wardrobe got any brighter over the course of the week. Lark kept fishing things out of Iris's closet, because apparently Iris was the go-to-girl in the family for boring clothes.

It was fine. Iris's class was fine. Ms. Shonubi was nice. The other kids were fine. But it all felt so empty, and still she could not get comfortable anywhere.

"You're really twitchy this year," Mira commented on Friday.

"I guess," Iris said.

"I don't remember you being so twitchy last year."

"The chair's uncomfortable," Iris said.

"You were twitchy in art. And music."

"Those chairs were uncomfortable too."

"Maybe you have back problems," Jin offered. "My mom has back problems and has a special pillow to sit on. You could bring a special pillow with you?"

"My dad has back problems too, so he uses one of those standing desks at work," said Oliver. "Maybe you could use a standing desk?"

"Yoga's really helpful too," said Mira.

"And Pilates," Oliver added. "My dad loves Pilates. He

says it builds his core muscles."

"There's no such thing as core muscles," Mira said.

"There are! They're around the stomach and back and stuff."

"I am pretty sure you are making that up."

"Am not!"

Iris stuck her chin in her hand and tried to hold still. There is nothing to make you more twitchy than a group of people talking about how twitchy you are, and Iris suddenly felt like she was made of worms.

"Do you want me to ask my mom where she got her pillow?" Jin asked. "It's a good temporary solution while you work on your core muscles."

Mira rolled her eyes. "Come on. Everyone's getting in line."

Ms. Shonubi's class had specialists after lunch every day, meaning that on successive days that week Iris had gotten to enjoy the confused looks on the faces of the music teacher, the drama teacher, and the art teacher at seeing her by herself, without a Lark in sight. *I know,* she wanted to tell them. *I don't get it either.*

Iris felt even more useless in these classes than she usually did. If her separation from her sister was supposed to bring out some previously undiscovered talent in playing the glockenspiel or using watercolors, it had not, at least not that first week.

But on Friday they had the first meeting of media, and that was the one class where Iris didn't feel completely useless. Maybe that was because the media specialist, Mr. Ntaba, was the only specialist who never had trouble telling the girls apart. (The music teacher had taken to calling them both Maguire just to avoid any errors, while all the other kids got to have first names.)

This year he sat them all down and cleared his throat and launched into the speech he gave on the first day of school every year, and for a few minutes Iris did not feel twitchy.

"The library," he explained to them, "might look ordinary to you, but that, my children, is just a facade to fool the board so they don't cut my budget. And they would do that if they knew the truth: this is a magical land where every one of you can find exactly the book you need at any given time—even if you don't know you need it. Every one of you can find the book that will change your life."

In kindergarten, Iris had taken all his words to be exactly true—maybe not that the library was magic, exactly, but that it was something like magic. What year was it when she knew that such things didn't exist? She couldn't remember. But still, it was nice to sit here and listen to him talk and believe it again for a little while.

"Someday this year you might feel some odd tugging at the center of your chest and you will find yourself standing among the shelves of this here library for reasons you barely understand, and all you have to do is say, 'Mr. Ntaba, I am looking for the book that could change my life,' and I will find that book for you. I am your fairy godmother, but with books." He said this line every year, and no one ever laughed at it, not even Dexter Atwood.

But really, that was exactly what Mr. Ntaba was. At least for Iris. One morning in third grade she'd felt some odd tugging at the center of her chest and found herself standing among the shelves of the media center. She did not say, "Mr. Ntaba, I am looking for the book that could change my life," because even in third grade she was not the sort of person who said that kind of thing. But he handed her a book nonetheless:

Amazing but True: Facts to Astonish You

"Here," he said to her. "Iris Maguire, you look like a girl who could use some astonishment."

Somehow he knew that Iris was not someone to be astonished by tales of great quests or mythological creatures or even wizard school. She pored over the book and found herself . . . maybe not astonished, but certainly intrigued. And that was good enough.

Did you know hippo sweat is red? Did you know cows kill more people every year than sharks? Did you know that the smallest mammal in the world is called the bumblebee bat, and is about the size of a half-dollar coin?

With Mr. Ntaba's help she went through various phases. Weird animal facts. Collective nouns. Even accidental inventions. Play-Doh was invented by a scientist trying to make a wallpaper cleaner! Someone once tried to create a new soda and then left it outside with the stirring stick in it and invented Popsicles! And of course presidential pets. Did you know Thomas Jefferson had two pet bears that he kept on the White House lawn? That Theodore Roosevelt's son put a pony in the White House elevator? That Benjamin Harrison once chased his pet goat, Old Whiskers, down Pennsylvania Avenue?

On the second day of fourth grade Mr. Anderson asked the class to contribute topics and a list of possible answers for a trivia game. Other kids came up with things like Dog Breeds, and Spider-Man Enemies, and Things I Am Allergic To. When Mr. Anderson got to Iris's sheet, his white eyebrows went up, he cleared his throat, and then he read, "Presidential Assassination Attempts."

That was before Iris understood that there is a difference between the things you have in your head and the things you present to the world—that sometimes you have to fit yourself into certain shapes, ones other people can easily name.

But none of that mattered when it was just you and a

book. Today, when her classmates were browsing the shelves, Mr. Ntaba asked Iris, as he sometimes did, "Have you found it yet?"

He meant something to astonish her. And she certainly had been astonished of late, but not in the way he meant.

"Not really," she said.

"But we will, Iris. Do not doubt my powers."

"I don't."

"In the meantime, if you see anything astonishing, let me know, okay?"

"I will."

He studied her for a moment. "I saw your sister earlier. Is this the first time you guys haven't been in the same class?"

She swallowed. "Yeah. It's weird."

"Do you know why that happened?"

"Principal Peter thinks we need to grow as individuals or something."

"I see. And do you agree with him? That you need to grow as individuals?"

She shook her head.

"I think I have just the thing." He disappeared for a moment and then came back with a big bright picture book. "It's about Ruth Bader Ginsburg. The Supreme Court justice. She disagrees with people all the time."

The book was called *I Dissent*. Iris flipped it open and saw the text *RUTH HAS DISAGREED, DISAPPROVED, AND DIFFERED.*

"This looks good," she said, heading for a chair.

"Iris, wait." He leaned in. "I know it's going to be lonely for you without Lark. But you can do it, okay?"

Iris stopped. And swallowed. She was not twitching at all; she was utterly still.

Lonely. It was the word her father had used, and she hadn't thought much of it at the time. It was a feeling, she realized, that she'd never really had before. It was the sort of feeling that belonged to people in books and movies, not a real-life feeling.

But that was before, when she and Lark didn't have separate classes, separate activities. When she lived constantly on two planes—the one with everyone else, and the one hidden underneath it where she and Lark lived together.

Lonely.

Iris looked at the floor and blinked once, twice. Everything blurred. Then she swallowed again and looked back up at Mr. Ntaba.

"I will," she said.

CHAPTER TWELVE

The Crow Girl, Take One

The giant crow continued to linger near their house. Lark, who was always too busy with the world inside her head to notice anything on the outside, did not notice, but Iris did. She kept meaning to point it out to Lark, but she never quite did.

And I knew why.

Once, when the girls were seven and heading to the car, Lark stumbled and dropped some crackers. That was Lark for you—she never seemed to quite see any of the things that were right in front of her face. She stumbled and she spilled and things flew everywhere, always.

But because it was Lark, when she stumbled and spilled, magic happened.

As the girls were heading for the car, a crow swooped down and ate the crackers. While Iris and her dad backed away, Lark just stood there and watched the bird alight and pick at the crumbs, and sometimes the crow looked up and eyed her right back. Friend or foe?

Lark was a friend, of course. And the next day she brought some Cheerios with her and *accidentally* trailed them all the way to the car. Two crows were there in an instant, taking turns so one could eat the Cheerios while the other observed the family.

They must have liked what they saw, for Lark kept dropping her snacks and the crows kept coming. This went on for a year, and soon the crows were flocking around Lark whenever she left the house.

They ignored Iris. They were not ever confused over which girl was which. Yes, crows can pick out faces—but they can see beneath the surface of things.

The girls were identical, but not the same.

After that, the crows started to leave presents in return.

One day Lark found a small silver washer by the birdbath.

A few days later, a screw.

After that, the tab from a pop can.

Seven-year-old Iris was suspicious. What were these crows doing? Why would they leave her sister these things? Did normal crows act this way? How did you know if a crow was abnormal?

And normal or abnormal, what did they want from her sister?

So Iris did what she did. She researched crows. And she discovered that crows are incredibly smart, that some of them even use tools. She discovered that they like shiny things, and that sometimes they bring these shiny things as gifts for people. These things were normal.

She also discovered that in some cultures, crows are considered a bad omen. And, as if to make that point even more clear, she discovered that the collective noun for crows is a *murder*.

Now, crows are much-misunderstood creatures. Humans, as a rule, are suspicious of things they do not understand, and crows are much smarter than anyone would like them to be. When your whole self-identity is wrapped up in being *the* species that can use tools, you don't really like it when you find out some bird is way ahead of you.

Crows remember things. And not just the things that happened to them—generations of crows have been known to avoid a spot where one crow was killed. For some reason, people find that unsettling.

If you cross one crow, another will hear about it. People call this gossip. But is it gossip if one member of a flock warns her fellows that someone is dangerous?

Is it?

Still, for Iris, none of it boded well.

So she told Lark. Bad omens! Freaky memories! A murder!

Lark thought it was cool.

She started collecting the gifts, though Iris did not think she should bring them inside. They were garbage, probably full of germs. Who knew where those things had been? But Lark only laughed. Maybe these things were garbage once, but to the crows they were treasure, and now they were treasure to her, too. She put each gift in a plastic bag and labeled it with the date and location, and kept the whole thing in a big plastic snap case under her bed. Sometimes she sorted them by date, sometimes by their location in the yard, sometimes by size. "Look," she'd giggle, "now I'm the organized one!"

As they grew older, Iris stopped being scared that the crows were up to something nefarious—omens were not real, of course, and one should not read too much into collective nouns. And yet, somewhere in the back of her head, some suspicion lingered.

And if Iris was suspicious of the crows, they seemed even more suspicious back. Like they knew she didn't like them, and they hated her now, and would hate her for generations to come.

Once, Lark tried to get Iris out to feed the crows with

her. "Let them see you doing it! They'll think you're on their side, then."

Iris was not sure if that was something she wanted them to think. "They won't like me."

"They'll like you if you feed them," Lark assured her.

"I don't think so. I think their hatred for me transcends snacks."

"That's silly."

"I don't see the point."

"Just . . . try, Iris? Please?"

Fine. It was important to Lark that Iris and her bad-omen murder of crows got along. So she went into the backyard and spread peanuts around the birdbath.

"Look at me! I'm a friend of the birds!"

"Iris, don't be sarcastic. They won't like it."

It was nowhere in any of the information that crows were particularly earnest. In fact, Iris was quite sure they were not.

But still, it was important to Lark, so Iris fed the crows with her for a week. Apparently, they did not like sarcasm. They continued to ignore Iris's existence, which was fine with her. She was happy to ignore them, too.

But they loved Lark.

Crows like shiny things.

Now Lark's collection had dozens and dozens of items in

it: buttons and bits of glass, a Barbie-sized glass slipper, paper clips and fishhooks, little stones and shells, silver necklace clasps, broken light-bulb pieces, a little ring, a blaster from an unspecified action figure, a crystal Lego, unidentifiable metal thingies, and even a small pebble shaped like a heart.

In fourth grade Mr. Anderson had had them do show-and-tell. Usually Lark tried to avoid it, as she did not like either showing or telling. But then she got the idea that if she brought in her crow collection, she wouldn't be so scared.

And when she got up to show her treasure chest, for once she didn't shrink in front of the class. She didn't exactly grow, either—she still didn't look at anyone, was still hard to hear—but this time it didn't seem like it was because she was terrified, but just that she was completely absorbed in the collection. She stood and talked about crows and showed her favorite gifts and told everyone how crows were so much smarter than everyone thought, how they told one another about danger, how they remembered for generations. She wasn't shrinking at all; she was herself. And for a moment Iris found herself slightly fond of the crows.

But something happened. Something popped in Tommy Whedon's mind and he murmured, "Freak." And everyone around him laughed. Both things hit Iris at once—the insult and the laughter. And then she saw them both hit her sister.

There is a special talent that some kids have to whisper

things that every kid in the class can hear but the teacher can't. It is a strange ability, and it's hard to imagine how it's really useful in the broader world, but if you are a mean kid in a fourth-grade classroom, it is everything. Tommy Whedon had this talent.

Mr. Anderson did not hear a thing, but Lark did, and red spread across her cheeks like a plague and she closed the plastic box holding her treasure and withered.

What was Iris to do? On the one hand, her sister was in distress, and she should comfort her. On the other hand, the person who'd caused her this distress was sitting two rows behind her.

Iris spun her head around and snapped, "You're a mole rat, Tommy."

But Iris did not have Tommy's magical ability, and kind Mr. Anderson heard, and looked at her as if she had disappointed him. And at recess Tommy told Iris she was nasty and ugly and bossy and no one liked her, and Lark didn't talk for the rest of the day. Somehow their parents got wind of the "mole rat" comment and Iris got a talking-to about name calling. Meanwhile people whispered *Freak* and *Crow Girl* at Lark for the rest of the year.

Iris blamed the crows.

That weekend, a crow left a small silver charm shaped like a moon right next to the birdbath. Lark put it on a string and wore it on her wrist for weeks; eventually her parents bought her a little chain for it so she could keep wearing it.

"This means I'm Crow Girl," Lark said to Iris. "But it's a secret."

Now the collection was under the bed, safe from other people's eyes. But the crows hadn't left anything since the silver moon. Lark still left food and checked the yard faithfully, because she was faithful, even if crows were not.

Sometimes Iris had nightmares of a whole murder of crows swirling around her sister, cawing *Freak* and *Crow Girl*, so many of them they darkened the sky, so many of them she couldn't see Lark anymore. Then she shouted and clapped her hands and they dispersed. But Lark was gone.

They were just nightmares, just Iris's mind spinning shadows into monsters. She knew that.

Still. She was fine if the shadows stayed away.

CHAPTER THIRTEEN

Camp Awesome

On Monday after school Lark headed down to the art room and Iris rode the bus to the library for the next exciting stage of growing as an individual. She had not been to the public library since the day the school envelopes came, when they'd stood outside Treasure Hunters and met the mustard mole man. Indeed, she'd forgotten all about the store, and him. She had so many other things to worry about, most immediately the next ninety minutes of her life.

Her bike was waiting for her there in the bike rack, just as they'd planned, so she could bike home afterward. This would work until it was winter, at least, and maybe by then her parents would have gotten over this ridiculous idea.

Until then, though, she was going to have to grin and bear it.

Or at least bear it.

She walked into the community room of the library to find the eyes of seven other girls move to her. At school she'd been ignored for being utterly boring; now she was walking into a group of people who didn't even know the most important thing about her, who didn't even know what was missing. And suddenly she was being examined, not for being a matching set, but for who she was alone.

As if that was interesting at all.

She slid in next to a pale girl with cat-eye sparkly glasses and curly black hair piled on the top of her head. The girl wore a black-and-white polka-dotted sweater and a Raven-claw T-shirt and gave Iris a big grin.

"Hannah!" she whispered, as if it were a very important secret.

"Iris," Iris whispered back.

"Ah." She nodded knowingly. "Like the messenger goddess."

"Yeah," Iris said. It was true. Iris was the name of Hera's messenger in Greek myths, and she was also the goddess of rainbows. Lark always found this hilarious, because if Iris Maguire were going to be the goddess of anything, it probably wouldn't be rainbows.

"I like your dress. *Wise* choice," she said meaningfully.

With Lark still dressing like she came from a colorless world, Iris had decided she needed to bring a little spark back to things, so today she was wearing the dress with the dubious-looking owl. Iris was no less dubious than she had been the week before.

"Thank you. I like your shirt."

"Are you Ravenclaw too?"

"I don't think so." She wasn't. Lark had made her take the test once. She was all Gryffindor, which Lark said was completely obvious because she liked to run headfirst into battle and had no common sense.

A suspiciously cheerful pink-cheeked college-age girl bounced in front of the room, long brown ponytail bouncing with her. She clapped her hands excitedly and announced she was named Abigail and she was Camp Awesome's counselor, and it was her job to help show them awesome things and, more importantly, show them how awesome they were.

Abigail announced they were going to start off with a game of Two Truths and a Lie, a fun get-to-know-you exercise, in Abigail's words. But Abigail said everything as if it had an exclamation point afterward, so it was more like Two Truths and a Lie! A fun get-to-know-you exercise!

In Two Truths and a Lie, you introduce yourself and say three "fun facts" about yourself—except one of those things is a lie and everyone has to guess which one. (!)

For some reason, Iris had no trouble spotting the other girls' lies.

Hannah did not go to circus school.

Preeti had never stuffed ten olives in her mouth on a dare.

Amma had never had a pet frog.

Novalie had never been to Disney World.

Gabrielle had not been on *Kids Baking Championship*.

And Iris had no trouble thinking of lies about herself: *I have thirty-seven fish! I can play the harmonica! I'm on the robotics team at school! My school has a robotics team!*

But truths were harder. They were slippery things: they needed to be caught and held tightly so they didn't fall away.

"I uh . . . have thirty-seven fish, my dad is living in London for the year, and I have an identical twin."

"That's the lie," exclaimed one of the girls—Morgan, a brown-skinned girl with freckles, who had never plotted a coup. "That you're a twin."

The other girls nodded.

Iris gaped at them. Wasn't it obvious? "No, I do have a twin sister. Lark."

Morgan leaned back in her chair, wide-eyed. "That's so cool."

"What's it like having a twin?" the girl on her other side

whispered. It was Emily—a skinny suntanned fourth grader in a softball T-shirt and baggy gym shorts, who was not allergic to people.

Iris didn't have a better answer for this than she did the week before. "Good?"

Ten minutes into camp and she'd proven herself uninteresting.

"Do you guys dress alike?"

"No."

"Did you ever switch places?"

"No."

"Does your mom ever have trouble telling you apart?"

"No."

"Huh," Emily said.

"I didn't think people would think that was my lie," Iris said. "I thought thirty-seven fish was kind of an obvious lie."

Next to her, Hannah leaned in and whispered, "I have twenty-six snails."

Iris looked at the table. That had not come up in Two Truths and a Lie. Hannah, apparently, had so many interesting things about her that having over two dozen snails was an afterthought.

"I started with two," Hannah continued, "but then . . . you know snails."

Iris did not know snails, not like that. But she certainly

was going to look it up later.

Now that the get-to-know-you exercise was over, Iris started rummaging through her backpack looking for her pen while Abigail bounced around the room passing out composition books and talking about something Iris realized she should probably be paying attention to, but wasn't.

"What's wrong?" Hannah whispered.

"I can't find my pen!" Iris said.

Hannah started slightly, as if she was not expecting Iris to sound so upset about office supplies. "I have pens," she said in soothing tones, handing one to Iris. "Lots of them. It will be okay."

"Thank you," Iris said. "I just . . . I don't usually lose things."

"Oh." Hannah nodded knowingly. "Portal, probably." And with that she gave Iris a quick smile and turned her attention back to Abigail.

The composition books were, Abigail said, courtesy of Camp Awesome, and the girls should always have them out while camp was in session and should feel free to write anything they wanted—any thoughts or feelings or ideas or inspirations or motivational phrases, anything that came to them. And most days they'd begin with "journaling," which Abigail explained was the process of spending time writing personal things in your journals. Why she couldn't just say it that way, Iris didn't know, but adults, apparently, were fond of making up verbs to suit their own purposes. And thus she opened up her new composition book and wrote:

> Adults like to make up verbs to suit their own purposes.

At Abigail's instruction the girls set to work decorating their composition books, and soon the room was full of the smell of glue sticks and Sharpies, the snip of scissors and the low mutterings of girls talking to themselves here and there. For inspiration, Abigail showed some of her own notebooks, on which she'd pasted a series of motivational phrases cut out of magazines, like a self-actualized ransom note.

Iris flipped from her blank cover to the sentence she'd written on the first page. She squinted at it, and then added the next line:

> Journaling

She tapped the pen on the paper and then wrote:

> Gifting
> Friending

And of course, from her dad:

Dialoguing

The words looked funny in the ink from Hannah's light blue pen. It wasn't the right color and the writing didn't flow. Iris liked her own pens: weighty, with a smooth gray exterior, flowing dark blue ink, a good grip, and a thick enough tip that the words you wrote looked like they mattered. Her parents had gotten a set for her for Christmas the year before; they even had a silhouette of an iris imprinted on the cap. But her pen was gone.

Next to her Hannah was drawing some intricate flower design on the cover of her book, while on her other side Amma was cutting out a model's eye from a magazine ad. Iris flipped back to her blank cover and stared at it, while everyone snip-squeaked-stuck around her. This should not be hard, she told herself. It was just a notebook.

But it was hard.

Amma looked up and caught Iris watching. "Do you want some eyes?" she asked, motioning to the growing pile of cut-outs in front of her. "I have a lot of them."

"Oh, thanks. I just . . . wouldn't know what to do with them. I don't really know what to do at all."

"Whatever you want!"

"I know, but . . . I don't want not to like it." Once you

drew a line in a gold Sharpie, that was it: that line was on your composition book for the rest of time.

No one else seemed to have a problem committing themselves. Amma was making a pinwheel shape out of the eyes, which was not something that would have ever occurred to Iris. Hannah's flowers had morphed into peculiar birds, the kind a witch might send out to look for you if she were so inclined. Preeti was adding whiskers to a giant silver cat; Novalie was turning glitter blobs into sparkly monsters; Emily had covered her pages in rows and rows of reveling stick figures; and Gabrielle had pasted phrases onto hers— Iris saw ONCE UPON A TIME and WHEN ROBOTS DREAM and MAGIC SCATTERED EVERYWHERE.

Lark would have loved it.

They all looked so studious, so determined, so focused. They looked like girls with purpose. It wasn't like Iris didn't have a purpose—she did, but Being Lark's Twin wasn't something you could paste on a journal. So Iris sat there, staring at the blank cover, chin propped in her hands.

"What's wrong?" As if magically summoned by Iris's not-Awesome mood, Abigail was before her, gesturing toward Iris's blank book.

"Oh," Iris said. "I'm not good at art."

"But! It's not about being good at something. It's about being yourself!"

"I just . . ."

Abigail eyed her, ponytail swinging slightly in a nonexistent breeze. "Don't think of it as art. Sometimes art is a lot of pressure. Just think of it as crafting. Crafting is for fun!"

When Abigail moved on, Iris flipped back to the page in her book and wrote down:

Crafting

CHAPTER FOURTEEN

Alice

After camp was over, all the girls gathered in the lobby waiting for rides, shifting a little on their feet, not quite sure where to stand. It was only the first day, and no one knew yet how the girls would arrange themselves over the course of the camp—a series of open circles, or in tight sharp immovable shapes. One way or another geometry would have its hold on them, but for now they all shuffled and giggled and looked curiously into one another's bright open faces.

As for Iris, she had no ride to wait for, so she slipped past the group on the outskirts of the lobby and wandered outside. She knelt down and spun the lock on her bike chain, but then stopped, stood, and squinted down the street. It was hot out still, too hot to bike up the hills between the library and home.

Across the street, a teenager yelled something in front of the candy store. Like most of the other stores on Upton Avenue, that one had been there as long as the girls could remember, with its toxically bright awning and giant sign in curlicue letters reading Treatz, as if an *s* were just too ordinary a letter to describe the wonders that lay inside, as if the regular conventions of language simply weren't sufficient for this particular store. There was the butcher shop, which advertised ostrich, which apparently people were supposed to eat. Iris found this too disgusting to consider further; Lark had once said she wanted to find the secret ostrich farm and liberate all the prisoners. There was a store filled with what her mother called bric-a-brac—that meant useless things like fancy dish towels and tiny vases and impractical plates that their mom said were decorative but the girls guessed were what you would use to serve the ostrich.

Lark loved that last store: she liked to walk into it and admire the goods inside as if she herself were searching for the perfect vase (which Lark said fancy people pronounced *vahz*) to accent her living room, the ideal decorative plate for the sort of person who wanted to decorate with plates. She walked around examining each trinket as if she were the interior designer for a grand castle. She'd turn over figurines while the store clerk watched warily. Lark didn't even notice, but Iris did; Iris could see the clerk's eyes turn over the twins as if decorating a castle with a whole room of girls.

And then there was the new store, Treasure Hunters, with the weird mustard mole man. It looked like it was open now, though no one was walking in or out. The chalkboard easel on the sidewalk no longer read We Are Here, but rather:

ALICE, WHERE ARE YOU?

(I know what you are going to ask. Yes, this is how it always happened.)

Iris squinted, as if the words might rearrange themselves into something sensical, something like Open Till Eight or Huge Sale on Tiny Teacups. But they did not.

ALICE, WHERE ARE YOU?

Iris chewed on her lip, eyeing the sign. And then crossed the street to the store.

Iris was not in the habit of going to antique stores, but if you'd asked her what one might look like, she'd probably have described something a lot like the interior of Treasure Hunters—dimly lit, little chimes ringing as soon as you walked inside, and stuff everywhere. Like your grandmother's attic, if you had the sort of grandmother who kept things. Iris's grandmother was not this sort—the only things she kept were books on decluttering—but she could imagine that this sort of grandmother did exist.

You would not know from the inside that the store hadn't been around long. Sometimes you pull a book from the library shelf and you suddenly feel like you've woken it up from a long sleep: the book opens tentatively; the pages turn slowly and stiffly, as if only dimly remembering that that was once their function. This is how the store felt.

There was furniture everywhere, odd art on the walls, vases big and small, a whole display case full of decorative plates. Treasure Hunters was where you went, apparently, when you wanted used bric-a-brac. One wall was full of clocks. On one bureau was a collection of creepy old dolls, the sort of dolls with stiff dresses and perpetually dazed expressions that people buy for children and then inform them the dolls are not to be played with. Some adults do things like that.

A few moments after Iris entered, the mole-faced man, now in a mustard vest and plaid shirt, emerged from a room in the back and moved behind the tall glass counter.

If he remembered Iris at all, his face didn't show it. Perhaps he did not recognize her when she wasn't in *a matching set*. The only thing on his face was suspicion, though that was a feeling Iris could relate to.

It's strange when you're the only customer in a store and a man in mustard clothing is watching you. You can't just turn around and leave, because that would be weird. But it's weird that you're there in the first place: you're an eleven-year-old girl, and the mole man knows an eleven-year-old girl doesn't belong in an antique store by herself, and you know it too but neither of you is going to say anything. And you can't say, *I don't know why I'm here either but your sign was weird before and it just got weirder, and now I want to know where Alice is too, and it is not nice when things get lost.*

Instead you're going to walk around and pretend to browse for whatever is a normal amount of time for a normal person to be in a store for normal reasons, hoping desperately the mole man doesn't speak to you, and then smile and nod and rush out and never come back.

"May I help you?" the mole man asked.

So that did not work. Iris turned to him, sticking her chin up in the air. "Yes, you can. I was wondering what your sign meant."

He looked around at the store. "Which sign?"

"The chalkboard one. Outside."

His eyes narrowed. "That is not for you."

"But . . . it's on a public sidewalk!" She blinked. "It's a *sign*!"

"Actually, that sidewalk is store property."

"But—" She stopped. He was squinting at her like she was the bottom line of an eye chart. "Never mind."

"I shan't. Are you looking for anything in particular *inside the store*?" He articulated these last three words very carefully.

"Um . . . just . . . dolls," she said, waving at the creepy collection above her, as if she was actually interested in them.

"Ah, yes, to be sure. Well, those are not for playing with."

Right. "So . . . who's Alice, anyway?"

"How do you know about Alice?"

"It's on the sign! On the public sidewalk!"

Her eyes fell to a glass bowl on the counter. It was filled with water and had something floating in it. She took a step closer. The something appeared to be a slice of cork with a needle stuck in it, and it was spinning in a circle.

Iris knew what this was. Once, she got a book on homemade science experiments from the library, and she did them in the backyard until her homemade volcano burst all over her dad's hydrangeas. One of the experiments was about making your own compass, and this looked just like that—a magnetized needle floating in a bowl of water. But it was not the sort of thing she expected a grown-up to have, and definitely not a shopkeeper.

"Can't you just buy a real compass?"

"I beg your pardon?"

She nodded toward the bowl. The needle was still quivering on its axis, as if searching for something.

The man's face scrunched up. "Well, that is an adorable whimsy. A compass! I never! Children are so imaginative."

"That's not a compass?"

"No! What an absurd idea!"

Iris straightened. "That is how you make a compass. I've done it!"

"Oh, I'm sure."

"I have! You magnetize the needle! It's science!"

"Right, of course. Science."

Iris's mouth opened and closed a few times. "You don't believe me?" she finally said.

"Oh, naturally I do. Yes, you made a compass! With science! Brava!"

He didn't believe her. That was clear. Iris gaped at him. She didn't know which was more angering: that he didn't believe her or that he didn't know anything about science.

"So . . . what is that, then, if it's not a compass?"

"It's magic, of course!" he said. And then covered his

mouth with his hands dramatically. "I shouldn't have said that."

Iris threw up her hands. "All right!" It was definitely time to go home. She opened the door, the chimes singing, and added, "I hope you find Alice, whoever she is."

The man glanced down at the not-compass. "As do I."

Iris's sojourn to the antique store hadn't satisfied her curiosity at all, but at least now, finally, something interesting had happened to her, something she could share with her sister that wasn't gray mush and uncomfortable seats.

And so, that night the girls sat on Lark's bed, while Iris fiddled with Esmeralda's tail and told her story.

"Remember the antique store?"

"Oh, the one with the chalkboard sign? 'We Are Here'?"

"That one. Well, the sign's changed. I saw it leaving the library today. It says 'Alice, Where Are You?'"

Lark sat back against the wall. "Wow."

"I know."

"That is not a good sign for a business either."

"I know."

"I wonder what it means."

"Well, I went in and asked."

Lark grinned. "Of course you did."

"And that weird guy was in there. And he wouldn't tell

me! He asked me how I knew about Alice."

"Um, because it was on the sign?"

"Yeah! That's what I said. He acted like I'd invaded his privacy or something."

"Iris, I feel the antique-store guy may be a touch odd."

"He was also doing the compass experiment—you know with the water bowl and the needle? Except he insisted it wasn't the compass experiment and he has never heard of the compass experiment."

"Okay . . ."

"He told me it was magic."

"Wow."

"Yeah. There's a bunch of creepy dolls in the shop, so I really hope they aren't magic too."

"Creepy, like how creepy? Creepy like they might be watching, or creepy like they might come alive and kill us all?"

Iris considered. "Somewhere in between, I think. Like they might be watching us and considering whether or not they want to kill us all."

"They have to wait and see how we act. Whether we're worth saving—"

"Or not." Iris added darkly. "So, what about art club? How was it?"

"Not bad, actually. We talked about a real painting for a

while. Ms. Messner showed us all the things it was doing with light and everything. And look"—Lark grabbed a framed photo of the two of them at Valleyfair—"art has positive and negative space, right? Positive space is the focus and negative space is the background. So in this picture we're the positive space and everything around us is negative space."

"That's for sure."

"But the negative space is part of the art too. So we're going to do projects with negative space this week."

". . . I don't know what that means."

Lark giggled. "Me neither!"

"So who's in the class? Are they okay?"

"Um . . ." Lark bit her lip. "It's fine. The Naomis are in there. Dexter. Not Tommy! And um . . . other kids? I wasn't really paying attention to them. What about Camp Awesome? Did you figure out what it was for, exactly?"

Iris sighed epically. "I'm not sure it's for anything. I mean, we have journals, that's all I know. So we're going to spend each day *journaling*."

She hit the verb-made-out-of-a-noun a little hard, but Lark did not react. Lark was used to making things out of other things.

"Can't you do that at home?"

"I don't know." Iris pulled at a thread coming out of the owl's eye. "Apparently it's more awesome to do it in a group.

Today we just decorated the journals."

Lark sat up, face bright and open. "Ooooh, what did you do?"

"Um, nothing."

"Iris!"

"I couldn't think of anything! There were all these glue sticks. It was a lot of pressure."

"We could do it now."

"No. That's okay."

"Why not? I have stuff." She spread her arms out to indicate the entire room, possibly the world.

Iris opened her eyes wide in mock surprise. "What? You have art stuff?"

Lark poked her. "Come on, let's do it."

"I just don't feel like it."

"Boring." But she didn't ask again, as Iris knew she wouldn't. "So what about the other girls? Are they nice?"

"I don't think they like me."

"Iris . . ."

"I mean it."

"Did you talk about assassinations again?"

Now it was Iris's turn to laugh. "Not this time. "

Lark wrinkled her nose. "Mr. Hunt would probably love it if you did that. I think he really likes murder-related stuff."

It was the first she'd mentioned her new teacher since the

previous week, and Iris hadn't asked about him. It was so unfair that she got the nice teacher and Lark was stuck with someone who scared her so much she couldn't even come up with any hobbies—Iris couldn't bring herself to mention it.

"Is he still being an ogre?"

"Yes. I have to give a book report next week."

"Out loud?"

Lark nodded.

"Uh-oh."

Lark liked books, but she did not like talking about them in front of the class. Or about anything else. She turned bright red and looked at the floor and her voice got quieter and quieter and she seemed to shrink down into a miniature Lark, one who was way too tiny to give book reports or even attend school safely. It is hard to watch your sister shrink. By winter last year Mr. Anderson had started to forget to call on her on oral report days. *Oh, Lark, we ran out of time! Just give me a written report.*

"He's so loud, too. His voice is like—" She threw her hands out in the air. "And we started doing math drills. Like we all stand up and he throws problems at us and if we get them wrong we have to sit and the person who's left standing wins. So we're supposed to want to win, like that's motivating. I don't want to win! I don't want to play. I don't see how doing math while someone yells at you is an important skill." While Lark talked, her cheeks were getting redder and redder. "And everyone else likes him fine. Tommy Whedon loves him. Tommy wins math drills."

"Tommy Whedon," proclaimed Iris, "is a blowfish."

A slow grin spread across Lark's face. "I thought he was a mole rat."

"He's both. He's a blowfish and a mole rat. He's a blowrat. Is he bothering you?"

"Not really." Lark glanced at her sister. "You're not going to, like, do anything, are you?"

"Not if he's not bothering you. The good thing is, if Mr. Hunt is really an ogre and he collects your heart, Mom and Dad are going to be really sorry."

Lark sighed ruefully. "That's comforting, anyway."

"We tried to tell them. But they didn't listen. And now..."

Lark slid down to the dollhouse and picked up one of the girl figures from her moon campfire.

"Mom, Dad," she said, waving the doll around. "My fifth-grade teacher is an ogre."

Iris slid down next to her and picked up the other girl doll. "I told you. I told you Principal Peter didn't do a background check."

Lark cleared her throat and picked up the mom doll. "Now, girls. Don't let your imaginations get control of you."

"You know these girls and their imaginations!" said the

dad doll, in Lark's other hand. "Well! I'm off to London!"

Iris laughed. The real Iris, not the doll.

"Bye, honey," said Lark/Mom. "Oh, girls. Monsters aren't real. That's very silly. Now excuse me. I need to go do something in the spider room." And the mom doll trotted down the stairs and headed for the haunted room.

"But," the Lark doll called after her, "what if he takes my heart?"

At this, Iris put her doll down and looked her sister in the eye.

"He can't take your heart," she said firmly. "You're Lark Maguire. You're the girl who defeats the ogres."

CHAPTER FIFTEEN

Meanwhile . . .

I n the heart of Minneapolis, just off of downtown, sits
one of the preeminent contemporary art museums in the
country. It began as a room in the mansion of lumber baron
T. B. Walker, which he designed in order to make the best
pieces of his substantial art collection open to the public,
and then he expanded it to fourteen rooms, and then eventually he built his own museum.

That, too, was the sort of thing very rich people did back
then.

Eventually the museum devoted itself to preserving and
creating modern art—not just painting and sculpture, but
performance and film. And then the head of the Walker Art
Center decided to expand the gallery to the outdoors, where

art and weather could interact over Minnesota's changing seasons, where people could interact with art, where kids could climb on sculptures and birds could perch atop them and dogs could frolic around them. Now the Minneapolis Sculpture Garden is home to more than forty outdoor sculptures across eleven acres, but the most famous one had been there from the beginning.

The sculptor Claes Oldenburg liked spoons. And really giant sculptures. And so when he was commissioned to make a fountain sculpture for the garden, he planned one of a giant spoon stretching over a small pond.

His wife, Coojse van Bruggen, looked at the plan and said, "Needs fruit." And thus *Spoonbridge and Cherry* was born.

The spoon with the cherry perched atop its bowl became the iconic symbol of Minneapolis. Its value was astonishing. Not that anyone could ever sell it. Not that anyone could ever steal it.

How could you? It in itself was the size of a giant truck, weighing about seven thousand pounds. You would need trucks, cranes, a crew of people to move it. And the garden was under constant video surveillance.

On the night the sculpture disappeared, the video showed a man entering the garden, a small briefcase at his side. Then the video skipped, and when the image clarified, all that could be seen was the small pool.

Spoonbridge and Cherry was gone.

CHAPTER SIXTEEN

Parts of Speech

So, all too quickly, the school year settled into its inevitable rhythm, and what had once been inconceivable soon became everyday reality. For Iris, the very structure of the school day—once comforting—felt oppressive. Every day would be like this. Reading. Gym. Math. Lunch. Specials. Science. Social studies. Bus. Camp Awesome. None of it with Lark. All of it feeling like she was this weird twitchy ghost.

Mostly she tried not to talk to anyone, as there didn't seem to be anything worth saying, and weird twitchy ghosts did not talk. But she couldn't always help it. For instance, each day right before lunch they had Pod Time, which involved some sort of discussion or activity with your *pod*—the collective noun for students in a cluster of desks in Ms. Shonubi's room. Today in Pod Time everyone was supposed to name a place they wanted to visit and tell the group why. This would, Iris suspected, be one of those assignments that seemed innocent on its face but would eventually lead to some kind of Pod-based project involving poster board and glue sticks and uncomfortable conversations about who should do the lettering and Iris having to find a way to correct people when they got the state flower wrong without them thinking she was a know-it-all, or, worse, ignoring her and getting the state flower wrong anyway, and either way someone telling her she was too *bossy*. Because you just can't win with group projects.

But, for now, Jin was explaining how much he wanted to go to Orlando to see the Wizarding World of Harry Potter and ride on the Incredible Hulk Coaster, and Mira said that her grandparents wintered down there, by which she meant they spent winters down there so consistently that it was a verb, and so Iris surreptitiously got out her Awesome journal and flipped open to the verb page and added:

Wintering

She bit her lip and studied the list. Snippets from her dad's work calls ran through the back of her head. The calls were way too boring to pay attention to and tended to be conducted in a language that sounded like English but none of the words were used in the right way. But now those words had a use:

Incentivizing
Workshopping
Bucketizing

"What are you doing?" Oliver asked.

"Me?" Iris looked up. "Nothing."

"This is Pod Time!" Mira said. "I don't think you're supposed to be writing things down."

Meanwhile, Oliver had leaned all the way over and was reading her journal. "'Crafting,'" he read. "Actually, that's not a made-up verb. It's a verb already. To craft: to make something with care and skill."

Iris narrowed her eyes. "What, do you read the dictionary for fun?"

"Maybe."

"Anyway," she said, straightening, "I know it's a verb like that. But not like Abig—not like this girl was using it. She meant crafting, like doing crafts. There's already a way of saying that." He looked at her blankly. "Doing crafts!"

He frowned. "But if you're making those crafts with care and skill—"

"No! It doesn't work like that. In the world of *actual words* used in the *actual right way* you don't say 'I crafted' and leave it at that. You have to craft *something*."

"Guys," Mira whispered.

"Oh." Oliver adjusted his bow tie sagaciously. "It's a transitive verb and they're making it intransitive. You should put an asterisk by that one, like—" He reached for her journal.

"Hey," she said, sweeping the journal shut. "That's private!"

He raised his eyebrows. "Your list of made-up verbs and one transitive verb used incorrectly is private?"

"Guys!" Mira's voice was a hiss now. "We're supposed to be discussing places! Also you guys are being really really boring."

"Maybe you could go to a dictionary theme park," Jin added.

Mira snorted. "Grammar World!"

"There could be a haunted house with whiches," Jin said, giggling. "Get it? Not witches, but whiches?"

"That would be Homophone World," Oliver corrected.

"You could ride the train at the Railroad Conjunction!" Mira said.

"Yeah, the *but* train," Jin said.

Iris tapped her foot on the floor. She did not want to go to a dictionary theme park. And she certainly did not want to go anywhere with Oliver, who would probably put asterisks on the rides and explain that they were not really roller coasters but intransitive coasters, whatever that meant.

If Lark had been there she could have tapped a message to her about the whole conversation and Lark would have rolled her eyes in solidarity. Or, Lark would have tapped out her own syntax puns that were way better than these, and Iris could have rolled *her* eyes in solidarity. But now she had to sit and suffer in silence, both actual and figurative.

If someone annoys you in class but your sister isn't there to tell about it, did it really happen?

"How's it going over there?" Ms. Shonubi called.

"Fine!" Mira said, glaring at them. "What about you, Iris?" she said pointedly. "Where would you want to go?"

With a sigh, Iris closed her journal. "Um, London, I guess."

"London, England?" Oliver asked.

"Obviously. Is there another one?"

"There's one in Canada. And Ohio. I also read atlases for fun."

(What Oliver said was true. Iris looked up other Londons later and made a list in her Awesome book. There were also ones in South America and Africa and all over the United States, including a London in California that wasn't a town but rather a "census-designated place," whatever that meant. Like, there's a guy out there who looks at a map and says, *I hereby designate this a place!* And all the other areas of the map are like, *Can we be places too?* And the guy says, *Nope, sorry. Maybe someday, if you dream.*)

"Well," Iris said, "I mean London, England. My dad's living there right now."

Jin's eyes went big. "Your parents got divorced?"

Iris blinked. "No."

"Are they getting divorced?"

"No, he's just working there for a while. Then he's coming back."

Iris glared at Jin. Her parents weren't getting divorced. It was just her dad's job. He was coming back. When their parents had sat them down to tell them that this was happening, that he was just going to be out of the country for a few months and it was just part of his job and it would go by so fast and he would call them every day and be home before they knew it, they'd talked quickly and brightly and confidently, words tumbling out of their mouths like polished stones.

But now Iris had to wonder if they'd been talking like that to distract the girls, like waving something shiny in front of their faces so they'd miss the monster crawling toward them. Grown-ups pretend that if they don't talk about things, kids won't know they're there. But you do know, at least you know *something* is there: you can see the weird blank space where the things they aren't talking about are supposed to be and you can see that something is lurking just behind it but you know you are supposed to pretend you haven't noticed anything.

"My dad's coming back," Iris said definitively.

Jin gasped. "You had a premonition!"

"No. Not a premonition. His assignment ends in December."

Oliver turned to Jin. "I think it was a premonition too," he whispered.

"I heard that!"

"Can we just do the assignment?" Mira squeaked.

That afternoon, Iris didn't see Lark before getting on the bus to the library, though she wasn't sure what she would say if she did. Part of her wanted to tell her everything Jin had said and watch her sister for any sign that she believed it was the truth—but she couldn't do that to Lark. Why plant a seed like that in her sister, who had enough to worry about as it was? Especially since the seed had already sprouted into something tangled and awful inside Iris's brain.

So when she walked into Camp Awesome, the thing was with her—no longer growing but still twisting into something more and more menacing. But it was her secret; no one noticed a thing. Abigail beamed at her as if seeing Iris was the best thing that had happened to her all day.

Which could not possibly be true.

Hannah and Morgan both greeted her cheerfully, and she tried to look cheerful back. This took some thinking. What sort of thing did cheerful people do? Well, they smiled, so Iris tried that. They said hi, so Iris tried that, too. They asked friendly questions like *How are you?* and made nice comments like *I like your journal cover* and *That's a cool* Twins *shirt*. But Iris couldn't quite make those words come out, as there were so many of them and there was a thing in her brain and it seemed likely she might put the words in the wrong order.

Today's game was another get-to-know-you exercise. Abigail told them to *circle up*, and informed them she was in possession of a magical invisible ball—and here she held her hands out at beach-ball width, and shouted, "Catch!" and thrust her hands toward Emily. Emily just stared at her.

"Oh! Let me get my ball!" And Abigail ran behind Emily and mimed picking up her beach ball, then shouted, "Catch!" again, and threw it at Gabrielle.

Gabrielle did catch the ball, and Emily said, "Oh!" so Gabrielle tossed the invisible ball to her. Iris didn't blame Emily for being confused; why they couldn't use a real ball was beyond her, unless Abigail had spent all her budget on glitter glue.

The game was that they would toss the "ball" around, and

when someone threw the ball at you, you introduced your-self with your name and an adjective that started with the same letter as your name.

At that very moment, a whole alphabet's worth of adjectives popped in Iris's head, from Admirable Annalise to Zesty Zinnia—every letter but the one she needed, *I*.

Iris's brain stopped. The ball went around. One girl caught it, said her name, and then threw it, and the other girl repeated that name and said her own.

"I am Awesome Abigail!" (Throw.)

"Awesome Abigail . . . Amazing Amma!"

"Amazing Amma . . . Playful Preeti!"

Slowly, she regained the power of thought, and slowly some *I* adjectives popped to the front of her mind, all of them unacceptable. She wasn't going to say *intelligent*, because that's not the sort of thing you're supposed to say about yourself. There was *invisible*, but that was ridiculous, as Iris was standing right there and everyone could see her. Same with *imaginary*. And she did not wish to be *icy* or *icky*. Everyone had a name—Genuine Gabrielle, Maleficent Morgan, Haunting Hannah (here she made a ghost noise)—and then Nice Novalie hurled the invisible ball at her and her mouth opened and her mind turned to fuzz and what came out was:

"Indecisive Iris."

Silence. Iris's insides turned to slime.

To make it worse, she'd done it wrong. She hadn't followed the rules. She was supposed to repeat Nice Novalie, but she'd gotten so fuzzy she'd forgotten. Games have rules and you are supposed to follow the rules—that's how games work. And Novalie, Novalie was so nice that she just whispered, "Repeat my name" at Iris super quietly. But Iris was already hurling the invisible ball at Abigail again and it was all much, much too late.

Then, of course, Abigail wanted them to use the game to learn one another's names, so she pronounced "Energetic Emily!" and then threw the ball to Emily, who this time caught on and said, "Maleficent Morgan," giggling a little bit, and Morgan said, "Haunting Hannah," who then announced, "Indecisive Iris!" and this went on for a full five minutes.

When camp was over, Iris ducked out ahead of everyone else and went to the library computers and searched for *I* adjectives, intending to write them down in her journal in case this sort of thing ever happened to her again. Instead she ended up with a list of adjectives she could not use.

She was neither *illogical* nor *imaginative*; she did not wish to be *inexperienced* or *irresponsible*, *immature* or *infantile*; she did not feel *impressive*, *important*, or *impulsive*; and she really hoped she wasn't *immoral* or *irksome*. She certainly was a little *impatient* and maybe *irritable*, but they didn't sound like things she should advertise. And sometimes *impassioned*, but that hardly characterized her. *Igneous* was a kind of rock. Mostly the adjective that best described her was *itchy*.

She had been doomed from the beginning. Even the dictionary knew it.

Iris picked up her backpack, which now felt much heavier than before, like someone had snuck in a bunch of reference books while she wasn't looking, and wandered out of the library.

CHAPTER SEVENTEEN

Mr. George Green

I wonder what would have happened had Iris just biked home after Camp Awesome that day. Maybe she never would have gone back to Treasure Hunters again, and this story would have had a different ending. But there was something twisted in Iris's mind, and her brain was still focused on producing adjectives at random. Lark would ask her about her day and she would only be able to say, *Inane! Illogical! Isolating!* She had no stories for Lark; all she had were these useless adjectives and that poisonous seed from her discussion with her pod, desperate to spread.

And there was still the sign in front of the store:

ALICE,
WHERE
ARE
YOU?

So, again, she crossed the street to Treasure Hunters.

She stopped in front of the sign and studied the words, as if there might be some sense in them if she looked at them long enough, as if Alice herself might pop out and reassure Iris that she was all right, that nothing bad had happened to her, that girls did not ever walk off the edge of the earth never to be found again.

Out of the corner of her eye she caught a flash of black right above. A large crow had settled on the tree branch and was fluffing its wings and strutting and cawing loudly.

"What?" Iris said, craning her neck. She was in no mood.

The crow fluffed its wings some more and cawed again. Whatever it was saying, it did not sound like a compliment.

"You're loud and rude," Iris said.

She turned and was about to head into the shop when something small hit her on the head. As the big crow pranced around the tree branch, the acorn it had dropped on her bounced onto the sidewalk and rolled away.

"Hey!" Iris yelled.

The crow let out a weird croak and picked up another

acorn, so Iris glared at it and then escaped into the shop.

She really, really disliked crows.

As the bells on the front door chimed above her, Iris took in the shop. Today, she was aware of the way the sun touched the dust as it danced in the air. She was aware that the shop was darker than any other she'd been to, as if it had opted out of the light available to it. She was aware of the smell— of old things and something else, something earthy. And she was aware of the clutter of things everywhere, all of them with their own histories and stories to tell.

She was so aware of all these things that she was only dimly aware that the thing in her brain was untwisting, that her mind had stopped burping out adjectives fruitlessly, that she didn't feel itchy or uncomfortable or even indecisive.

So she began to look around. The shopkeeper emerged from the back room, today wearing a rust-orange crew-neck sweater with a yellow-and-orange plaid shirt underneath and brown corduroy pants.

He stopped when he saw her. "Oh, it's you again."

"Nice to see you, too!" she said brightly. "You don't like kids very much, do you?"

"On the contrary, I adore children. As long as they stay very still and don't touch anything."

In a way, Iris empathized with him, as she did not particularly like people touching her things either. Still, on principle, she ran her finger along one of the vases.

The not-compass was gone from the counter, replaced by a large brown Idaho potato perched on some kind of stand with wires coming out of either side, like a tuberous Frankenstein. The wires fed into something that looked like an ancient typewriter, and as Iris watched, one of the keys depressed and typed an *s*. And then the typewriter was still.

"Is that magic too?" she asked drily.

Again he fixed her with a meaningful look, as if daring her to react. "Yes, of course. What does it look like?"

"It's a potato battery." She had done that experiment too.

"I see. Yes, it is a"—he made quotes with his fingers—"*potato battery.*"

Just then, another key pressed on the typewriter: *d*.

"There's no need to be rude," Iris said. "You're the one telling me it's magic."

"And you, young lady, are telling me it's a *battery* made out of a *potato*." He gazed at her as if she were the most ridiculous person to have ever walked the earth.

Her parents would have been horrified by the way she was talking to this adult, but he did not seem to mind particularly. And there were so many adults in her life whom she couldn't tell how ridiculous they were acting; it was refreshing to have one for whom she could. "Is that what it's supposed to do?" she asked as another key was pressed: *x*.

The piece of paper under the roller showed that, so far, the typewriter had produced nothing but lines and lines of random letters.

"Not at all," he said. "But I am ever optimistic. Now, what may I help you with? Perhaps you'd like directions to a hardware store where they sell real batteries?"

Before Iris could say something sarcastic back, she caught some slippery movement in the shadows and started slightly. She did not believe in ghosts, of course, but if they did exist, this would seem like the exact kind of place they'd want to hang out.

But it was not a ghost at all. Back in the corner by the old clocks sat a long-haired calico cat, blinking impassively at Iris.

The cat was beautiful—she had a bright white belly and soft orange and gray spots with little tabby stripes rippling through them, wide green eyes, and big white whiskers that stuck out on either side of her face grandly. She looked as if she had many important things to say and that if you paid proper attention she just might say them to you.

"You have a cat?" Iris asked.

"Oh," he said. "Sometimes. Is she here?"

"She's"—Iris looked over at the grandfather clocks; the cat was batting at the minute hand on one of them—"yes." She glanced back at the shopkeeper to see whether or not he noticed what the cat was doing. It did not seem the sort of thing he would be happy about.

"That's Duchess. There's nothing I can do about her, I'm afraid. Cats cannot be controlled." He said this as if it were the worst possible thing he could say about any creature.

"Well, she—" Iris looked back again. The cat was gone. "Wait, she was just there."

"Pay no attention to her comings and goings." He leaned in and whispered conspiratorially, "That's what she wants you to do."

". . . Okay." She glanced back into the shadows for some last sign of the cat, but it was just gone.

"Now, may I help you with something?"

This would be the time to say, *No, thank you*, and go home. But in here it felt like all the clocks in her own life had stopped, and she really did not want them to start again.

"I just wanted to . . . look at the books?" she said, motioning to the bookshelves.

"Hmmm." He studied her carefully. "That seems reasonable. I'll tell you what; I will even let you touch some of them. The ones on"—he pointed—"those shelves. None of the rest of them. I imagine that pleases you, Miss . . . ?"

"Um, Iris. Maguire."

"A pleasure, Miss Maguire. I am Mr. George Green. You may browse." He smiled magnanimously, then added, "That bookshelf."

As Mr. George Green turned his attention to the typewriter, Iris wandered over to the wall he had indicated, gently laying a finger on various antiques along the way. When you got over the creepiness of the whole place, there were interesting things in there: a display case of swords, another of ornate pocket watches, a box of magazines with browning pages. But it was the books that called to her. They were leather-bound and gilt-edged with golden letters pressed on the spines, and they looked as if they contained real truths.

Mr. George Green did not seem to have much knowledge of actual kids and the things they might be interested in, so she wouldn't have been surprised if the bookshelf he'd given her permission to look at was full of early-twentieth-century philosophy textbooks or gardening treatises. But oddly enough he'd sent her to some rows of actual kids' books. Among them was a colorful atlas-sized hardback called *A Child's Guide to Our World*.

Iris opened it, turning the yellowed pages carefully. The copyright page told her it was from 1947. It could have belonged to her great-grandparents.

The book was like the shop, dusty and enticing, filled with entries about LUMBERING and THE DARK AGES and WONDERS OF THE SKY and of course MAN (by which it meant PEOPLE). It speculated that Mars might have plants, said that the universe had no beginning and no end, counted ninety-eight elements, and promised that a plan for world government was on the way. There were only four kingdoms of life, and it informed readers that it was hard to say what exactly "light" was.

Iris studied flags for countries that no longer existed, maps missing countries that existed now, dinosaurs that never existed even though people at the time thought they did. She knew, intellectually, that knowledge evolved and sometimes people believed the wrong thing. People had once thought the sun revolved around the earth.

Still. It was one thing to know that and another to look at a book from more than seventy years ago and read the contemporary equivalent of someone saying the earth was flat.

She wanted to run to Mr. Ntaba and show him the book, have him give her assurance that everything she'd learned the past few years was an actual fact, that some girl seventy years from now wouldn't be reading the books he'd given her, mesmerized by how wrong they were.

Whatever child had owned the book in 1947 had written notes in pencil here and there, circled entries, made little stars, even doodled. There was a sheet of lined paper pressed into the pages where the girl (Iris was sure it was a girl) had written *Nevermore* and drawn ravens all around. Occasionally she'd doodled on the pictures themselves—the Tyrannosaur was given angel wings, and George Washington now wore a big flowered hat as he crossed the icy Delaware River.

How long had Iris been there when Mr. Green cleared his throat and announced the store was closing? She had no idea—it really had felt like time had stopped, like the store was the sort of place where that could happen.

She popped up, and his eyes caught on the book she was reading.

"You like the real world, then?"

She nodded.

"You are a very practical girl, aren't you, Iris?"

She straightened. "Well . . . yes. I am."

"You don't often meet girls who are so practical. Most of them are so"—he searched for the word—"impractical."

"Well, I don't know if—"

"Yes, it is nice to meet such a sensible girl. You can come look at books anytime you wish, sensible girl."

"Thank you?"

"Just that shelf, though."

"Okay."

Iris flipped through the book one more time. There was so much she hadn't read, so many facts from the strange and dusty world of the last century. And the girl who had owned it—was she a grandmother now? Did she know that light had properties of both a particle and a wave, and that Jupiter had dozens of moons?

And there—on the inside cover, that girl had written her name.

THIS BOOK BELONGS TO ALICE.

Iris stared at the letters until she felt Mr. Green's eyes on her. Pretending like it was nothing at all, she closed the book and put it back on the shelf.

When Iris finally got home, she discovered that her sister was sitting on the step outside the back door, hugging her knees to her chest, eyes red.

"What's wrong?" Iris asked, running to her. "What are you doing out here?

"I lost my key," Lark said. "I'm locked out."

Iris's face went hot. "Oh, no."

"I don't understand where my key is," Lark said. "I checked my backpack this morning and it was there. How could I have lost it?"

"Maybe it's on the counter? Or it fell on the floor?"

"No! No, it's not." She looked up at her sister. "I said I checked my backpack this morning and saw it." Lark's eyes were flashing.

"I . . . uh . . . I know. I just thought, maybe—"

"You thought maybe I'm not remembering right? Maybe

I don't even know what day it is? How come when *you* lose something it's completely impossible, but when *I* do I probably left it on the counter?" Lark's jaw was set now, and that was trouble.

Iris looked at the step. "Sorry." She didn't mean any of it as an insult. It was just the way of things, that was all: Lark lost things and Iris found them. Lark was too busy making campfires on the moon to keep track of things, and it was better to be the person who made campfires on the moon. Anyone could keep track of stuff.

"Why were you so late? I've been out here forever."

Iris opened her mouth. Why was she so late? Because they'd talked about London in Pod Time and then Jin had planted a seed, and because they'd played a get-to-know-you game at Camp Awesome and she was Indecisive Iris. She was late because she'd wanted to be in a place where the clock stopped for a while, and because she'd been looking at a book of old facts that weren't facts anymore at all. She was late because she felt like a pinball being bounced around against her will, and pinballs cannot control when they get home.

"Camp . . . went late," she said.

Lark squinted at her and Iris looked away.

"I was worried," Lark said quietly. "You're supposed to be home before I am." Her voice tightened. "I thought you must have gotten hit by a car, or—"

"No, no. No." It felt like something was grinding up her stomach. She was supposed to be the one who made Lark feel better, not the one who left her locked out of the house and terrified. Everything was all wrong.

"Can we go inside, please?" Lark asked.

Iris pressed her lips together and nodded, blinking away tears.

"See? No key," Lark said when they got inside, motioning around the kitchen.

"It will turn up," Iris said.

Lark whirled around and glared at her. The grinder in Iris's stomach slowly churned.

"I have homework," Lark muttered, and turned on her heel and went upstairs.

Iris collapsed into a chair and put her head in her arms.

When her mom came home a half hour later, Iris had removed her head from the table and was trying to do a math worksheet. It actually made her feel a little better— these were problems she could solve, over and over, a whole worksheet of them.

Though apparently none of that showed on her face.

"What's wrong?" her mom asked, settling in at the kitchen table.

Iris looked at the table. There was nothing to do but just

say it. "Are you and Dad getting a divorce?"

"What? No! Why would you ask that?"

Iris folded her arms around her chest. "Would you tell me if you were?"

"Honestly, honey, I can't even answer that because I have no idea what I would be doing."

For some reason, that was the most reassuring thing her mom could have said. "Okay," Iris whispered.

"Where did you get that idea?"

"Someone at school. He thought if Dad was in London you guys might be getting divorced."

Her mom's lips disappeared. After a moment, she said, "Well, it is an unusual situation. But your father had to go. I can see why you might worry that something was really wrong, and we should have worked harder to make that clear. I'm sorry."

Iris didn't know what to say. She'd spent so much energy being mad at her parents lately, and now her mom was acting perfectly reasonable and even apologizing. What was she supposed to do with that?

"Did you tell Lark you were worried about this?" her mom asked.

Iris shook her head.

She leaned back. "Good. She'd spin it into this whole *Parent Trap* thing where your dad took you to England and I kept her here and you didn't see each other ever again until you both mysteriously ended up at the same summer camp."

"Wait, why am I the one going to England with Dad?"

"Because Lark would send you to the interesting place."

This was very true. "I have another question."

"Shoot."

"Is there stuff you learned at school that you found out later wasn't true? Like everybody believed one thing and they were wrong?"

"Well"—she blinked at Iris—"sure. I mean, you know about Pluto, right?"

Yes, Iris knew about Pluto. Once upon a time there were nine planets in the solar system, and schoolkids memorized them in order: Mercury, Venus, Earth, Mars, Jupiter, Saturn, Uranus, Neptune, Pluto. And then, a little before the girls were born, it was announced that Pluto wasn't a planet anymore. There are eight planets, that is all. That hunk of ice out there? Pay no attention to it.

"Also," her mom added, "as far as anyone knew, there were only, like, five dinosaurs. Five kinds, I mean."

"Which ones?"

"Oh, let's see . . . the T. rex, of course. Stegosaurus. Triceratops. Pterodactyl. And the brontosaurus. Which was always my favorite. And I think doesn't exist anymore?"

Iris shook her head. "I don't think there's a pterodactyl, either."

"Really?"

"No. They're called pterosaurs now. And I don't think they're really dinosaurs at all."

"Hmmpf."

"So . . . when you learned these things weren't true, did it bother you?"

"Well, I just learned about the pterodactyl, so I'm going to need time to adjust to that." She tilted her head. "The Pluto thing was weird. It was just in the newspaper one day: Scientists Declare Pluto Not a Planet Anymore. I guess I never thought that that was a mistake you could make, you know? But then you realize the whole idea of a planet is made up by a bunch of people in a room anyway, and . . ." She shrugged. "And I did like the brontosaurus. It seemed like the nice dinosaur amidst all the ones with the teeth and claws and spikes, like if you got accidentally sent back to dinosaur time, that would be the one that you'd want to run into."

"But . . . isn't it weird?" Iris pressed. "That all of these things you learn can be wrong?"

"Sure! I mean, when I was a kid you were supposed to eat margarine, which was like . . . fake butter. It was supposed to be so much better for you. And then one day it was like, no, this is basically death in a stick. And suddenly we were supposed to eat butter again. So you can be doing what everyone tells you to do to be healthy, and then that's the thing that's bad for you."

"So what do you do?"

"I guess . . . we just do the best we can with the information we have, you know? And stay open to the idea that there's a lot we don't know."

Iris didn't have any trouble being open to the idea that there was a lot she didn't know. Every day was about all the things she didn't know.

It would just be nice to be able to believe in the things she did know.

"Honey, what's this about?"

Iris swallowed. "Weird day."

Her mom leaned in and took her hands in hers. "You can tell me anything, okay? And ask me anything. You know that, right?"

"Yeah," Iris said quietly. Her mom squeezed her hands, and that, at least, felt true.

Later, Iris knocked on Lark's door softly. Her sister was on her bed, Esmeralda on her chest, reading *Harry Potter and the Prisoner of Azkaban* for possibly the hundredth time.

"Hi," Iris said.

"Hi," said Lark hesitantly.

"I'm sorry," Iris said. She was. Very sorry. She shouldn't have been so late, and she shouldn't have dismissed Lark. She was supposed to be the one person who didn't do that kind of thing. "I'm really sorry."

Lark put down her book. "It's okay," she said.

"Can I come in and read with you?"

"Yeah."

A minute later Lark had scooted over on her bed and Iris had tucked herself in next to her. And here, again, was a place where time did not seem to matter, a pocket in the world to crawl into.

CHAPTER EIGHTEEN

The Edge of the World

There is one more story I should tell you.

When baby Iris and baby Lark were both finally home from the hospital, their parents were given strict instructions to keep them inside and isolated as much as possible until the end of April. There was some particular virus that flew around in the winter that caused most people to get bad colds but could be devastating for a premature baby's lungs. Consider it like a quarantine, the doctors said.

So for five months the girls and their mom stayed inside, only leaving the house for their doctor appointments. Lark had to go more often because of a condition that meant sometimes her lungs and heart just stopped working for a little bit. So she was attached to a monitor that beeped every time she stopped breathing or her heart stopped beating.

"We were supposed to wait to see if your body would figure it out and reset itself," their mom said when she told the story, "so when the alarm went off we were supposed to count to ten, then wake Lark up."

"What do you mean, wake her up?" Iris asked.

"Oh, well. Gently at first. Like, rubbing her face. And if that didn't work, maybe squeeze her arm."

"And what if none of it worked?"

"Then . . . we were supposed to do CPR."

"How do you do CPR on a baby?" Iris asked.

"Very carefully," her father said.

Their father could never manage to wait the full ten beeps before waking Lark up. "I made it to four once, though," he told them proudly.

The alarm used to go off all the time. The wires got crossed or the leads fell off and the thing would start beeping and Iris—herself a fully functioning something-is-wrong-with-Lark alarm—would shriek and both parents would run to their bedroom and find the machine broken but Lark was fine and eyeing them curiously, as if making scientific deductions about the effects of repeated loud beeping noises on fully grown humans.

Everyone wanted to come over and see the new babies,

and no one seemed to believe that the doctors' warnings could be legitimate. *Oh, I just have a little cough,* they'd say. *You guys are so paranoid!*

Their dad escorted his own aunt out of the house after she sneezed on Lark and insisted it was just allergies.

"It was a long winter," their mom said.

When the girls were two, that cold virus hit and got into their delicate lungs and the girls began to cough and wheeze, and they were both whisked off to the emergency room. There, a nice doctor with long, curly brown hair listened to their lungs and gave them each a small heating pad shaped like an animal—Iris a gray bunny, Lark a calico cat. Two hours later Iris and the bunny (named Bunny) were sent home, but Lark and the cat (named Esmeralda) were admitted and kept overnight. It happened again when they were four—each girl got a mask strapped about her nose and mouth and inhaled some medication that tasted like tinfoil. And Lark was admitted again, bringing Esmeralda with her.

Iris didn't remember much of any of this, though she knew that Great-Aunt Carol used to talk a lot about how her allergies flared up in winter. Iris remembered her parents standing over Lark with a stopwatch counting her breaths— they must have done it for her, too, but she had no memory of that. And she remembered the emptiness of their room when Lark was in the hospital overnight, of crawling up into the top bunk to go to bed and feeling like without Lark there on the bottom it might just float away. And the painfully barren feeling of a Larkless house, as if her sister had just disappeared into thin air. She remembered that whenever she got a cold, her parents would splash disinfectant everywhere. *Be so careful not to give it to your sister.* She remembered that when Lark was at the hospital, one parent was always home with her, and Dad (or Mom) would sit on the couch with Iris and they would read books or watch movies and Mom (or Dad) would tell her that her sister just needed a little help getting better, but she would come home so soon.

By the time the girls were in elementary school, colds were just colds, and they could all go around sniffling without getting doused in disinfectant.

Until they were eight.

They both got the cold—really, the whole second grade had it. The girls stayed home from school for three days, sleeping and reading and playing board games and trailing Kleenex everywhere. Their mom doled out spoonfuls of orange medicine and sympathy. On day four, they both went back to school a little sniffly, but no cough.

Then that evening Lark complained that her head felt like it was going to explode. She had an impossible fever and could not look at lights and could not touch her chin to her chest, and these were *emergency symptoms* and required her dad packing Lark up in the night and taking her to the hospital while Iris and her mom waited at home.

And then Lark wasn't coming home; she was staying there. The *emergency symptoms* belonged to an actual emergency, and one that would not be over soon.

They'd left for the hospital so quickly they'd forgotten Esmeralda, and on the morning of the first day Iris took the stuffed cat from her sister's bunk in order to give it to her mom to take to the hospital.

But she squeezed it to her chest and it smelled like Lark. So she grabbed Bunny and gave it to her mom to bring to Lark.

Two days came and went and Lark was still not back. They did not know when she would be home. A dark shadow circled around their house and held everyone tightly. Their parents spoke in bright words to Iris, as if the shadow weren't there, but it was clear that something terrible had wrapped its slithering way around them and begun to squeeze.

It was *meningitis*, caused by an infection that had slipped in while her body was busy with the cold, like the shadow that had slipped into their house while no one was looking.

Meningitis was an inflammation of the brain, caused by either a virus or an infection. It could be fatal. No one had ever explained any of that to Iris, though; she'd had to look it all up herself.

It was the end of the world. You always know when it's the end of the world, no matter how bright people try to make their words. Iris knew. And she did not understand why her parents were pretending it wasn't. Did they know the truth and were they keeping it from her, or did they just not see it?

And which was worse?

What do you do when the world is ending and the adults are acting like it's not happening?

They sent Iris back to school, and she tucked the stuffed cat in her backpack to keep her company all day.

Day 3, day 4, day 5, day 6. *No, you cannot visit. I'm so sorry.*

Day 7, day 8, day 9.

Her mom would be at the hospital during the day, her dad at night. Before he left he'd sit on the bottom bunk with Iris (he did not trust the top bunk) and tell her stories. Iris would listen, clutching the stuffed cat close.

One night her dad told her the story of the Pied Piper, a musician who was called into the town of Hamelin to rid it of a snake infestation. The piper played his pipe and led all the snakes away, but when he asked for payment, the towns-people refused. So he played his pipe and led all the children of Hamelin away. No one ever saw them again.

That night Iris had a nightmare of a townful of chil-dren disappearing into thin air—everyone but her. She ran through empty houses calling for her friends, but no one answered. They were all gone.

The nightmare warped, got worse. The Pied Piper played his pipe and all the children marched out of the town and off the edge of the world. Sometimes Iris marched with them; sometimes she could only watch; sometimes she knew what was coming and couldn't do anything to stop it; sometimes the edge just came. No matter what, she woke up terrified.

It was not the only nightmare. From the night Lark was rushed off to the hospital, Iris had dreams of robbers in black stocking caps and masks and black-and-white striped shirts scaling the walls of her house and climbing in the windows, of a fire blazing through the house quicker than they could run, of monsters under the bed and in the closet and just outside the door, of long dark slithering things hissing at her. She dreamed of vampires, of zombies, of werewolves in the bright full moon, of real wolves circling and baring their teeth, of monstrous birds, of bone-fingered witches reaching for her, of demons slipping under her skin and taking hold of her.

And then Lark came home, clutching Bunny close.

It was over.

She would be fine.

But she looked as if something had tried to sip the life from her. It wasn't a monster; Iris knew that. It was just biology.

Because things like that happen. Sometimes the world is monstrous. Sometimes, for whatever reason, an infection slips under your skin and takes hold.

Wash your hands. Cover your cough. Keep your hands away from your eyes and mouth. Douse yourself and people near you in sanitizer. Don't share food. Eat plenty of fruits and vegetables. Don't go outside with wet hair. Get lots of sleep.

These things are supposed to protect you. Except sometimes they aren't enough, and that is when the monsters come.

Memory tells us funny lies sometimes. Iris remembers her nightmares as a fact of her childhood, can't remember a time without having them, a time where falling asleep at night didn't feel like jumping into a pit of rattlesnakes.

But it's not true. These nightmares started the night Lark went to the hospital.

And when Lark came home, Iris's nightmares did not stop, though her sister was keeping the bottom bunk weighted down where it was supposed to be, and one night in the middle of a dream where every child disappeared from the school but her, she heard the sound of Lark climbing up the bunk-bed ladder.

Iris told her the story of the Pied Piper and the children of Hamelin, and how they just walked out of town and never came back again.

So Lark rewove the story. "But when they got to the edge of the world," she whispered in Iris's ear, "that's when they grew wings and flew away. The Pied Piper could only watch. The children couldn't go home again, but they lived in the sky and the birds kept watch over them. The end."

It was a good story. Maybe it was better to have wings and hang out with the birds than to be in a town with people who'd cheat someone out of money. Maybe the kids would have grown up to be that sort of people too, but now the birds would help them be different.

The next night when Iris awoke from a nightmare—vampires, this time—Lark slipped into her bed and collected the pieces of the dream and reshaped them: that swarm of vampires that menaced her were all vegetarians, no more dangerous than Bunnicula.

And when the sun came up Lark told her about all the ways an ordinary girl could defeat a vampire.

They remember Lark's bestiary as just something that happened too. It was Lark—of course she had her own monster book.

But it didn't just happen. Lark told Iris stories, and then at some point Lark started drawing pictures, and then she wrote out facts about each monster, and soon she was collecting them all into a book—a monster bestiary.

"We need this," Lark had said. "We're the girls who defeat the monsters."

So it was Lark who named all the monsters for Iris, gave them shape and form and powers, and, most importantly, gave them weaknesses. And once you can look at a monster head-on, once you know the sound it makes, the precise threat it poses, the way it can be defeated, then you can look straight into the dark places and not be so afraid.

And at night, sometimes, your sister crawls into the top bunk with you, bringing Esmeralda, and you sleep tucked in with each other.

Sometimes that, alone, keeps the monsters away.

CHAPTER NINETEEN

Freakenstein

So life proceeded this way through September, as the temperatures dropped and the leaves began to turn red, orange, and yellow. Iris did not go back to Treasure Hunters after Camp Awesome because she did not want to be late again, though she always looked to see if the sign had changed. (It had not.) Whoever Alice was, Mr. George Green had not found her yet.

So she was always home when Lark got home from art camp (even though Lark never again lost her key), full of talk of negative space and perspective and color theory, while Iris had no stories to tell. Iris had no color theory, no perspective. Everything remained gray and mushy. And everywhere she went she couldn't escape the feeling that she was the wrong girl.

Class was no exception. Her pod had its own rhythm and Lark would have gotten it; Lark would have slipped into it, added to it. Iris just sat and listened. And Ms. Shonubi was nice; she read to them every day and let them pick out whatever book they wanted during independent reading time. She gave the class nonconfrontational word problems and fun science experiments and talked about history like it was an adventure. She would probably have loved making dollhouse rooms and cataloging gifts from crows if she'd had a chance.

In other words, Iris was the wrong girl for her.

Maybe she would have been fine in Mr. Hunt's class. She didn't mind oral reports. She liked telling people how things were. She didn't really mind math drills—they were orderly, at least.

But Lark did.

She minded a lot. The book report went terribly—Mr. Hunt kept telling her to *look up* and *talk louder* and *have confidence* and *work on her presentation skills* and that he would call on her more to help her *practice speaking in front of her peers*, which he then started doing, and every time, every single thing Lark knew flew from her head like a scared bird and she could not answer.

"I have to just tell them," Iris said, sitting on Lark's bed one Sunday night after Lark had spent some time fretting about an oral report she'd have to give on Thursday. "Mom and Dad. The experiment failed. It's not working."

"Don't," Lark said softly.

"But I have to! I'll tell Principal Peter. I'll tell Mom. We said we'd try it, and we tried it, and it's not working, and I'll tell them that, and then they can switch you out and everything will be okay again."

"You can't," Lark said.

"But—"

"Iris!"

Iris stopped.

"Iris. It's not going to help. It never helps. They'll just tell you that we need to try *more* and *harder* as if I'm not trying as hard I can, and I just can't take that."

"But that's why I'll do it."

"They'll still think it. They'll still think I'm just not trying."

"But—"

"Iris. No. It won't help. They won't listen to us."

And Lark held her eyes and tapped out *Please*, and there was nothing Iris could do but nod and agree.

Because she was the one who listened to Lark.

* * *

The next afternoon Iris was in media—the one class where she didn't feel like the wrong girl. For that one period every Monday and Friday she could sit in a chair without feeling like she didn't quite fit in it correctly, that she was not made in the right way.

Mr. Ntaba seemed to be on a picture-book biography kick with her, specifically biographies of girls and women who were told they couldn't do something and did it anyway. This was clearly supposed to inspire her, though she wasn't exactly sure how. But the stories were good.

On this particular Monday, he called her to the desk and handed her a book about Alice Roosevelt, Theodore Roosevelt's daughter, who, according to the title, was the one thing in his life the future president could not manage. Iris chose not to take Mr. Ntaba's selection personally.

"I picked this one for you. I think you'll like Alice."

Alice, where are you?

Iris flipped open the book, looking at pictures of this girl running and bouncing her way through her life, Teddy Roosevelt chasing after her. She said she wanted to "eat up the world."

"Thank you," she said, taking the book and heading toward a beanbag, wondering what it would be like to want to eat up the world.

"Oh, hey," Mr. Ntaba said, "tell Lark I hope she feels better."

Iris stopped. "What do you mean?"

"She wasn't here today when her class had media. I assumed she was home sick?"

"I—I don't think so? We came to school together." Iris could feel the red climb up her cheeks. It was possible that Lark had gone home sick, that her mom had come to pick her up. That had happened before, but when they were in the same class, Iris was able to watch these things happen as opposed to just hearing about it from the librarian.

Which was rather embarrassing. Part of being twins was that you knew more about what was going on with your sister on a daily basis than the school librarian did, no matter how much you liked that librarian.

This was where ESP could have come in handy. Iris could have thought, *Psst, Lark, are you okay?* And Lark would have thought back, *I had a sore throat and Mom came to get me but I feel better now. How are you?* And then no one would have had to worry.

Iris grabbed the book and paced around the library, while all around her, her classmates were happily reading and not worrying about their twin sisters. Mira and some of the other girls were grouped around a table looking at a book and whispering to one another. Jin was paging through a big book on space travel, and Oliver was, in fact, reading a dictionary for fun. Other kids were lolling in the beanbags and huddled in corners. The library clock ticked slowly on.

Iris huffed and went back to the desk. "Mr. Ntaba? I want to go find out what happened to Lark. Can I go to the office?"

This sort of thing really wasn't done in school—students didn't go wandering out of class, at least as far as Iris knew. There were rules, protocols.

Normally, she would have been prepared—she could have explained exactly why all those rules and protocols did not apply to this particular situation, and also why they were ridiculous in the first place and should probably be immediately stopped before they did actual harm, and didn't Principal Peter have a pattern of making poor decisions anyway?—but she was not prepared. The words did not come. All she could do was look up at Mr. Ntaba and say, "Please?"

He frowned. "Iris, I'm sorry. I can't let you leave class without a very good reason."

"This is a very good reason."

"I know that it's a very good reason *to you*, but to the people I'd have to explain myself to, it's not a very good reason."

"But—"

He held up his hand. "But I can call down to the office. Would you like me to do that?"

She nodded and he disappeared into his office behind the library desk.

This is what he discovered:

Yes, Lark had gone home sick. Ms. Snyder in the office had a note for Iris from her mother but hadn't delivered it yet due to the untimely escape of a kindergarten class hedgehog.

"Did Ms. Snyder say anything else?"

"No."

"Nothing about what's wrong?"

"No, but Iris, if it were serious, I'm sure someone would have come and gotten you."

"Can I go get my note, please?" she asked.

There must have been something in her voice, or something on her face, because Mr. Ntaba gazed at her and then nodded. "All right, Iris. But"—he leaned in—"no shenanigans."

It was probably a joke, though Iris was not in the mood for jokes. Nor was she in the mood for shenanigans. Still, she flashed Mr. Ntaba a smile as if he were very funny indeed, and as if she certainly could be trusted to go to the office and come right back and the very idea of her stopping along the way and engaging in any kind of shenanigans was utterly laughable.

Which was true. Iris had one mission and one mission only—to find out what had happened to her sister. But when she got to the office, Ms. Snyder was at the front desk talking to someone on the phone about trapping small animals. Nodding at Iris, she handed her the note from her mother and waved her away. As Iris walked out, unfolding the note, Ms. Snyder's voice trailed after her. "No, no, not like that! This is a kindergarten hedgehog! We need Mr. Prickles alive!"

Iris—
Lark has gone home sick for the day. I've already dropped your bike off, so you can bike home from camp as always.
Love,
Mom
P.S. No arguing.

Iris stared at the note, mentally sputtering. *Love, Mom? Love, Mom?* What kind of a way was that to sign off? What kind of a note was this, anyway? Notes were supposed to contain information; that was the whole point of leaving a note for someone. This had no information at all. *Home sick.* What kind of sick? There were so many ways to be sick. You could feel queasy, you could have a sore throat, or you could have *emergency symptoms* and be rushed to the hospital.

You can bike home after camp as always.

After camp! She was just supposed to go to camp, like nothing was wrong, like her twin sister wasn't home with a queasy throat emergency.

The rational explanation was that of course Lark was fine. If her mother could breezily write *you can bike home*, then there was no emergency.

Unless something was wrong and they weren't telling Iris.

They didn't want Iris to worry. So they wouldn't tell her and she'd just tra-la-la fiddle-dee-dee her way to Camp Awesome, because everything was awesome, and not find out until nighttime that something was really wrong.

She wasn't even going to get started on *No arguing*.

In short, there was no part of the note that didn't make Iris furious.

She glanced back into the office, but Ms. Snyder was still on the phone and didn't look like she wanted to hurry up her conversation so Iris could call home.

Thwarted by a hedgehog.

With a huff, Iris crumpled up the note and headed back to the media center. All she wanted to do was run into someone who was in Lark's class and could tell her what had happened.

And she did.

She ran into Tommy Whedon.

Why Tommy was wandering the halls by himself when there was protocol, she did not know. Iris didn't want to acknowledge he existed. Still, Lark had said he hadn't been bad this year, and right now he was her only option. So maybe she could just ask—

And then Tommy stopped, his face twisting. "What?" he snapped.

Iris stiffened. "Nothing," she said icily. Apparently her decision had been made for her.

"You're a psycho, you know that?"

Iris crossed her arms. "Excuse me?"

"You are. I think you have anger issues."

"You're a troll, Tommy. The most ridiculous kind. You just sit in caves and burp and bother people."

"I thought I was a mole rat."

"You are. You're a troll, a mole rat, and a blowfish."

His eyes narrowed. "Psycho and Freakenstein. You guys make a great team."

"What did you call my sister?"

"Freakenstein! She's a huge freak. She's, like, possessed or something."

Iris went cold. "What do you mean?"

"She puked in class today. It was so dis-gust-ing. Just puke, everywhere. I don't know what projectile vomiting is, but if it's a real thing, that's what she did."

Iris exhaled. Vomit was not good, but it was the sort of thing that happened to you and you got better. It did not require a trip to the emergency room, unless you vomited for more than twenty-four hours or ran a high fever.

The questions tickled at her throat. Was Lark running a high fever? Any other symptoms? But she was not going to seek comfort in the cold blowfish eyes of Tommy Whedon.

Just then, he puffed out his cheeks and started making gagging noises. And for one half of a millisecond Iris thought he might be sick, might actually vomit.

But then he leaned over and pretend puked on the floor.

Iris whirled around and stomped away.

Shenanigans.

CHAPTER TWENTY

Superpowers

On the bus, Iris perched herself next to Natalie and Jenny, two of Lark's classmates, and got the full story. Apparently, while Iris's class was doing free reading time, Mr. Hunt's class was dissecting owl pellets.

Iris knew what owl pellets were, but apparently Lark had not known. Lark probably thought they were special owl food you bought at the store to convince owls to be your friends.

Owl pellets are not special owl food from the store. Owls do not eat pellets from the store, or anything else from a store. They are predators and eat small prey animals. In fact, they swallow these small animals whole, and then regurgitate the undigestible parts. In the form of a pellet.

The class assignment was to pick the bones of the prey out of the pellet and reconstruct the skeleton of the animal it once was. Which is a thing you can do with owl pellets. Natalie and Jenny said that Mr. Hunt seemed really excited about the whole thing, which of course he was. Ogres are notoriously excited by things involving digestion.

To Mr. Hunt, this was probably a cool hands-on exploration of nature. To Lark, it was a horror show. Not only did Lark not like the food chain, but she did not like anything involving bodies, especially things coming out of bodies. And she especially *especially* did not like anything involving bodies or things coming out of bodies at school. It had taken her until third grade to be able to go to the bathroom at all during the school day. Once in fourth grade Mackenzie Bradford vomited in class, and Lark cried out of sympathetic embarrassment.

And now it was Lark who had thrown up.

"It was pretty gross," Jenny said.

"Like, grosser than owl pellets," Natalie said.

"Which are really gross," Jenny said.

"Maybe she vomited up her prey," Natalie said.

Jenny giggled. "We could reconstruct her breakfast!"

The girls moved on to reconstructing their own adventures with owl pellets, and Iris sat back against the cold bus seat. Now that she wasn't worried about Lark being rushed to the hospital, now that she could picture the whole scene, now that the girls were telling her how utterly gross Lark throwing up had been, Iris understood the real consequences of Lark getting sick today.

She would be mortified.

Iris was aware that the owl-pellet activity was designed for educational purposes and not specifically to traumatize her sister, and yet if you went to an ogre meeting and the agenda were Find a Way to Torment Lark Maguire, you might come out of it with something much like this project.

The last thing Iris wanted to do was go to Camp Awesome today. She wanted to go home and talk to Lark and try to save her from the ocean of embarrassment she was probably drowning in right now. But her mom had told her to go, and as much as she wanted to go home, her mom would be mad if she did, and Lark did not like it when their parents were mad at Iris.

So she went.

Camp Awesome had continued to be an intense experiment in making Iris feel less than awesome. She understood how the activities might make some girls feel awesome, and indeed the rest of her campmates seemed to really enjoy everything they did. Collages, duct-tape art, collages with duct-tape art. Glitter glue and fabric paint, pom-poms and google eyes. Macramé and mobiles, stickers and slime.

Beading. Journaling. Icebreakers and warm-ups. Get-to-know-you games. Get-to-know-you-better games!

She still couldn't seem to find her way in at Awesome, or figure out what to say to all the other girls. At some point she'd written down all their names in her journal and then made a chart with everything she'd learned about them.

For instance:

Amma:
5th grade
Truths: fencing and gymnastics.
Lie: had a frog, but it died
Journal cover: circle of eyes
Favorite color: purple
Favorite food: cupcakes
Adjective: amazing
Favorite book: Rise of the Jumbies
Favorite movie: MOANA

It would seem like if you did this long enough you would figure out how to act in front of someone.

It would seem like it.

Today when they walked in they found that Abigail had hung pictures of female superheroes all around the room. There was Batgirl, Supergirl, Wonder Woman, Captain

Marvel, Black Widow, the girl and the mom from *The Incredibles*, the green lady from *Guardians of the Galaxy*, the Powerpuff Girls. They all looked ready to fight crime, conquer evil, and be as awesome as possible.

"Who's your favorite?" Novalie whispered to Iris.

"Um, Batgirl?"

Novalie nodded. "I like her too. I like her better as Oracle, though."

"Yeah," Iris said, pretending she knew what that meant.

Abigail bounced in front of the room wearing a Wonder Woman T-shirt. "Today we're going to talk about superheroes!" she proclaimed, as if that weren't entirely obvious.

"You should have Moon Girl," Morgan said.

"I don't—who's Moon Girl?"

"Moon Girl is the smartest person in the whole Marvel Universe. She's way smarter than Bruce Banner. She's a nine-year-old black girl with glasses and she's friends with a big dinosaur. I'm going to go as her for Halloween and bring a dinosaur stuffed animal."

"There's a black-girl superhero?" Gabrielle asked.

Morgan nodded enthusiastically.

"Coooooooool."

"I should look that up, Morgan!" Abigail said brightly. "Thank you! Now—"

"What about Batwoman?" Preeti asked.

"Well, she's right—"

"That's Bat*girl*!" Preeti said. "What about Bat*woman*?"

"Or She-Hulk," Morgan said.

"Or Thor. Thor's a woman now too," Novalie added. "My brother's mad about it, but he's a big jerk."

"Superman's in China," added Preeti. "But he's still a guy."

"Ms. Marvel's Muslim!" Amma exclaimed.

Abigail squinted at the girls as if they might be playing a trick on her. Her eyes fell on them each, one by one, and they just stared back expectantly. Except for Iris, who just shrugged.

"Well," Abigail said, clapping her hands together. "You guys sure know a lot about superheroes! That's awesome! When I was a kid, we weren't really supposed to like them."

"Why not?" Morgan asked.

"Well, I mean, people thought they were for boys."

Preeti frowned. "Which boys?"

"Just . . . boys. In general. *Star Wars*, too."

Hannah piped up now. "What about Rey?"

"They didn't have Rey back then. But they had Leia."

Hannah gasped. "General Leia!"

"Well . . . no."

"So, what were you supposed to like?"

"Um, princesses, mostly."

"Oh!" Morgan said. "Have you read *Princeless*? She's a princess but kind of a superhero also. She's black too," she added to Gabrielle and Amma.

"*Princeless* is great," Preeti added.

Iris could not follow the conversation, but she wrote the books down, for Lark's sake.

"Have you read *Princess Academy*?" Morgan asked. "It's super feminist. My mom says so."

Hannah scrunched up her nose. "General Leia was a princess at first. So you can obviously like princesses and *Star Wars*."

"Well"—Abigail sputtered—"it was just different. Like toy shelves were either pink or blue, so there were toys for girls and toys for boys."

"My mom says pink used to be the color for boys," Morgan said.

"Also," added Gabrielle, "why would you tell half your customers they shouldn't buy your stuff? People weren't very good at selling things."

All the girls nodded, and Iris nodded with them. This made sense to her.

"Well," said Preeti, "you still can't find girls on superhero stuff. Black Widow's never on Avenger stuff, and Wonder Woman isn't on Justice League stuff. Except the Chobani yogurt tubes."

"Yeah," said Hannah. "I got a whole set of *Last Jedi* figures for my birthday that didn't have Rey in it. I wrote a letter to Target to complain."

"You can't find Ms. Marvel on anything," said Amma. "I would want all the Ms. Marvel things."

Iris watched her Awesome-mates. Even the girls who were quiet in this conversation were nodding along. All these girls were passionate about things. They knew things, things that other people cared about. What did Iris know? Besides collective nouns for animals, emergency symptoms, and presidential assassinations?

"It's because they think boys won't buy it if there's girls on it," Morgan said.

Gabrielle shrugged with the wisdom of a sixth grader. "Some boys make fun of stuff for being girly. And they tease boys who like that stuff. So being a girl is bad, apparently."

Morgan nodded solemnly. "My mom says that's the patriarchy, and it hurts boys, too."

Abigail stood at the front of the room like she'd come in to give them all a lesson on the solar system and they'd invented their own rocket ship. "Well. It's good you girls know so much about superheroes! I wasn't expecting . . . so, I'm going to change plans a little. We're going to start today with some journaling, and then we'll do sharing. So, here's your prompt: If you could have any superpower, what would it be, and why?"

Iris deflated slowly. She should have seen this coming.

"But, before we start," Abigail chirped, "let's make a list of superpowers."

Abigail went to the whiteboard while all the girls around Iris shouted out suggestions:

Invisibility
Strength
Mind reading
Flying
Being stretchy
Embiggening
Ensmallening
Speed
Supersmarts
Deadly throwing accuracy
Turning into animals
Beast mode
Teleportation
Jedi mind tricks
Archery
Fighting
Time travel
Interrogation
Stealth

It was something, watching all the girls together. There was a collective energy that kept building in the room, some invisible force connecting them. One girl would shout out a word and the others would look to her and grin. They didn't need an invisible ball anymore.

All but Iris, who had not figured out how to plug into this particular grid. So she sat at the table and copied down all the superpowers in a page in her notebook, as if record keeping were a job that everyone wanted her to do, as if she had a role in this at all.

There were a lot of superpowers to be had in the world, a lot more than she'd even imagined. So, as the other girls started writing in their journals, Iris looked down the list and tried the powers on.

It was obvious what Lark would pick: invisibility. Lark would be ecstatic if she could just go wherever she wanted without anyone paying any attention to her. She could sit in class without the ogre ever making her do math drills, and when it was time to give an oral report, no one would be able to find her. Maybe if she vomited in class the vomit would be invisible. Or, if it wasn't, she could blame it on Tommy Whedon. And sometimes, if she felt like it, she could pretend to be a ghost and float things in the air and knock over trash cans and open and close doors. Lark would like that.

And maybe while the rest of the class dissected owl pellets she could reassemble mouse skeletons. Probably nothing would put the ogre off the owl-pellet exercise like seeing the mice skeletons reassemble themselves.

But Iris did not want to be invisible. She felt that way now, and she did not like it at all. Nor did she want to be able to read minds—that was the sort of thing that probably seemed like a good idea until you actually tried it. She did not want to fly in the air with a murder of crows and drop shiny things in people's backyards. She did not want to embiggen, or become the size of a wasp. Sure, it would be nice to be supersmart, and interrogation powers might have their useful moments. But these things didn't just happen to people in real life. Sure, there was Batman, who apparently became a superhero by being impossibly rich and working out a lot, but Iris didn't think that happened to people in real life either, or more people would do it.

She had other problems. She couldn't go back in time and save Lark from vomiting, or keep Principal Peter from hiring the owl-pellet-loving teacher in the first place. She couldn't protect her sister from the mortification that was surely burning her up while Iris sat here.

Really, all she wanted was to be able to organize the world in a way that made sense, and that was not a superpower. Though it felt as impossible as one.

They went around the table and the girls shouted out their answers—Amma, embiggening; Emily, beast mode; Gabrielle, flying; Hannah, flying; Morgan, supersmarts; Preeti, turn into a cat.

Abigail said she wanted to be superstrong, strong enough to lift a truck, strong enough to lift all of them up if they needed. She winked, and the girls cringed at the metaphor.

But when they got to Iris, she just shook her head. "I don't know."

"What did you write?"

Just a list. "I didn't, really."

"Okay, Iris. Novalie, what about you?"

For a while, Abigail had been pushing her to try. Now it seemed even Abigail had given up. Even Abigail didn't have that kind of superpower.

CHAPTER TWENTY-ONE

Reconstruction

After Iris got home, she ran right up to Lark's room, where it looked like a tiny tornado had hit the dollhouse world.

"I threw up in class today," Lark said when she entered. She didn't even look at Iris.

"I know," Iris said.

"In front of everyone."

"I know."

"How do you know? Was everyone talking about it?"

"No! I asked Jenny and Natalie on the bus, because Mom left me a note that you'd gone home sick, that's all."

"Did they laugh?"

Kind of? "No, definitely not."

"Everyone in class laughed. Except Mr. Hunt. He got all red and weird and sent me to the nurse's office. Did they tell you what we had to do?"

"Owl pellets."

"Do you know what those are?"

"Well . . . yeah."

"Well, I didn't know. I thought it was, like, owl food or something. So when I found out, I was like, I can't do this; I'm going to have to pretend to be sick or something. But I couldn't tell Mr. Hunt I was sick—what if he knew I was pretending and he got mad at me? So then I thought, you know what? I'm just going to do this. How gross can it be? And I'm standing there looking at this . . . thing, and I have my little knife, and everyone else is cutting into theirs and pulling out bones."

While Lark talked, Iris made her way over to Lark's bed, grabbing Esmeralda and holding her tight.

"And I can't do it. I can't put the knife in. And meanwhile all these skeletons of these poor animals are reconstructing themselves. People are, like, guessing what they have. A bunny! A frog! A mouse! And all I can think is that maybe the process will keep going and the animals will take on flesh and fur and come back to life and then I can open the window and send them all to freedom. And then Mr. Hunt says,

'Lark, is there a problem?' And everyone turns to look at me. Everyone. And Tommy says something about Crow Girl, I don't even know what. So I just plunge my knife into the pellet and pull out this little bone and—"

She mashed her lips together.

"I tried. I did! But none of the other kids seemed to mind at all, like maybe they were grossed out at first but then they all kind of got into it. Like it was a game. Like a kit from the Science Museum, only it's not a kit from the Science Museum at all. It was a real bone. It was so tiny."

"I know."

"What's wrong with me?"

"What? Nothing."

"Something's wrong with me. Everyone else is fine. Everyone's fine with the math drills and the mouse remains. But I'm not. I threw up in front of everyone." Her eyes were red now.

"There's nothing wrong with you!" Iris's voice had edges, and Lark blinked up at her. "There's nothing wrong," she repeated softly. "You thought it was gross and you got sick. It happens."

"Why does it only happen to me?"

Her eyes were looking up at Iris desperately, as if Iris could give her an answer and make it all okay.

Iris swallowed. "It happens to you," she said, talking

slowly, "because most people look at a bone and see a bone. You see the whole story."

It was true. Lark saw backward in time—the beginning, the middle, and the terrible end. Everything had flesh, everything had feelings, everything had a story, and she felt for everything. Once upon a time there was a mouse who lived in a field. And then the owl came. The end.

Iris sat down next to her sister and Lark tucked her head into her shoulder. They fit like this. After a moment, she put her hand on Lark's knee and tapped three times on her leg. It was their code for something, something like *I am here* or *I love you* or *Iris and Lark*, or something that was a combination of all those things.

Lark exhaled loudly and then tapped three times back.

"So . . . what are you doing?" Iris asked, nodding to the dollhouse. It was undergoing major renovations. The whole family was sprawled on the floor and Lark had taken apart the campfire room in the attic. That room had been there the longest of any of them, and Iris could not help but feel a twinge. She'd liked roasting marshmallows on the moon.

Lark sat up. "I'm making boxes," she said, motioning to the origami pile.

"For what?"

"It's an attic, isn't it? This is where they keep things."

Iris shifted. Lark had not made rooms like normal rooms in some time.

"What kind of things?"

"Things they want to put away."

". . . Like what?"

"Just things."

"Okay."

"Things that go in brightly colored boxes. You know."

She did not. "What about the family?"

"I think they should each be in their own rooms."

"The girls, too?"

"They have to be."

"Why?"

"Because someone decided it was supposed to be this way, that's why. Someone made a decision and now everyone's just locked in their own room and they can't get out and find each other. They should never have split up in the first place."

"What about Baby Thing?"

"Except Baby Thing. Baby Thing stays with the Lark doll so she can watch over it."

It wasn't the first time Lark had done something like this. For a while last year the dad character had been strapped on a table in a mad-scientist room, next to a duct-tape mummy-cyborg, which was also strapped to a table. Each had a tiny tinfoil cap strapped to his head, and the caps were connected to each other by a wire. Making it easier, Lark explained, for the brain to travel directly from the dad figure to the cyborg-mummy figure once the mad scientist flipped the switch.

"Did I do something?" their dad had asked when he saw it.

"Never open the door to strangers," Lark had responded darkly.

Now Lark picked up the Iris doll and considered her. "At first I was going to put you in the bird room so you could fly. But then I realized you should probably be in the armory."

"That doesn't sound too bad."

"I trust you the most with the weapons. Mom will be onstage with the chickens. Dad . . . maybe a picnic in the bear habitat."

"That might be dangerous."

"Well, you know Dad. He probably wouldn't notice the bears."

"Don't you think he'd be in the disco room?"

Lark smiled a little. "He wishes. That's why he is trapped."

"And what about you?" Iris said, picking up the Lark doll.

"I'm not sure yet. I think she's in the attic."

The attic was bare now—all signs of the moon and the starry black night were gone. All that was left were bits of paper and paint and drops of glitter here and there, the ruins of the former landscape.

With a thoughtful frown Lark stared into the attic, considering. Then she started placing the little origami boxes in there, strange bursts of bright clean color against the post-apocalyptic room

"Aren't you going to decorate the room first?"

"No, I'm just going to leave it like this."

"But it looks . . ." What? Not just bare. It looked ruined. Lonely.

"I know," said Lark. "But it's the attic. That's how attics look."

"Well, then, shouldn't the boxes be more broken down?" Something about the bright colors of the origami papers made it all look worse.

"No," Lark said. "This is what I want."

And that was the end of that. Lark never minded when Iris gave suggestions, because Iris never minded when Lark didn't take them, and Iris never demanded to know why. Their parents always wanted Lark to explain why she'd put the chicken on the stage or the dog in the cat room or pasted a whole hallway entirely in cotton, and sometimes she had an explanation—*because she's doing a one-chicken show*—and sometimes she didn't. Or, Iris suspected, she had an explanation, but not one that could be explained. The dog was in the cat room because it felt right to Lark to do it that way, and that was all that really mattered.

"So why are you—she—in the attic?"

"She's looking for something."

"In the boxes?"

Lark scrunched up her face. "I don't know yet. Probably."

There were times when Iris and Lark knew exactly what the other was thinking; there were times they talked in secret languages that no one else knew. And there were times where it seemed like they didn't speak the same language at all.

"I'm sorry about school," Iris said.

Lark nodded slightly. "Me too."

Iris watched her sister fill the attic with brightly colored origami boxes, and after a while Lark's face relaxed and her eyes cleared and her cheeks dimmed from red to pink. She sucked on her bottom lip as she carefully folded paper into perfect little boxes—she did it so swiftly and elegantly, like it was what the paper wanted to be most in the world and all she had to do was help it get there—and then put boxes in the attic, moved them around, and took them out again.

It seemed like it was going to take a while.

So Iris went downstairs to find her mom frantically searching through piles of paper in the kitchen. There had been a lot of frantic searching for things since their dad had left.

"I can't find the"—she waved her hand around as if by disturbing the air the missing word would pop out—"electric bill."

"It will turn up," Iris said brightly.

"I just . . . I don't know where anything is anymore."

Tell me about it, Iris thought.

"Maybe whoever's stealing stuff took it," her mom muttered.

"Huh?"

"Oh, there's some crime ring, people taking stuff from museums around here. It's all over the news. I don't seriously think they took my electric bill, though."

"Okay. Um, Mom, I want to talk to you." Iris slid into a chair and looked up at her mother with her best serious expression. Their last serious conversation had gone so well, after all.

"Oh, yes, of course." Her mom glanced at the piles, and then sat at the breakfast table across from Iris, clearly giving her daughter her full attention, clearly banishing all thoughts of lost electric bills and the disasters they might portend. Iris had her best serious expression and her mom had her best listening expression, and there they were, both of them, doing their best. "What's up?"

"I think Lark should move to Ms. Shonubi's class."

There. A practical solution to the problem. They had done their best, they had tried, but clearly it wasn't working. Clearly it was a mistake. Lark getting sick in class proved that. Yes, it was terrible for Lark, but it had one positive benefit of showing their parents that this idea was a terrible mistake.

Her mom blew air out of her mouth. "Honey. We talked about this."

"I know, but we should talk about it again. She doesn't like Mr. Hunt."

"I understand that, but that's not a good enough reason. It's not even a month into the school year. Lark might like him just fine if she gives him a chance."

"That's not going to work. She thinks he's an ogre."

Her mom sat back and exhaled deeply, one of those cleansing breaths they tell you to take before standardized tests. "I wish I knew whether you meant literally or figuratively."

"You mean, whether she really thinks he's an actual creature of myth, or whether she just thinks he acts like one?"

"Exactly."

"I don't think there's a difference."

Mom just shook her head. "You guys and your stories."

Iris flushed. "I'm not making this up. And neither is Lark."

"It's just the fourth week of school and you've decided your fifth-grade teacher is a monster."

"Not mine. Lark's. She doesn't like him. He makes her do math drills in front of the class."

Her mom tilted her head. "Sweetheart, I don't think that makes someone an ogre. I think that's just what teachers do."

"She threw up in class today!"

"I know that. I went to pick her up, remember? But that's hardly the teacher's fault."

"She threw up because he made her do something that grossed her out. They were dissecting owl pellets."

". . . Is that owl food?"

"No." Iris explained what they really were.

"Oh. Well. Your sister is unusually sensitive to that kind of thing," she said, looking vaguely grossed out herself. "But that doesn't make the teacher an ogre. I'm guessing a lot of the students found it really interesting. Wouldn't you?"

"She doesn't like him," Iris repeated, ignoring her mother's inarguably true statement.

"Is this really about Mr. Hunt? I know it's hard on you guys, being separated."

"No. I mean, yes, it's hard. But . . . it's not that."

"Look, things are tough on Lark. You and I know it. Living in the world's going to be a little harder on her than it is on other people. But she still has to live in the world, you know? And not every teacher is going to be just right for her. Or for you."

"Yeah, but—"

"Iris. Love. Do me a favor. I know you guys have a . . . flair for the dramatic. But could you just try to rein it in right now? I don't think its going to be helpful for Lark this year. She needs to be practical. And so do you."

Iris swallowed. She *was* practical. That was the entirety of her personality. If she wasn't practical, who was she?

"Don't get me wrong, I love how creative you girls are. Your imaginations are wonderful. But sometimes a teacher is just a teacher, doing his best. And Lark is going to be stressed and anxious without you there, and maybe it's not the best thing to encourage her . . . flights of fancy. Maybe it's better to just show her that things are . . . normal."

"Normal," Iris repeated.

"Yes, normal. Getting assignments you don't like is normal. Getting a teacher you don't connect with is normal. Getting sick in class. These things happen. It's part of life and something we all have to deal with. Lark, too."

"But . . ." But what? But Lark *was* dealing with it. The point was she shouldn't have to. The point was Lark wasn't normal, and shouldn't have to be. Lark was Lark. Didn't anyone see that?

Her mom reached across the table and took her hand. "My girl. I love how you take care of your sister. You are so brave and loving. But don't forget to take care of yourself, too."

This was not the point at all. The point was Lark and how Mr. Hunt was not *the right fit* for Lark and wasn't it important to try to find *the right fit* for your child's emotional well-being and if maybe you had a teacher right down the hall who was *the right fit* and Mr. Hunt was *the wrong fit* then it was only logical to move Lark down said hall. It was only *practical*.

"Please know your father and I would never make you two do something that we thought would be bad for you. And the decisions we make might not always make sense to you, but trust that it's not because we don't care or aren't paying attention. We do care, and we are paying attention." She looked down at the table. "Look, honey. We're all going to have to pull together. All three of us. I'm trying, I am, but it's hard without your father here. I'm on my own."

Iris could not talk. She just stared at the table.

"Honey, I know you don't understand, and I am sorry about that. Just concentrate on yourself. And with Lark"— her mom glanced out of the window for a second—"just don't let your sister get so stuck in her head she gets lost there."

Iris had trouble doing her homework that night. Even the math problems didn't seem to line up the way they usually did. Instead of answers following questions like clockwork, everything was like a question leading to more questions.

Perhaps this was what it was like when you were not practical.

There was something else, something sitting there in the back of her mind. She couldn't figure out the shape of it, let alone what to call it, but it cast a long shadow over every-thing.

So she threw down her pencil and went to check on Lark.

Lark had been quiet during dinner, like she was still fold-ing boxes in her head. And she looked slightly green, and rather like she should be sleeping as opposed to trying to set the world record for origami box folding. But she was not sleeping—she was still in front of her dollhouse. The attic room was completely filled with the bright yellow, purple, pink, green, red, and blue cubes, and dozens more spilled out over the table and the floor beneath. But against the ripped-out hull of the dollhouse attic, the colors looked sad somehow.

Meanwhile, the Lark doll was sitting on a pile of boxes with her back turned, staring out the window, Baby Thing lying on a box next to her.

"What's she doing?"

"She took a break from going through the boxes."

"I can see that it would take a while. The family should maybe consider having a garage sale or something."

Lark grinned a little. "They hold on to a lot of stuff. No one else even comes up here."

"Did you figure out what she's looking for?"

Lark shook her head.

She worked for a while more while Iris sat and watched,

and then it was time for bed, so Iris said she hoped her sister felt better; she said she was sorry about the owl pellets, she was sorry about the ogre; she said if anyone made fun of Lark, she—Iris—would personally lock them in the janitor's closet. And not the one on the second floor, the one in the basement. Where no one could hear their screams.

And still she sat there, watching Lark rearranging the boxes in the attic so they were organized by color while the little doll stared out into the sky and her mother's words flew about the room:

Don't let your sister get so stuck in her head she gets lost there.

CHAPTER TWENTY-TWO

Meanwhile...

The grand Minnesota Zoo sits in a suburb south of the Twin Cities. About twenty miles, as the crow flies.

The Minnesota Zoo opened several decades ago, its founders having envisioned a new kind of zoo—no more animals trapped in small iron-and-concrete cages serving life sentences for the crime of being interesting, staring out at the families gaping back at them, waiting for the occasional little girl or boy with a big heart who would look into their eyes and see the sadness there and take a little bit of it away with them.

No more of that. This would be a new zoo, one where animals had room to roam, one where they *lived*—not in cages, but in carefully constructed habitats, scrupulous facsimiles of their natural environments, the next best thing to actually being there.

I have to say, they did a good job.

Here the animals had space; here they had grass and trees and water; here they were separated from people by glass partitions or simple fences instead of cages. Here a state-of-the-art monorail transported visitors across the nearly five hundred acres of land. It was revolutionary, and soon other zoos around the country decided that there were other options for their animals besides close quarters and misery.

Today the Minnesota Zoo is a leader in conservation, working to save endangered rhinos, wolf pups, Asian wild horses. Prize exhibits include the African penguins, the Amur tigers, the Canada lynx, and of course the rare and wonderful beluga whales—Peanut and Aphrodite.

The zoo is usually crowded in September, and if you want to be near the whales when no one else is, you need to be at the gates at eight a.m. with the school groups in their matching T-shirts and the parents with strollers.

So on this morning no one was at the top of the tank to see the man clutching a large brown briefcase as he stared down into the pool watching Peanut and Aphrodite swim. And they missed quite a sight. For the man placed the briefcase on the concrete, opened it up, and pulled out three items not normally found in your average briefcase: a pair of industrial gloves, a tightly sealed mason jar filled with some kind of shimmering light, and a foot-long walleye.

Quickly he put the gloves on, careful to tuck them under his sleeves, opened the mason jar, delicately rubbed the contents on the walleye, then dangled the now-shimmering fish over the tank.

The white whales had already had their seven a.m. breakfasts of herring and smelt, as they did every day, and they normally would not eat again until lunch. But Peanut was not going to say no to a good snack if offered. So, as it had been trained to do for years, it rose up out of the water and gulped down the fish, Aphrodite—more wary, perhaps, of the change in routine—lingering underneath.

If anyone human had been watching, it would have seemed like time stopped for a moment. The whale was perfectly still, mouth around the fish. Then the man leaned forward and placed his hand on the whale's smooth head.

And in a blink, the whale was gone.

Just gone.

But if anyone had been looking carefully—anyone besides me, that is—they would have seen the man place a long white figurine in his briefcase, snap it shut, and stroll away from the whale tank.

CHAPTER TWENTY-THREE

The Fortress of Solitude

The plan was that Lark would stay home from school for two days to "recover." No one specified whether it was her health or her dignity that needed recovery. Whichever it was, Lark looked like she needed it. She looked like a plant someone had forgotten to water.

Their mom was going to work from home in the mornings, but she needed to be at work in the afternoons, so Lark would go into the office with her and read and do homework, and perhaps with a couple of days of quiet all the uneasy things inside her would settle, and Lark would unwither.

Perhaps.

As for Iris, when she got to school she stalked around the fifth-grade wing listening for whispers of her sister's name. Gossip always skittered around the school like spiders: you needed to stomp on them early before they mutated and took over the whole place.

But she was too late. It seemed like all the fifth graders were stopping to ask Iris if Lark was okay, and in Iris's agitated state it was impossible to tell who meant it and who was snickering behind their concerned masks. Everyone was talking about Lark, and no one seemed to be talking about the ogre who had caused this whole event. No one was talking about the barbaric practice of making elementary schoolers piece together regurgitated prey.

So Iris was already in a black mood when she went into her classroom, and of course the kids in there immediately pounced on her as if she were the prey.

"Is Lark okay?"

"I heard she projectile vomited!"

"I heard she turned green."

Iris stuck her head in the air. "She's fine, thank you," she said as primly as possible. "People don't actually turn green, you know." Lark had been a little green-tinged, but that was different.

Summoning as much dignity as she could, she set herself down at her desk, where her pod mates were eyeing her like she herself might regurgitate prey at any moment.

"So, did you, like, feel it when she threw up?" Jin asked.

Iris glared at him.

"Jin." Mira said. "This is not the time."

He sunk in his chair. "I—just wondering—"

"No!" Mira said. "Does she look like she wants to talk about psychic powers? I'm sure this was very stressful for her."

"Vomiting can be a reaction to stress, you know," Oliver said. "Maybe Lark was under stress."

"She should try chamomile tea," Mira said.

"Is that a pet-psychic thing?" Jin asked.

"Chamomile," pronounced Oliver, "is a plant."

"It's a person thing. My mom makes tea. It helps me when I'm stressed."

Jin rolled his eyes. "What could you possible be stressed about? You're a girl."

Mira and Iris both turned on him. "What?"

"Girls aren't stressed!" said Jin.

Oliver shook his head solemnly. "That's not true. My sister is the most stressed-out person you'll ever meet in your life. She's more stressed out than Superman."

"Why would Superman be stressed out?" Mira asked. "He's Superman."

"Superman," Oliver said, "is always stressed. About

everything. I think he has an anxiety disorder."

"He's got a point," Jin said. "You don't go hang out in a palace made of ice called the Fortress of Solitude because you feel really chill about things."

"Ha!" Oliver said. "Chill!"

"That's ridiculous," Mira said. "My aunt sees pets with anxiety disorders all the time and they're nothing like Superman."

"That," Oliver said, "is a logical fallacy."

"You're a logical fallacy!" Mira snapped. "You guys are being insensitive. Again." She turned to Iris. "Is Lark okay?"

And now they were all looking at her not like she was a curiosity, not like they might snicker as soon as she turned around, but like they cared.

Iris blinked. "She's not really. She's super embarrassed." Normally she would have lied and said Lark was fine, why wouldn't she be fine? But somehow in the face of all of this pod sympathy, she couldn't manage to lie. "Everyone laughed at her," she added quietly.

Mira exhaled. "Those jerks."

Jin shook his head slowly. "People are awful."

"The worst," Oliver agreed. *"Repugnant."*

"When is she coming back?"

"Thursday, I think." Though Lark had an oral report scheduled for Thursday and would probably do everything in her power to stay home.

"We should do something nice for her," Mira declared.

"I agree," proclaimed Oliver. "I don't know her, but you're our pod mate, and Lark is your sister, so she's like our sister. Our pod sister. And you know what they say?"

"What?"

"Always stand behind your pod sister."

"Superman would," Jin agreed.

Iris didn't know what to say. No one had ever really taken her side before, other than Lark herself.

Just then Ms. Shonubi called Iris's name. There, standing in the doorway, was the ogre.

"Iris," Mr. Hunt said after she followed him into the hallway, "I wanted to know how your sister was."

Iris gave him her best haughty look. "She's . . . recovering."

"Good. That was . . . I'm very sorry that happened to her. Anyway, I know she won't be back for a couple of days. I wanted to give you her homework so she doesn't worry about getting behind. There's an astronomy project due Thursday, but she knows about that."

He was acting very nice, a fact Iris tried hard not to acknowledge in any way. "Okay."

"Is she all right? Lark?"

"I'm sure she'll be okay. Eventually."

"I see. Well, please tell her I hope she's feeling better."

He shifted, looking as uncomfortable as Iris felt. "I . . . ," he started, scratching his face. Iris waited. "Yes, I hope she's feeling better."

He was very nervous, for an ogre.

Now that Lark was with their mom, there was no reason for Iris to go home right after camp, no reason at all for her to stay away from Treasure Hunters and the old books and the small pocket away from time. And the sign, still there.

When she walked in—and there, the smell; and there, the dust in the air; and there, the silence—Mr. George Green was already at the glass counter, hunched over another experiment. This one was a pyramid made out of dowels with a small doughnut-shaped magnet hanging in the middle and long magnets strapped to the base. The hanging magnet was swinging around the pyramid, bouncing around and spinning.

He smiled when he saw her. "Miss Maguire! I was afraid you weren't going to return!"

"Oh." Iris could not help but be flattered that he remembered her, though she supposed not many eleven-year-olds came into Treasure Hunters. "I was busy."

He put his hand to his chest dramatically. "I was afraid it was something I'd done. I've been told I am 'a little strange.'"

"No! I mean, no."

"Well, I am glad. You must live near here?"

"Sort of. I mean. Yes, but. I go to this . . . camp. At the library after school every day. And I bike home, so—"

"So, you have time on your hands to explore the wonders of antiquing."

Iris's eyes popped open. "Yes, that's exactly it," she said, hoping she sounded convincing.

"And"—he motioned to the contraption on the counter, a sly smile spreading across his face—"I suppose this is science too?"

"Well, yeah? Those are magnets, right? So it's just the different polarities making it spin. . . ." The doughnut continued to bounce and spin, and as Iris looked more closely, she realized the whole thing was set upon an antique map of Minneapolis, and the whirling doughnut was moving back and forth over it as if in a frenzy of indecision. "What are you doing, anyway?"

"It is a finding spell," he said. "Or an attempt at one. As you see, the magic seems to be a little confused. But I will persevere! Or perhaps," he added with a sly grin, "I should use 'science.'"

"You might be a little strange," Iris said. He winked. "Can I look at the books? . . . Just on the one shelf, of course," she added quickly.

While Mr. George Green turned his attention back to the

magnets, Iris settled back into Alice's book and the world as it was in 1947.

Last time she'd just browsed through the brittle yellowed pages of the book, reading its brittle yellowed facts, but now she went through looking for Alice's pencil marks.

Really, it didn't make sense that this was Mr. Green's Alice. Iris could not tell if he was thirty or sixty, but he didn't seem 1947 old. But maybe this book was old for Alice, too. Maybe she read it, marveling at the dusty facts, just like Iris was.

Now that Iris was looking more carefully, she realized that this Alice had spent a lot of time with this book, and not just drawing wings on dinosaurs. In the entry for SCIENCE they kept saying *man* for *person* and *he* for *they*: *A scientist is a man who studies science. He records his observations. He does experiments. A psychologist is a man who studies the minds of men. The sociologist studies man's way of living in groups of men.* Alice had circled every *man* and every *he*. There were a lot of them.

Some of her notes felt more random. Under BIRDS she'd underlined everything about flying. (It seemed clear what her superpower would be.) Under MUMMY she'd written, *It Lives!* Next to CAT she'd written, *Travels through clocks!* Above OPERA she'd scrawled, *The Phantom Is Coming for You!*

It was the entry for MAGIC that was most curious. Alice

had underlined *Magic is tricks performed by magicians for entertainment* and added several exclamation points. And then in the margins she'd added, *Magic has a cost.*

Iris took out her journal and wrote this down. And then added some of the other notes:

It Lives!
Travels through clocks!
The Phantom Is Coming for You!
Magic has a cost.

When she went back to the BIRD page to look for any other notes, she noticed that Alice had drawn on top of the existing full-page illustration under the BIRD entry. She'd given some of the birds speech bubbles—the sparrow said *cheep* and the mallard said *quack* and the mockingbird said *ha-ha.* But it was the drawing on the crow that caught her eye—there was something hanging out of its mouth. Iris squinted at it. It looked like . . . a necklace.

Iris carried the book over to Mr. Green. "Was this book Alice's?"

"How do you—"

She thrust the inscription on the front in front of him. "Is this the same Alice?"

His eyes widened. "How could this be? Where did you find this?"

"On the shelf."

"This is a mistake. I need to put this back in her room."

"Her room . . . where?"

"I would not have imagined this was hers. Alice was not interested in—hmm."

"Who is she?"

". . . My sister."

Iris took a step back. "Oh."

Mr. Green did not look like a mole anymore. His eyes were big and sad and oddly focused, like he was watching a parade of ghosts. "Yes," he said, taking the book. "She was my sister."

"Could I—could I ask you a question?" She should not do this, she knew. He clearly did not want to talk about it, and talking about it was poking him in a bruised place. And yet Iris poked. "Here, on the bird page."

"Yes. Alice had . . . quite an imagination."

"It's the crow I'm wondering about. Do you know why she'd draw . . . a necklace hanging out of a crow's mouth?"

His eyes flickered, hardened as he stared at the page. "Alice had a friendship with crows when she was a girl. They liked to bring her gifts. You are a sensible girl and I know that must sound like odd behavior to you, but crows—"

"Are collectors," Iris breathed.

He exhaled. "Yes. Alice was enchanted with them. That's

the sort of girl she was."

"What happened to Alice? Where did she go?"

And there, his eyes filled with ghosts again. "She disappeared," he said.

CHAPTER TWENTY-FOUR

The Wolf in the Closet

I ris nearly stumbled backward.

"This will be hard for a girl like you to understand," he continued, "but Alice was not a sensible girl. Everything was a story to her. She longed for magic, but if she'd had it . . ." He shook his head. "She couldn't have handled it. She couldn't even deal with the mundane world. Her imagination—she saw monsters everywhere."

"I do understand," Iris said quietly.

He nodded at her. "The things that would be nothing to people like you and me, Miss Maguire, they hurt her deeply. Such a sensitive girl, you understand. Slings and arrows. Doom everywhere."

"But what happened?"

"She was sixteen. It was hard enough for her when she was a child, but then it got worse and worse. She was becoming . . . untethered. One afternoon I put her in my study so she was closer to me, and when I went to check on her I opened the door to find her . . . gone."

"Did she run away?" Iris breathed.

"It would not have been possible. She was just gone."

Off the edge of the earth, never seen again.

"So I look for her wherever I go," he finished.

The magnet still spun and swung within the pyramid, jittery and panicked, like a disoriented prey animal trying to find safety.

If something happened to Lark, maybe it would be Iris making compasses out of water and batteries out of potatoes and calling them magic.

She had watched a show about hoarders once, people who kept things. Sometimes, it was because they'd lost something. Sometimes, they needed things to hold on to. Maybe that was why Mr. George Green had a store of old things that he called treasure.

"What about the crows?" Iris asked, though she did not quite know why.

And now his face changed; his eyes met hers; his voice hardened. "Well, yes, Miss Maguire. What about the crows?"

"I . . ." What was she supposed to say? He thought she was practical.

"It is sensible to see the truth of things, even if the truth strains credulity," he said, as if reading her mind.

She did not say anything.

"Alice was such a softhearted girl, you understand. She loved animals. And they loved her. And yet, when I look back . . ."

"What?"

His lips twitched. "You will think me irrational, I am afraid. But . . . I do not trust the crows. That's all I will say."

As Iris biked home, her thoughts whirled. She was not conscious of the route she took home, of whether her legs ached on the big hill, whether the fallen leaves crunched beneath her tires.

No, she was not being rational either. Mr. Green thought she was sensible; meanwhile a great murder of crows was swarming around in her mind.

No, she did not believe in omens. No, she did not believe her nightmare about the crows taking Lark would come true. She did not believe in such things.

But you do not need to believe in something to be afraid of it.

Now, something else in the bag of things she could not

tell Lark. The bag was straining from the weight. But she couldn't tell her—it would have been hard to explain that she'd been at the shop at all, given she hadn't ever told Lark she'd been back in the first place. Lark had clearly almost seen the lie last time, and if she started talking about the shop again, Lark would look more closely at her words, take them apart, and see the lie underneath.

And then the rest of it. The magic, the sister, the crows. What would she say?

Alice, where are you?

Lark had dismantled more of her dollhouse during the day, and when Iris went into her room the mom, dad, and one of the girls were lying on the floor like toppled statues. Iris took a step closer to examine it, but Lark interrupted her.

"Baby Thing is gone," she said, motioning to the dollhouse.

"Like, it doesn't live there anymore?" Knowing Lark she'd decided it got carried off by a bear and was now being raised as one of its own.

"I mean the doll. It's missing." Her voice cracked, and she added, "I looked everywhere, I promise."

Iris flushed. "Oh, no," she said. She did not say *It will turn up*. Nothing had turned up, not the bracelet, the ogre, the pen, the key.

Not Alice.

As for the house, the attic was still full of boxes. But much of the rest of it was gone—the bird room, the bear habitat, the disco room with its hanging sparkly ball and bedazzled walls. Lark had taken the bedroom on the second floor and she'd done the oddest thing imaginable—changed it into an ordinary dollhouse room. In a way.

It was a girl's bedroom, just a garden-variety room. Lark had made wallpaper, big white daisies stenciled on a pink background, and unearthed the original dollhouse furniture, with a dressing table, bureau, and four-poster bed covered in a comforter with one giant daisy in the middle. The room reminded Iris of Abigail, somehow. Doll Lark sat at the dressing table, staring into the mirror.

The little room next to the girl's room had once been the bathroom, way back when. Now Lark had covered all the walls and one of the doorways in shiny black paper, so the only entrance was from the girl's room. That door was shut, but right behind it stood the only object in the room—a wolf figurine.

"It's her closet," Lark said. "I need to put clothes in there and stuff, but I have to make them."

"But—"

"There's a wolf in the closet."

Really, it was obvious.

"She doesn't know it's there," Lark continued, "but she knows something's there. She's terrified to open her closet door. She just won't do it."

"How does she get her clothes?"

Lark shrugged. "She can borrow clothes from her sister. Anyway"—Lark gave her a half smile—"she's been wearing the same thing for three years."

There was something behind Lark's words, something lingering behind the closed door. And Iris did not know how to get the door open.

"So . . . what are you going to do with the rest of the house?"

The other bedroom was still hulled out, but Lark had left the first floor intact, so now the house consisted of the attic with all the boxes, the girl's room, a wolf in a closet, an armory, a haunted room, and the stage with the chicken on it. The house had gone from quirkily strange to terrifying— even the chicken stage now seemed menacing in context. The only thing normal was the girl's bedroom, but even that didn't look right anymore. It was too put-together and normal against the nightmare house—aggressively normal, the sort of room girls had in TV shows in which the rich parents had hired an interior decorator and never allowed the children to eat in there or play in there or read or sleep or talk or breathe. Aggressively normal, in a way that said things were *absolutely not normal.*

She considered. "I don't know. Maybe a panic room? I've never had a panic room."

"And is that where the rest of the family is?"

"No. They're just gone. Looking for the baby, I guess."

Iris swallowed. "Even me?"

Lark lifted her head, her gray eyes meeting Iris's. "It's not really you."

"Well, sometimes it is."

"No! You'd never leave me."

It wasn't until later in the night that Iris realized that when Lark had said, *You'd never leave me,* the *me* was the doll. Which meant that even though the absent doll wasn't Iris, the girl alone with the wolf was Lark.

It was hard to sleep after that.

CHAPTER TWENTY-FIVE

The Compliment Box

A t school the next day, Iris could not stop thinking about Alice. About the sensitive sixteen-year-old girl who had grown less and less—what was the word he'd used?—tethered. About the crows around her.

What was it with the crows? What did they see in girls like Alice? In girls like Lark?

Of course, it could be a coincidence. It could be that the girls were both animal lovers, and prone to shiny things themselves.

Anything more would have to be magic.

And there was no such thing.

Lark was the girl who defeated the monsters—the Pied

Piper, the ogre, the vampires, the trolls. She was the one who taught Iris how to be safe. So what was Iris supposed to do when Lark invited them in?

Lark would be back in school tomorrow, and Iris did not know how she was going to do it. For Lark, if you threw up in class, the only proper course of action would be to transfer schools, and possibly states.

If this were a Disney movie, Iris and Lark would switch places now—Lark would happily enjoy Iris's pod and get into arguments about superheroes and anxiety disorders while Iris stared down the snickering masses in Mr. Hunt's class while demolishing them in math drills. But in her heart of hearts Iris still could not believe that people couldn't tell them apart: they were identical, but not the same. They'd get caught. She didn't know what the punishment was for identical-twin-related fraud, but it was probably pretty dire.

And life was not a Disney movie.

What life was, though, Iris no longer felt sure.

It Lives!

Travels through clocks!

The Phantom Is Coming for You!

Magic has a cost.

It was this last one that stuck in her brain. The *Child's Guide to Our World* was clearly not interested in magic in the same way that Alice was: it spoke of magicians pulling rabbits out of hats and picking a card, any card. There was no cost to those kinds of tricks, except perhaps to the rabbit.

"Do you guys know what it means to say magic has a cost?" Iris asked her pod during lunch. It seemed like the sort of thing they would know.

"Oh, yes," Mira nods. "It's true for psychic powers, too. Whenever my aunt does a reading on a cat, she gets a headache."

"True," said Jin. "In lots of stories you can't just do magic. You have to give something up or else it takes something from you. Like Mira's aunt gets sick. Or maybe you need to give up some blood or something."

"Not in *Harry Potter*," Oliver said. "You can just do spells."

"Yeah, but it does have a cost," Jin said. "There are dark wizards and stuff. There's no cost to do spells, but, like, there's a big cost to magic existing. There's a Dark Lord and Death Eaters and this whole war, and most of the good guys die."

Oliver regarded Jin for a moment and then began to nod slowly and gravely.

"Not everything's in your dictionary, Oliver," Mira said.

"Well, I'm going to write that in, and then it will be," Oliver said.

Iris stared at the page in her notebook: *Magic has a cost.* What did Alice mean? Was it the crows—a cost to them giving her gifts? Or something else? Was that why she'd disappeared?

Magic has a cost. There was magic to Lark, and it made it hard for her to live in a world of owl pellets and Tommy Whedons and math drills.

And there was magic to their sisterhood. There was. She'd always known it, on some level, but now it was clear that no one else understood what they had. It was rare and special. And now everyone was trying to take it away.

And that was the cost.

But she wasn't going to let them. She was going to hold on, with everything she had.

She was going to fight back.

First, she needed to know more. About Alice, about just what Mr. George Green was not saying. There was something behind his words, something he was keeping from her.

But, before she could go to Treasure Hunters again, there was Camp Awesome to endure.

Every day when she walked in, Iris felt a little worse than the day before; by the end of the semester she was going to be oozing into the room like a pile of insecure goo.

Yesterday Abigail had had them decorate shoeboxes for what she termed *SECRET REASONS*, and today the shoeboxes were lined up on the table at the side of the room, each one labeled with the name of the girl who had made it.

Iris had done her best. She'd taken paper and colored markers and written out things she knew to be true and pasted them on the box. *Grover Cleveland was the only president to get married in the White House. The collective noun for ducks is a* paddling. *There's no word that rhymes with orange.* It was something, anyway.

There was a stack of brightly colored note cards in front of each girl's place. Gabrielle immediately started separating hers out by color, and Hannah spread hers out into a rainbow. Iris just stared at hers, feeling like Lark in a math drill.

"Now that you girls have really gotten to know each other," Abigail said, "I think you will all agree that each girl in here is awesome in her own way."

A couple of the girls giggled, and Abigail took that as affirmation. Iris just flushed.

"So take some note cards and write the name of each girl on top of one. And then write down a compliment for the girl. Tell her what makes her awesome. When you're done, you'll slide them into the boxes. You'll all take home your boxes tonight, and whenever you need a reminder about how awesome you are, you'll have it."

Abigail beamed like the sun.

Iris sank in her seat. This was going to be a disaster. She'd barely said a word at camp besides "I don't know" and "I couldn't think of anything." What were the girls going to say about her?

Iris, you are awesome because you sure don't know much.

Iris, you are awesome because you can't think of anything.

This wasn't her. She knew that. She'd never been this way before; it was like she was playing this role here and she couldn't get out of it. Whatever the other girls put in her box, it wouldn't be about her; it would be about this other-Iris, the one who possessed her when she crossed the threshold of the community-room door.

As for her own compliments for the other girls, she had no idea what to say. She'd been observing them all as if behind glass this whole time.

While the other girls worked on their note cards, Iris got out her journal for inspiration and flipped to the chart she'd kept about them. Would anyone notice if she used the adjectives the girls used about themselves? *Novalie, you are nice. Amma, you are amazing.*

"What are you doing?" Hannah asked.

"Uh—just checking something . . ."

Hannah's eyes flicked over the journal page where Iris had been keeping her chart. "You've been writing down everything we say?"

"I guess?" Though it was rather obviously true. This was the thing that other-Iris said. "I guess." She never guessed.

That was the point of trying to know things—so you didn't have to guess.

"Why?"

"I just—" Why? What was she supposed to say? She had no good reason at all. Because she couldn't decorate her journal. Because she didn't even know what kind of superpowers she wanted. Because she liked the other girls. Because she didn't know what to say to them. So instead she wrote things down.

Something like that, she guessed.

Hannah peered at Iris through her glasses. "Are you some kind of spy or something?"

"What? No."

"Like from Camp Not-Awesome or something?"

"No."

"That stuff is private."

"I'm not going to show anyone!"

A couple of the other girls looked up at them, and then back down at their cards.

"But—it's still private. How would you like it if I wrote everything you said down?"

She probably wouldn't. She knew she wouldn't. But then, she never said anything.

"I just . . . I want to keep track. So I know who you are."

"But that's not who I am. That's just . . . stuff. You could know who I am by, like, talking to me? But you don't want to talk to anyone, do you? You're too good for that."

Words choked up into Iris's throat. Hannah's usually bright, open face was twisted in—was that anger? And it looked all wrong, like getting glared at by a daisy.

Iris closed her journal. "I'm sorry," she whispered.

Hannah narrowed her eyes, as if she doubted it, she doubted it very much, and turned away.

Iris stared at her cards, cheeks burning.

Around her, the other girls were starting to get up and slip their cards in the boxes. Hannah stacked hers and banged the edge of the pack on the table, perhaps a little more firmly than was strictly necessary, and then got up haughtily and went to the boxes.

Iris watched as Hannah slipped a card into her box. Maybe it would say, *Iris, you are a spy*, or *Iris, you are creepy*, or *Iris, you should go to Camp Not-Awesome*.

This was not going to end well.

The other girls were sitting back down and talking and laughing together as Abigail grinned like a mad scientist whose preposterous experiment had suddenly come to life.

Iris's own cards were half blank, and so she scrawled messages—*Amma, I think it's awesome you know how to fence; Morgan, you know lots of interesting books; Hannah, the monsters on your notebook are so cool*—all these girls who were so good at things, who had stuff to say, who were not creepy at all.

Now the girls were *circling up*, and starting a sound-and-motion exercise, and Iris hurriedly slipped her alleged compliments into the array of boxes, when there was a knock on the door. And another. Everyone else was too absorbed to hear it, but it didn't matter, because whoever was knocking just opened the door anyway.

A tall overly-polished-looking man in a business suit stood in the doorway, surveying the group. "Is there someone in charge here?"

Abigail turned around. "This is a private class. Is there something I can help you with?"

"I'm afraid the noise from your group is making it difficult to concentrate. Could you ask your girls to keep it down? They're making quite a ruckus."

The girls all stopped and stared at him. Iris sank into the shadows.

"We were not making any kind of ruckus," Abigail said.

"There's no need to be rude. I'm just asking that you control your girls here. And if it continues, I'll have to talk to the library board."

Abigail drew herself up. "My girls can take care of themselves. Feel free to talk to whomever you like, and in the meantime, I ask you not to violate our space again."

From her corner, Iris was impressed. Abigail had lost her

bounce and her bubbles. Suddenly she was tall and firm and still, a warrior at the gates. *Do not mess with my girls.* This, Iris understood. This was the sort of awesomeness she could get behind.

After the man left, stalking out like he was heading straight for his man meeting, Abigail whirled around and faced the group.

"Girls, listen. There are people in this world who will tell you you need to dim your flame. That it's better to be nice all the time, and you should be ashamed for making noise. But you don't have to listen to them. You have a right to be loud! Do you hear me?"

The girls mumbled assent.

She put her hand to her ear theatrically and repeated, "Do you hear me?"

"Yeah!" the girls shouted.

"Do you hear me?"

"Yeah!" they all yelled at the top of their lungs.

"Now," she said, grinning, "let's make some noise."

Abigail waved Iris over and led the girls in some kind of collective stomping exercise, and Iris tried to stomp along with them.

Once upon a time, she was a girl who knew how to stomp. If Lark had been there, Iris would have had no trouble stomping; she could have made enough noise for her and

Lark both. If Lark had been there, Iris would have stomped up to Abigail and said that some people were not stompers and that did not make them less awesome.

But now she was not stomping, not really. It was like her legs didn't know how to do that. Maybe soon she'd stop being able to talk, or clap her hands, or make any noise at all. Maybe soon she'd just fade away.

CHAPTER TWENTY-SIX

Sisters

When camp was over, Iris snuck up to the top floor of the library with her compliment box and lifted up the box lid warily, as if all manner of flying snakes might leap out and bite her.

But there were no snakes, just a pile of folded-up note cards, along with some stray glitter blobs. Stiffening a little, Iris unfolded each of the cards and spread them on the table.

I like your freckles.

You are nice.

You don't say much but I bet if you did say stuff it would be funny.

You're nice.

Your sneakers are cool.

You're really nice.

And, clearly from Abigail, *Iris, you are awesome!*

And one that had her name on it but nothing else.

Iris had to hand it to Hannah—she could simply have not written a card at all, but then Iris might simply not have noticed and not understood the full extent to which she hated her. The best way to get Iris to see what a terrible person Hannah thought she was was to put in a blank card.

Hannah knew how to stomp.

Iris stared at the rest of her compliments. She should value them while she could: Hannah was probably telling all the other girls what a creep Iris was right now, and pretty soon there would be no more *You are nice* for Iris.

And really, she wasn't nice. She knew that. It was the one thing about her that was consistent from her not-Awesome life and her Awesome life, though perhaps she hid her not-niceness better at Awesome. Lark was the nice one. Iris was just Iris.

In fact, for most of her life people had told her she should be nicer. A preschool teacher. A babysitter, who did not understand how things in the house were done. A neighbor dad. A neighbor mom. A cashier at Target. Some kid at a lemonade stand.

But you don't just transform your personality. They could tell her, *Iris, you should be purple.* And she could try to be purple.

She could cover herself in purple paint. But eventually all that paint would wash off and she would still be Iris. Plus, all that paint would probably give her a rash.

You are nice.

Who was this strange girl, who was still not nice, but was not anything else, either?

And who was Iris, now, if she didn't know how to be herself anymore?

Her head was starting to hurt. She dumped the whole box into the garbage.

Then she left the library and crossed the street to the antique shop.

Mr. Green was behind the counter when Iris got there, along with Duchess, who brushed up against Iris's legs.

"Oh, don't pretend to be nice," Mr. Green snapped at the cat.

Duchess glared at him, then turned her back and strutted away, tail puffy and perfectly erect.

"Hello, Miss Maguire!" On the counter in front of him was a green plastic bottle of fizzing pop with a slowly inflating balloon over its mouth.

"What happened to Alice's book?" she asked, nodding to the shelves. There was a gap where the *Child's Guide to Our World* had been.

"I took it away. It will go back to her room. For when she comes back." He said this with such confidence, as if he was saying that the sun would set tonight and come up tomorrow, and the words squeezed Iris's heart.

"You still think she'll come back?"

"I know it," he said. "I am a powerful man, and I have a lot of resources at my disposal. Wherever she is, I will find her. I promised her that."

She took a step closer. She wanted to ask, *How can you be sure?* In a world where people could just disappear, how could you be so sure they would come back?

Or . . . was he sure with the part of him that did kids' science experiments and called them magic? There was no way to ask that question. So she watched the fizz in the pop bottle dance.

"I have a sister, too," she said, after a while.

"Ah. You do. Is she a practical girl, like you?"

"No," Iris said. Fingers of guilt pressed against her temples for a moment, but Iris brushed them away. Lark wouldn't mind her saying that. Lark would not want to be practical.

Would she?

"She's . . . she's had a hard year at school," Iris continued, playing with a strand of hair. "She always does, but this year is worse because I'm not . . . She doesn't . . . work like other people work. She gets hurt easily and feels everything and she's really creative and does the coolest stuff but she can't deal with math drills or owl pellets or loud noises. But crows love her. They were leaving her things for a really long time, but then they stopped and that hurt her too, and she just can't, like, throw up in class and have it be okay, and so she's terrified to go back to school but she has to go back and something bad is going to happen when she does. Someone will say something or not say something and either way it's going to be bad and I'm scared."

Iris closed her eyes for a moment so the wetness in them would not escape, in the way all those words had escaped from her mouth. She was like a fizzing bottle. She should not be saying all these things about her sister to Mr. Green, and yet she had no one else to say them to, and it was too hard to hold on to them. She could barely hold on to anything anymore.

Some practical girl.

But Mr. Green only nodded. "She's not made for this world."

". . . Not really."

"She's like Alice."

"Yes."

"But she has something Alice didn't."

"What?"

"You."

Iris stared at the ground. And there, that pressure again.

"I cannot help but wonder what I could have done differently," he said. "I believe in self-reliance, but, as you say, some people are not made for the world as it is. I should have been more attentive. I let her fancies get the better of her." He gazed at the bubbling beaker for a second. "But that will not be the fate for your sister, Miss Maguire. You take care of her. You protect her."

"I try." Once, she would have believed this. But she didn't even know who she was anymore. She had no adjectives.

"I wonder," he said, "if you are happy."

"Me?"

"Yes. Does the world ever seem too small to you, Miss Maguire?"

She bit her lip. What a question. No. It was way too big.

"It is like that for some of us. We must not worry so much about others that we lose track of ourselves. There are worlds to conquer, Miss Maguire."

Suddenly Duchess let out a long meow and darted over to the clocks. As Iris watched, she turned around and gazed at Iris, giving her one long slow blink.

Do I have your attention?

She did.

Are you sure?

Yes.

Good. Watch now.

The cat jumped on one of the tables and stretched all the way up to the face of the grandfather clock next to it. It batted at the minute hand once, twice, three times.

"Miss Maguire!" said Mr. Green.

"What?"

She glanced back at Duchess, but the cat was gone.

Travels through clocks.

"Where did she go?" Iris said. "I don't understand."

"Miss Maguire, your sister . . ."

"What?"

"Do not tell her about the magic." He gestured to the experiment on the table.

"Why not?"

"We do not want her to get lost."

There is the thing you never say out loud. No one wants to hear it; they just want to hear about mistaken identities and *Parent Trap*–style hijinks. They don't want to hear that the earth has edges, and that you fear that the person who is everything to you could fall off at any moment.

The truth is, Iris's Pied Piper nightmares had never really gone away. They'd just changed. Now the piper was leaving town with just one child in his wake—just Lark, who was so enchanted by his beautiful music she did not see Iris running out of the house yelling at her to stop. Iris knew that if she could just get Lark to *see* her, the spell would be broken and Lark would be saved.

But Lark did not stop, no matter what Iris did. The Pied Piper marched her right out of town. Whatever promises the flute was making to Lark, Iris could not hear them, could not understand. How could she save her from what she did not understand?

They were identical, but not the same.

She wanted to tell Lark; she wanted Lark to solve it for her. This was dream language, symbols, truths underneath lies. This was the language Lark spoke.

How do you say: *I have nightmares that I watch you go and I don't do anything to stop it?*

How do you ask your sister: *What is it about the music that you hear and I don't?*

How do you ask your sister: *What is it about that music that takes you away?*

As Iris biked home, Mr. Green's words swirled around in her head. *We do not want her to get lost.* Of course she was not going to tell Lark about the "magic" that Mr. Green seemed to believe in so thoroughly. She had not even told Lark she'd been visiting him.

Magic has a cost.

What would Lark think if Iris told her about the cat and

the clocks and the notes in Alice's book and the disappearing girl? What kind of story would she write? And what would she think if someone opened the door to magic being real?

What would keep her from walking right through that door?

As Iris turned down the street to her house, she realized she'd been at the shop longer than she'd thought, far too long, and the guilt burned at her stomach. It was late enough that her mom would be back from work, and Lark with her. She should have been there when Lark got home.

And yes, her mom's car was in the garage when she got home, and Iris prepared frantic apologies for Lark. Another flare of guilt when she saw her sister on the back step—had Lark been waiting outside for her?

The answer was no. No, she was not waiting for Iris at all. For near her, with its head in a giant bowl of Cheerios, was an enormous crow.

"Look!" Lark said. "It was in the birdbath when we got home! It—oh!"

Iris had pressed the button to close the garage, and the creaking of the door startled the crow and it flew away.

"Well, anyway," Lark said, "I talked to it for a while and then came back and got the Cheerios."

Lark sounded like a bird herself, chattering away. She

wasn't withered anymore; she was Lark again, and you could feel her happiness in your toes. Their mom appeared behind the back door looking like she'd found everything she'd ever lost.

"Did you see it, Iris?" their mom said. "It's so big! Maybe it was a raven? I wonder what the difference is."

"Ravens are bigger, usually," Iris said. "But that was still a crow. We don't have ravens in Minneapolis."

(Iris is right—ravens provide ill omens for the north of the state only.)

"That's my girl," said her mom with a grin. Whether she was talking about Lark or Iris, Iris could not tell.

Later, the girls sat on the floor of Lark's room, while Lark sorted together pieces for what looked to be the strangest dollhouse room yet. She had a ball of brown clay in her hands and was carefully fashioning it into something or other. Iris knew not to ask questions until Lark was ready.

"So, I've decided I'm not going to be embarrassed about throwing up," Lark proclaimed, studying the clay.

"Good."

"It's not my fault that the assignment was disgusting."

"Totally."

"This ogre's not going to get to me that easily."

Iris leaned back on her hands. "Poor ogre had no idea who he was messing with."

She could hear that there was something missing behind her own words, that the enthusiasm she should feel at seeing Lark act like *Lark* again wasn't quite there. But Lark was too absorbed to notice.

"I figure the vomiting just lulled him into a false sense of security. He thinks he's got me now. So he'll let his guard down."

"Basically," Iris said, trying to sound normal, "the vomiting was like your superpower." There's a species of baby bird that vomits goo at any seagull that tries to eat it, and the goo makes it so the seagulls can't fly and then they drown in the ocean. Iris had read about this bird, and it was the sort of thing she might have told Lark if Lark were a completely different person.

"I have a plan for the oral report tomorrow. I don't have to just stand there and talk. I'm going to make a diorama and bring it up with me so I can talk about that and that's not as hard, you know what I mean? I can look at it and not at Tommy Whedon's blowfish face."

"Is that what this is?" Iris nodded at the clay ball, which was starting to look more and more like *something*, though she could not quite tell you what. "What's the assignment?

"Astronomy. So I'm going to do Andromeda."

"The constellation?"

"Yeah, but I'm going to make a diorama of the myth,"

Lark said. "You know, the story behind the constellation."

Iris chewed on her lip. She could say, *Wouldn't it be easier to just do the assignment?* Because it would be easier—at least, easier on her. Less risky. But Lark probably thought she was doing the assignment; this was just how her brain worked. Astronomy = constellations = mythology behind the constellations = diorama of a girl getting eaten by a sea monster.

Andromeda was a princess in Aethiopia, the daughter of Cepheus and Cassiopeia. Queen Cassiopeia bragged that Andromeda was more beautiful than Poseidon's wife, and in Greek myths it's really a bad idea to say that you're better than the gods at anything, and anyway Poseidon had huge anger issues, and so Poseidon got really mad and sent a sea monster to ravage the town, and so naturally her parents chained her to a rock near the sea and offered her as a sacrifice to the sea monster.

Lark's diorama materials consisted of a giant rubber squid bath toy, a lot of blue glitter glue, a Lego Moana mini doll, some hot-pink duct tape, and her usual construction paper, paints, and clay.

"Are you going to draw in the constellations somewhere?" Iris asked. "So you can explain the actual stars?"

Lark wrinkled her nose. "That wouldn't make any sense. How can there be constellations when the story hasn't happened yet?"

"Well, the stars will still be there. Just . . . nobody's called them a constellation yet."

"Oh. Right. Still, it doesn't make sense."

"But . . . maybe you should do it so you have the astronomy stuff in there?"

Lark looked up at her. ". . . Do you think I'm doing it wrong?"

"No! This is really neat."

"Do you think the kids will laugh at me?"

"No!"

"I mean, this is talking about astronomy, right? There's constellations of the sea monster and Cassiopeia and Cepheus. I can say all of that."

"Yeah, okay."

Lark grabbed a tendril of hair and started to pull on it. "Do you think it's a bad idea?"

"No! I think it's a good idea."

"I mean, if I tell them the story that I know, and I'm just describing the diorama, then I won't get all . . . freaked out, you know?"

"Yeah! Yeah, I know."

Lark worked on her clay blob for a while more, while Iris thought of Alice's fact book, of the angel wings on the *Tyrannosaurus rex* and the flowered hat on George Washington. Maybe Alice gave presentations in school about the flight patterns of brontosauri and about sea monsters instead of stars.

"Hey, what about the antique shop?" Lark said all of a sudden. "Is the sign still there?"

"What?" For a second, Iris was afraid she'd said something about Alice out loud. But she hadn't—Lark just reached over to her mind and plucked things out sometimes, without even knowing it.

"You know? *Alice, where are you?*"

"Um, I'm not sure."

Yes, the sign was still there. But Iris hadn't said anything about Treasure Hunters since before Lark lost her key, and she had no idea how to start now. Iris was the one Lark trusted.

"Maybe we should bike over there this weekend," Lark said. "See what we could find out."

Iris knew that look in her sister's eyes, the one that saw the whole story play out. Alice had gone down the rabbit hole, through the looking glass, and only the intrepid twin sisters could find her.

Yes, she would love it. And Iris couldn't bring her there.

"Yeah," Iris said, for lack of anything else to say.

But Lark was already onto something else.

"Can you believe the crow came back? Finally?"

"No," Iris said. Of course the crow had been there for a

couple of weeks, but Lark didn't know that.

"I know it's silly but . . . it made me feel better. Like I don't need to be scared of ogres. I have a giant crow for a friend."

"No, you don't have to be scared," Iris repeated. "You don't."

"I'll just bring my Cheerios to school and then my giant crow will sit on my desk and no one will mess with me. That'll show 'em."

Iris hugged herself. She should feel better, she knew she should. All the strange birds were settling on their roosts. Lark was herself again, and that meant there was nothing she could not conquer. Even Mr. Hunt and Tommy Whedon, and the very literal nature of school assignments.

But why could a crow do what Iris couldn't?

CHAPTER TWENTY-SEVEN

The Andromeda Project

That night, Lark brought the diorama down to the kitchen and presented it to their mother, who oohed and aahed and texted a picture to their father, who would see it right when he woke up.

Lark never mentioned that it was an astronomy assignment, and Iris did not either.

Lark's diorama may not have been the assignment, but it was probably the best not-doing of an assignment in elementary-school history. Lark had made the background so it looked like a dark white-capped sea disappearing into a stormy horizon, and the purple squid bath toy looked like it was rising out of the waves toward the town, with one of its tentacles rising toward the chained Lego Moana/

Andromeda. Behind her rose the town, with the silhouettes of the huddled queen and king on the backdrop. As for Andromeda herself, she was wearing a red toga over her Lego outfit, and her thin arms were pinned against the gray craggy clay rock face by a pink duct-tape chain. Still, she wore her Lego smile, as if she were just off working in the cupcake bakery, about to go save some dragon eggs with Lego Ella and Lego Azari Firedancer. The effect was impressive: here the sea monster menaces the people of Aethiopia, its long purple tentacle reaching out toward the chained princess; here in the distance the people who have condemned their princess to this terrible fate are huddled in fear; but Andromeda still smiles confidently, sagely, as if she knows something. As if she has a plan.

In Greek mythology, Perseus rescues the princess on his way to defeating the Gorgon. In Lark mythology, that sort of escape would not be nearly enough. Andromeda would have a secret plan that would topple the whole monarchy, perhaps the gods themselves, and by the end the sea monster and Andromeda would be peacefully ruling the kingdom together, land and sea.

And Iris could not help but wonder, would Lark tell the whole classroom that?

No, probably not. She knew better. Just like Iris knew not to start talking about presidential assassination attempts in front of her classmates, Lark knew not to stand in front of a classroom and explain that the murdered wives of Henry VIII became vengeful ghosts and haunted him until he went mad and repented all his sins, or that the dinosaurs all escaped to a secret planet and lived there with Amelia Earhart. You learn these things, over time.

Or had she learned?

Lark was going to stand up in front of the class to give an oral report on Greek myths when she was supposed to do astronomy, and maybe she hadn't learned. School wasn't about being creative. It was about doing what you were told. Most kids learn that by fifth grade, but Lark had not. The best way to get by with someone like Tommy Whedon was to try not to draw attention to yourself at all.

And Lark was about to draw a lot of attention to herself.

It was Crow Girl all over again: Lark wanting the world to be one way, when really it was something else altogether.

And maybe that was why Iris's crow nightmare was so vivid that night. She awoke with the image of the gossipy, swarming crows overtaking her sister, and she could not go back to sleep. What if the project went wrong? What if Mr. Hunt asked her what it had to do with astronomy? What if Lark froze, and the kids laughed at her? And Iris wasn't there to help her?

Well, Iris would have to help her now. So she got up and padded down the stairs.

The diorama was sitting on the kitchen table where Lark

had left it. She'd put the lid back on so she could take it to school without anyone seeing what was inside. Lark liked to unveil things.

Iris took off the lid and studied the project. No, it wouldn't take much to make it work for the assignment—just talking more about the constellations themselves. Maybe she could even add a few details about constellations in general, and how they got named.

So Iris sat down at her mom's computer and made some notes—Andromeda was named a constellation by the astronomer Ptolemy in the second century, along with nearby Cassiopeia and Cepheus and Perseus (the hero who eventually rescued Andromeda) and the sea monster itself, called Cetus—and then printed up pictures of the constellations with illustrations of the figures drawn over them. Iris would not try to draw those herself—they would be all wrong.

But she could draw the stars. That way Lark could just point to them if Mr. Hunt asked. She could gather her thoughts, show the stars, maybe then refer to Iris's notes.

Then it would be fine.

So Iris took a gold Sharpie and carefully drew in dots for the Andromeda constellation, as well as Perseus and Cetus. She didn't have Lark's artistry, and some of the proportions might not have been quite right, but she did the best she could. Then she folded up her notes and printouts and

tucked them in an envelope.

And then Iris was able to sleep.

Of course, Lark overslept the next day, and the morning was too full of Lark-getting-ready chaos for Iris to give her the envelope full of notes, and when Lark finally came downstairs (dressed like herself again in an *Alice in Wonderland* T-shirt, puffy skirt, and purple-and-black leggings), Iris suddenly couldn't find the words.

It had seemed so simple last night: She'd just do a little extra work and have it there if Lark needed it. And of course Lark would be delighted—who doesn't want to have a backup plan?

In the bright light of day she remembered that Lark did not particularly love a backup plan.

So Iris slid the envelope in her own backpack. She'd wait until the time was right.

But the time wasn't right in the car, with Lark chatting happily away. Iris kept one eye on the diorama, which Lark hadn't opened yet, and another out the window. It seemed like there were crows everywhere this morning.

It will be fine, Iris reassured herself. It's just extra facts. Extra facts never hurt anyone. It will be fine.

And Iris kept telling herself that as Lark walked into school carrying her diorama as if it were made of fairy dust and wishes, and when they entered the fifth-grade wing they found Oliver, Jin, and Mira waiting for them.

"Hi," Iris said, glancing around.

Oliver gaped. "Wow," he said. "You're *identical!*" He looked as if none of the dictionaries in the world could have prepared him for this moment.

"Don't stare, Oliver," Mira said.

"Find your chill, Oliver," Jin said. "Hi, Lark."

"This is . . . my pod," Iris said. Casually, she rested her hands on the ledge in front of her and tapped out, *I'll explain later.*

"Okay!" Lark said cheerfully, wrapping her hands around the box. *Weirdo,* she tapped.

"We were waiting for you," Oliver said. "We thought we'd walk you to class."

"Me?" Lark said.

"Yeah, you're our pod sister!"

Oliver, Jin, and Mira all grinned, and Iris wanted suddenly to build a diorama for them all. They had planned this—the pod. They had planned to meet Iris and Lark outside the fifth-grade wing and welcome them with open pod arms, so Lark wouldn't have to walk to class alone after the whole vomit episode.

It was so nice. Like, really nice, not the kind of nice that old ladies in grocery stores and annoyed preschool teachers wanted you to be. Iris did not know what to do.

"What's that?" Oliver asked, pointing at the box.

Lark grinned. "It's a diorama. I have a presentation. It's Andromeda." She said it like it was no big deal, like Lark gave presentations all the time, with or without Greek mythology dioramas.

"Like the myth?" Oliver said.

Lark nodded happily.

"Neat. I made a Gorgon head out of Legos once," Oliver said.

"They should have Lego Greek myth sets," Jin said.

Lark's jaw dropped, like this was the best idea she'd ever heard. "They should! Can you imagine Athena coming out of Zeus's head?"

Mira shook her head ruefully. "You get to make dioramas? We never get to make dioramas."

Cool pod, Lark tapped.

I know, Iris tapped back, the undercurrent between them crackling just as it was supposed to.

But something was wrong. Iris had something to tell her and she could not just tap it out. She reached into her backpack and put her hands on the envelope.

"Can we see?" Oliver asked.

"The bell's about to ring," Iris said, squeezing the envelope.

"Just a peek!" Jin said.

As Iris's heart went into her stomach, Lark grinned and said, "Okay!" She lifted off the top of the box and displayed her creation for them, and as the whole pod made appreciative noises, her smile only got bigger.

She did not look inside. Maybe the stars would just disappear by presentation time. Maybe Iris had drawn them in magical disappearing Sharpie. Maybe Iris herself could disappear.

"I wish we did Greek myth projects," Jin said.

"Why are there stars during the day?" Oliver asked.

The bell rang then, and so Lark put the top back on, looking at Oliver like he was very random indeed. Mira yelped something about them being late and Iris motioned them on.

"I'll catch up," she said, grabbing Lark's arm.

"I can't be late," Lark whispered, shoulders slumping, eyes widening.

Iris breathed in. "Here," she said, handing over the envelope. "I made you this. It's just facts about constellations and some printouts with the pictures of all the Perseus constellations and stuff about Ptolemy and—"

Lark's face went from confusion to slow comprehension to something that looked very much like hurt. Iris's words shriveled in her mouth; she could feel herself shriveling with them.

Then red spread across Lark's face, just as it had the first day of school. Mr. Hunt leaned out of the classroom and called for Lark, but for a moment she just stared at Iris as if she could not quite understand what she was seeing. Then she grabbed the envelope, turned, and stalked into the classroom.

Iris skulked to her seat and spent the morning feeling shame bubble inside her like a lava pit. *Please,* she thought, *please let it be okay. Please.*

Then, about halfway through math, Iris's hand flew to her chest. She looked up and saw Mr. Hunt lurking in the doorway.

That burning inside her changed, suddenly, in the blink of an eye. It wasn't shame anymore, but it was still bright red and hot and poisonous. She stood up before Ms. Shonubi even had a chance to call her name.

"Iris," he said when they were standing in the hallway, hands folded and pressed against his chin, "there's a . . . I was wondering if you could . . ."

"What? What's wrong?"

"Your sister is in the nurse's office. I was wondering if you might go talk to her."

"What happened?" This was his fault. If he hadn't made Lark feel horrible, if he'd understood Lark like Mr. Anderson had, none of this would have happened.

"I'm afraid she got up to give a presentation and got

very . . . flustered. Some of her classmates—there may have been some reaction to the incident on Monday. . . . There was some teasing and she was very upset and ran out of the room."

Iris felt the heat rise in her cheeks, in her chest, in her fingertips. Hot tears burned in her eyes. Hot words rose up in her throat and burst out of her mouth. "You're an ogre!" she yelled.

Heat rises. Iris knew this. And so her words floated up in the air to the ceiling and then just hung there where Iris and Mr. Hunt could stare at them. He gaped at the words, and then back at her, as if maybe she was the ogre.

Iris turned and ran.

Lark was in Ms. Baptiste's office on the cot with a Barn-hill Elementary blanket wrapped around her shoulders. Her face was white with deep red splotches, and her eyes were swollen and red.

"You drew on my project," Lark said.

Iris's throat burned. She could not speak.

"You drew stars on my project," Lark repeated. "You didn't even draw them well. You're terrible at drawing."

"I'm sorry," Iris breathed. Her tears were burning her face.

"And your envelope? Your little facts? Your printouts? You think I can't look up stuff on the internet?"

"No, I—"

"I can, you know. I can look up stuff *and* write it down. And I can draw, too. I could have made these drawings." Lark pulled a piece of paper out of her backpack and crumpled it up, then threw it at Iris.

"I know."

"I could have drawn the stars on if I'd wanted to. But I didn't want to. I wanted to do it my way. Why doesn't anyone let me do things my way?"

"I didn't mean—"

"But you did. You thought my way was stupid, so you thought you'd save me from myself, is that right?"

It was. It was exactly right. Iris was crumpling like paper.

"So all morning all I could see was you handing me that envelope. And I just wanted to go home. I should have gone home. But I didn't—I couldn't. And then it was time and I took the lid off and I saw what you'd done. You didn't even tell me. You just left me to discover it! And Mr. Hunt kept calling me up and then people started laughing. And someone started making puking noises, and people laughed harder, and I'm holding this stupid stupid thing and—"

"Lark—"

Lark looked up at her. "If you don't believe in me"—and now the tears were spilling out of her eyes again, spilling everywhere. She did not finish the thought.

CHAPTER TWENTY-EIGHT

For Your Own Good

When their mom came and picked Lark up from school, Iris did not even try to go home with them. She just sat on the cot in Ms. Baptiste's office with her head in her hands.

This was her fault.

She wanted to go back and put her finger on the precise moment where things went wrong, so she could make sure never ever to do it again as long as she lived. And while it seemed like sneaking down in the middle of the night to fix the project might have been it, that if she pressed on that moment hard enough everything she'd done and everything she should do now would be clear, something whispered in the back of her mind: *That isn't it, you dear thing. Go deeper.*

But she did not want to go deeper. She didn't want to go anywhere. She just wanted to stay here with her head in her hands in the dark and quiet, possibly forever.

But soon Ms. Baptiste came to get her and gently suggested that it was time to go back to class.

Iris got up wordlessly, and then she noticed the nurse's necklace.

"That's a crow," she said flatly.

"Oh, this? Yes." Ms. Baptiste held up the silver bird dangling from her necklace. "I love corvids. They're so smart! Did you know they can use tools?"

"Yeah, I know."

"Did you know they can recognize faces? And they warn each other about dangerous people? If someone tries to hurt a crow, pretty soon other crows start attacking them *on sight*. Isn't that cool?"

"I guess," Iris said.

"I like it," said Ms. Baptiste. "They protect each other. It would be nice to have a flock, wouldn't it? Anyway, you go back to class. I'm sure Lark will feel better soon."

Iris nodded softly.

When she left the nurse's office, she did not turn right to go back to the fifth-grade wing. She had made a mess of everything, but now she needed to try to fix it. So she headed right to the office and told Ms. Snyder she needed to see Principal Peter.

Principal Peter was a shiny-headed, shiny-faced man who wore a big, shiny smile that showed off his shiny, shiny teeth. It was hard, sometimes, to look at him directly, but right now Iris fixed her gaze on him and did not blink.

"And what can I do for you, young lady?" he asked shinily.

She could do this. She could make it right. She could press her finger on this moment and discover it was the moment she made everything okay again.

She knew she needed to act correctly, that if she got emotional he'd dismiss her as a hysterical little girl. That is what it is to be a kid: adults don't take you seriously unless you act like you have no feelings.

Iris cleared her throat.

"I am here to talk to you about Lark," she responded, speaking slowly. She was sitting up so straight; her chest was out; her voice was steady even though some strange tendril of feeling was tickling at her throat.

"I see," he said. "As I'm sure you are aware, it wouldn't be appropriate for me to talk about another student with you."

"But—she's not another student. She's my sister."

"I am aware of that. You do look something alike!"

He laughed. Iris did not.

Breathe, Iris. Breathe. She had come in here mad before, and he had done nothing but question her attitude. So she was going to take deep cleansing breaths, just like Abigail had taught them, and speak to him, one reasonable person to another.

"I think Lark should be in Ms. Shonubi's class," she said reasonably.

"I am afraid there is no room in Ms. Shonubi's class."

"I'll switch with her. I'll be in Mr. Hunt's class."

He smiled a shiny smile, as if she were a first grader telling him she wanted to be a Jedi Knight when she grew up. "This is not a Disney movie."

"That's not what I mean." Breathe, Iris. Breathe. "I could take her spot, and she could take mine."

"Now, Iris," he said, leaning forward in his chair. "I'm sure you understand that we can't simply switch students for no reason."

"But there is a reason."

"Iris, you can trust us. We are working hard to make the best possible learning environment for her. Mr. Hunt has already spoken to the students who teased your sister."

"He did?"

"As you know, our school has a strict anti-bullying policy. That is part of our Believe in Barnhill program. But"—he leaned back in his chair, eyes never leaving her—"that policy applies to you as well. You called a teacher an ogre."

Iris went hot.

Principal Peter folded his hands together. "Now," he said,

looking a little less shiny, "do you really think that's appropriate?"

No. Of course she didn't think it was *appropriate*. Iris was not a sheep dropped into an elementary school, bleating all around looking for her ill-mannered herd. Right there in the front of the school handbook—the same thing the students had to sign at the beginning of the year—it said, *Do not call teachers ogres.*

Or it probably would next year.

"I believe I asked you a question."

"No!" Iris said, too loud, too fast. "Of course not."

"I am glad we agree. It is not appropriate at all. If anything like that happens again, we will have to discuss measures. Now, Iris. I know this is a difficult adjustment for you. I understand your emotions are high. We didn't expect this to be easy, but we do believe this is in your best interest in the long run."

"... We?"

"Your parents and I."

Her eyes narrowed. "It was your idea, though. You're the one who did this. You're mad at me for complaining to you last year and you're trying to punish us." She might as well say it. She was saying everything else.

"Iris . . ." He shook his head, as if she was the one who had disappointed him. "First of all, that's not how adults do things. Second of all, I am not 'mad' at you. But, yes, you do seem to devote a lot of emotional and mental energy to defending your sister, energy that could be better spent on learning. And how you do expect your sister to know how to stand up for herself when you're always standing up for her?"

Iris's mouth fell open.

"Third, I cannot have you believe this is some kind of retribution from me, or that this decision wasn't made with both of your very best interests at heart. It was your parents' idea, not mine, as I'm sure they'd be happy to tell you."

A chill hit Iris's body with the force of a massive wave. She sat for a moment, while the cold washed over her. It felt like someone had turned a dial in her brain and all she could hear was the hum of static. "I have to go," Iris said.

It had been her parents' idea.

It hadn't been Principal Peter at all, though he agreed to do it. And now Iris was mad all over again.

She could not exactly call her mother and yell, because her mother was watching over Lark, and she did not want Lark to hear any of this.

But there was another person she could yell at.

If she could find a way.

It was six hours ahead in London. This meant they mostly talked to their dad in the mornings before school, later on the weekends. By the time Iris got home from Camp

Awesome tonight, her dad would be fast asleep.

Still. He'd said when he'd left that the girls could message him anytime and he'd get his head to a computer screen as soon as he possibly could, and even though he wasn't there *with* them, they should always know he was there *for* them, and he would prove that by turning on the notifications on his Skype app so he'd always see them and could respond right away, and while Iris didn't know what exactly that meant, it seemed to mean something.

So Iris stomped up to the media center, to the one grown-up in the school who might look right at her and really *see* her.

"Mr. Ntaba—

"What's wrong, Iris?"

"I need to talk to my dad. Lark had to go home and—"

"You need to use the phone?"

"With the computer. I need to Skype him. He's in London."

Mr. Ntaba gazed at her, studying her. Iris looked back. He had known her for six years, and for five of those he'd seen her always next to Lark, and this year she was not, and he must know. He must know that even the Right Book could not help her now.

"Please," she said quietly.

A moment. A short nod. "Okay, Iris. You can use the computer in my office."

Soon she was sitting in Mr. Ntaba's office chair while he

loaded up Skype for her and watched as she signed into the family account.

DAD I NEED TO TALK TO YOU

And he wrote back right away, just like he'd promised:

Three minutes.

When his face popped up on the screen, Mr. Ntaba ducked back out front, and Iris turned to steel.

"I heard Lark had a bad day," her dad said. "Are you all right? Where are you anyway?"

No. She was not going to be distracted. "This was your idea."

"What?" he said. "What was?"

"That we're in different classrooms. It wasn't Principal Peter's idea at all. It was *your* idea."

Her dad's face hardened. "Yes. And your mother's. It is, after all, our job to parent you two girls. As your parents."

And there, everything was hot again. "Why didn't you tell me? Why did you let me believe that it was Principal Peter?" *Do not cry, Iris, do not cry.*

"Well, Iris," he said, his voice heavy. "I guess we thought you'd be upset."

"You lied to me," she said quietly.

"We didn't *lie.* You made an assumption and we did not correct that assumption. But if you had known it was us, we never would have heard the end of it. We wanted you to be able to focus your attention on making the best of the situation."

"Fine," Iris said. "If you did this, you can change it. It's not working."

"It's still September!"

"Just . . . call Principal Peter and tell him it's not working; tell him Lark should be in class with me."

"I know this is hard. I know Lark is struggling."

"Mr. Hunt is"—*don't say he's an ogre, don't say he's an ogre*—"not right for her. The worst bully in fifth grade is in her class!"

"Or it might be that your sister is struggling because she does not have you in class with her, and that is very new. There is going to be an adjustment period. We did not expect this to be easy at first, on either of you. Give her some time; let her find herself."

"She doesn't need to find herself!" If there was any kid in the whole world who had already found herself, it was Lark. "There's nothing wrong with her."

"No. No there's not. But maybe both of you need to learn to be okay without the other one."

"Why?"

"Because that's life! That's what growing up is. You can't depend on another person for everything."

"Why not?"

". . . Because."

Iris narrowed her eyes. He didn't have a good answer. He was just saying these things that you say because they sound good, because somewhere in time someone decreed that You Can't Depend on Another Person for Everything. What kind of an idea was that? It sounded like the sort of thing people who didn't have anyone to depend on said to make themselves feel better.

"This isn't just about Lark," he added.

"What do you mean?"

"I mean, Iris, that maybe you needed this too."

Iris sputtered. Where to begin? If she argued that, no, she didn't need this, she was accepting the *too* part. Which she was not accepting, not in the least. With one word, her father had swept away everything she'd said, like it had never happened, like they both had agreed that, yes, Lark needed this.

"Maybe you need to spend a little less time on your sister and a little more time minding yourself."

"I don't need minding!"

"Iris, you called a teacher a troll"—*Do not correct him*, Iris told herself. *Do not correct him.*—"Yes, I know about that! Your mother and I already talked. What were you thinking?"

What was she thinking? She hadn't been thinking! Wasn't that obvious? Apparently everyone thought she'd sat around and planned this, that she'd woken up in the morning and thought, *Hey, you know what would be fun?*

Nothing about this was fun.

"Iris, you have to stop treating everyone like it's you and Lark against the world. It's not healthy. And apparently it's going to lead you to insult teachers. Really, Iris, name calling?"

Her anger turned into something else, something slimy and slithering and thick. Before, she'd wanted to burst open, but now she felt like she might collapse inward like a dying star. And maybe it would be better.

"I didn't mean it," she said, voice a whisper.

This was failing, all of it. They were the ones who had done this, and yet she was the one imploding. If she had been with Lark, none of this would have happened, and she wouldn't have tried to fix Lark's project, and she would not have said the thing she said to Mr. Hunt, and everything would be okay.

No, she was not strong. No, she did not sound like someone who should be listened to. She was Invisible Iris, Immature, Impulsive, Insulting, Infantile. Inept. Inconsequential. She was the sort of person who could not be trusted, the sort other people made decisions for. For Your Own Good.

"Iris, I trust nothing like this will ever happen again."

"No," she whispered.

"That's my girl."

". . . Please, just move her?"

"Iris," said her father, "you will be okay. She will be okay. We want you guys to have the faith in yourselves that we have in you."

"I have to go," Iris said, and hung up.

Out front, Mr. Ntaba was talking to a second grader, perhaps showing her the book that would change her life. Inside the office, Iris leaned against his chair and stared at the monitor, blinking hard.

She'd made a mess of everything. And she couldn't clean it up.

Abigail had told them to make noise, to stomp around; she'd told them they were worth listening to. But Iris never had a problem making noise; she never had a problem standing up for herself. She could stand tall and firm and still; she could stomp around when she needed to; she could let her inner flame shine bright.

It was supposed to be the key. The magic. The spell that opened up the world to you. Be strong; be confident; stomp around. That was supposed to work.

But what happened when you did all of that and no one listened?

CHAPTER TWENTY-NINE

The Girls in the Glass Coffin

Though the day had been terrible, Iris did not dread going to Camp Awesome. It wasn't that she was happy about it either; she just felt nothing. She had spent all of her feelings for the day.

Anyway, she didn't want to go home. She couldn't bear to see Lark. And Lark probably didn't want to see her.

Iris took her seat, avoiding Hannah's eyes, and everyone else's for good measure. Abigail was standing in front, resting her hand on a big stack of picture books from the library.

"Well," she said, "we talked about superheroes and superpowers the other day. Today I want to talk about fairy tales! I got a bunch of fairy tales and folktales from these very library shelves!"

In her head, Iris let her head fall on the table with a loud *thwap*.

Amma perked up. "Do you have any from Somalia?" she asked, motioning to the pile of books.

"Um," Abigail said. "No."

"That's okay," Amma said cheerfully. "I'm used to it."

Abigail went on to chirp about how the Grimm brothers get all the credit for the fairy tales we know today but they didn't actually write them; they just went around and collected the stories.

Amma whispered, "Nobody thinks the Grimm brothers had anything to do with Somalian folktales."

Abigail did not hear. "I'm going to hand out books in a second, but first I want you guys to think about what fairy-tale character you identify with the most, and when you're ready, we'll go around the room, okay? Who wants to start?"

"What do you mean?"

It was Iris who had spoken, and she seemed just as surprised by it as anyone else.

"Iris!" Abigail looked like it was Iris's first word ever and she was delighted to be the one there to witness it. "What fairy-tale character do you identify with?"

She shook her head.

"Identify with! Feel is the most like you? Like maybe you really feel like you're a lot like Cinderella or Rapunzel or . . ."

Iris glanced around the room. All the girls were looking at her.

It was not exactly what she wanted to ask. She wanted to ask Abigail, what happens if you stomp and no one pays any attention? What do you do then? But she couldn't ask that, at least not without dissolving. So instead she said:

"But . . . that doesn't make any sense."

"How so?"

"How are we supposed to identify with fairy tales? Our lives aren't like fairy tales. Fairy tales have witches and curses and stuff."

Abigail grinned, as if Iris had said something delightful—though Iris was pretty sure she had not. "Well, that's where the imagination part comes in. Think about the biggest problem in your life right now. Go ahead. You don't have to tell me; just think in your head: What's your biggest problem at this very moment?"

You, Iris thought.

It wasn't true, but it felt good to think it.

"Now, take that problem and tell it in the language of magic!" She said that like it was a real thing, like that was a language one could speak. *Oh yes, I take French and Chinese and also I can ask how to get to the bathroom and the library in Magic.*

"I mean it," Abigail exclaimed. "Maybe the problem is a curse, like Sleeping Beauty had. Or a monster!"

An ogre. Lark would understand, but Iris just shook her head helplessly. All her monsters were Lark's. She could feel the other girls looking at her, and part of her brain was whispering, *Shut up and act normal!* But the rest of her just didn't care anymore. She wasn't normal. It was time to stop pretending.

Abigail tried again. "What do you like about fairy tales?"

Her cheeks flushed. "I . . . I don't like fairy tales."

"Why not?"

"Because . . . because girls in fairy tales are boring. Because stuff just happens to them. They don't do anything."

Abigail frowned. "I think—"

"You know, she's right," Morgan said. "They really don't. It's all bad things happening to them."

"Yeah," Preeti chimed in. "And they always get saved by men. What's up with that?"

Abigail blinked rapidly. "Well, Cinderella did something. She went to the ball."

"Her fairy godmother just showed up!" Morgan said. "Bibbidi-bobbidi-boo! Cinderella didn't *do* anything."

"Cinderella," agreed Preeti, "is not awesome."

Amma added, "If you'd brought Somalian folktales, I could show you some where the girls aren't boring."

Iris looked around. The other girls were all nodding thoughtfully, as if they agreed with her, as if Iris had finally said something interesting.

No, she didn't like fairy tales. She'd never liked them. Either the Pied Piper was punishing kids for the grown-ups' sins, or some girl was stuck in a tower because her parents took some cabbages. What was to like?

"Yeah," burst out Novalie. "Like any day you could find yourself in a glass coffin with weird dwarves staring at you, or trapped in a castle with this huge wall of thorns."

"And you're waiting for some guy to crawl up your hair," said Preeti. "That's, like, your only hope."

"Or kiss you," said Morgan, shuddering.

"It's basically a horror movie," added Gabrielle, with the authority of someone who knew these sorts of things. "Like you're just going along minding your own business and some witch hates you because you're pretty or some fairy is all ticked because your parents didn't invite her to your christening and then suddenly you've got witches after you."

Iris swallowed. This was exactly what it was like. Suddenly she felt like she was in a glass coffin, dwarves pointing and staring and whispering to one another, and she was helpless to do anything. She was trapped in a tower and someone was pulling on her hair and it hurt so badly. She was all alone in a dark castle dreaming of monsters and she tried and tried but she couldn't wake up, and there was no Lark to crawl into bed with her and tell her it was going to be okay.

All day she had not cried, and now, suddenly, the tears came to her eyes, stinging like poison. She pressed her lips together hard, trying to keep them from spilling out—she did not want to cry here, of all places—and out of the corner of her eyes she saw Hannah looking at her like maybe she wasn't the worst person in the whole world, like maybe Hannah knew just how she felt, and then the tears fell.

The other girls knew how she felt.

The other girls knew how she felt.

They felt the same way.

They felt the *same way*.

Edging her chair closer, Hannah slipped Iris a Kleenex. "I have lots," she said, "you can have as many as you want," and that did not help Iris's crying at all. Then a hand on her back—Amma, who had gotten up from her chair just to comfort Iris, and then Emily was on the other side of her squeezing her knee, and Hannah kept giving her Kleenex, one after another.

Then, a large sniff from the front of the class. Abigail, standing, watching the gathering group. "You girls . . . ," she said, eyes full. "You're . . . awesome."

Iris looked up and all of the Awesome girls were looking at her like they would be around her too if only she had any more sides. Preeti was rubbing her own eyes, and Iris wanted to say something, she wanted to tell the girls that she knew how they felt, that she felt the same way, that they could feel the same way together and that was better than feeling it alone. But she had finally gotten her crying under control and if she said that she might never stop.

And then Abigail exclaimed, "Gretel!" far more loudly than strictly was called for, and all the girls exchanged glances.

"Pardon me?" Gabrielle asked.

"In 'Hansel and Gretel'!" Abigail exclaimed. "Gretel's not boring. She kills the witch!"

Now, the other girls were looking to Iris to respond. To Iris! As if she was the expert on fairy-tale heroines and the relative boringness of the characters therein, as opposed to the one with the chapped cheeks and red stinging eyes

So she nodded. And wiped her face. And took a big breath.

And the other girls nodded too.

"Yes!" Abigail exclaimed. "Hansel goes in the cage, and the witch tries to get Gretel to turn on the oven so she can cook her! And so Gretel tricks the witch and says she can't figure out how. And so the witch finally leans into the oven to show her, then Gretel pushes her! A very clever plan. I might even say"—she raised her eyebrows—"an awesome one."

Everyone settled back in their seats then. Iris looked around the room, regarding her campmates. It felt like her chair had been at the edge of the room this whole time, and now that she'd pulled it into the circle, she could see what they really looked like. Gabrielle shot her a look that clearly said *I hope you're okay* and Iris felt herself smile a little at her.

"I like Cinderella," Emily whispered to Iris.

"That's okay," Iris said quickly, sniffing a little. "My sister loves Cinderella."

"Sometimes you want a fairy godmother, you know?"

"Yeah," Iris whispered back. "Yeah, I do."

CHAPTER THIRTY

Puzzles

Iris might not have understood what Abigail was asking, but I did not have any problem understanding it at all. And I do like fairy tales.

Iris had misunderstood the question. Abigail was not asking the girls whom they admired. She asked whom they identified with, a much different question.

I identify with all the Grimm fairy-tale girls, every single one. I always have. Those were the only stories I understood, and the only stories I knew how to tell. I did not know there were other possibilities.

And Iris identified with them too though she would never have phrased it that way.

Iris was in a glass coffin, trapped in a tower, alone in a castle fast asleep.

She dreamed that she'd undone the spell, that now she was fighting the monsters who had trapped her. She thought she was awake and yelling and stomping and people could finally hear her. But no. No one could hear her, and she couldn't make a sound. She was still trapped.

And she did not have a fairy godmother.

But it is something to know that all those other girls are in the room with you. Even if you are all in glass coffins. At least you aren't alone.

It is a terrible thing, to feel alone.

Now that September was at its end it was cold enough for fall to begin its spread through the trees. Some trees were still green and full, others bright red or orange or yellow, and a few were already bare.

One of the big maples in front of the library had lost its leaves already and was now a tangle of limbs and branches. As Iris walked out of the library, she saw that this tree was covered in crows.

There were dozens of them in that one tree, covering the branches as if the crows themselves were that tree's peculiar fruit.

And they weren't just in that tree. There were crows

everywhere—along the phone lines, in the other trees, perched on the roofs of the other shops. They were everywhere except in the immediate vicinity of Treasure Hunters.

So Iris darted across the street into the store.

"Are you quite all right?" Mr. Green asked when she walked in.

Iris shook her head. There was no point. Her face tended to hold on to the stain of tears for as long as it could.

"Would you like to talk about it?"

Yes. No. Yes.

She'd come here for a reason, though. Even if she wasn't quite sure what that reason was.

"My sister . . . Lark . . . she had a bad day at school. And I can't help her. There's nothing I can do."

"You feel powerless," he said.

She looked up at him and nodded.

"It is a terrible feeling."

"Everything's just so out of control," she said. "And there's nothing I can do about any of it. Nobody's listening to me. And maybe they shouldn't—I don't know. What happened today . . . it was my fault." She swallowed and glanced to the floor. "Maybe I'm bad for Lark."

There. The words were out now.

When you are trapped in a glass coffin, you have a lot of time to think. All these pieces had been floating around in the air just waiting for Iris to put them together. And now she had.

All day long this roiling goo of emotions had been churning inside her, morphing from one terrible beast to another, but now all of that had settled. Now the goo just sat there, heavy.

Her parents had told the school to separate them. At first her reaction had just been fury, but now the cold fact of it stared at her and she could not look away.

It used to be that they had better outcomes when they were together. Everyone knew it. That was the story. But somewhere along the line the story changed, and now, apparently, they were better off apart. Their parents believed it. Not just that: they believed that Iris was bad for Lark. That without her Lark would *find herself*. Which meant that *with* her, Lark was lost.

There was a time that this idea would have infuriated her. She would have run into Lark's room and spilled words everywhere, so many words they would fill the room and threaten to flood it. *Can you believe it? How absurd! How ridiculous. How dare they? How could they?*

But now she found herself wondering if it was true.

"Do you really believe that you're bad for your sister?"

"I don't know. I don't know anymore." He had said Alice's fate wouldn't be Lark's, but then, he also thought Iris was sensible. He could be wrong about anything.

He frowned. "I don't understand why people aren't listening to you. You are not some silly girl. They should listen."

"Well, they don't."

"Sometimes it can be easy to feel powerless in the face of other people's problems. Alice was a very unhappy girl, but it was important for me to remember I was not responsible for her emotions. I could not make her listen to me, alas. But I have been alive a long time, and I have learned something very important."

"What?"

"Power is yours for the taking. And once you have it, you never give it up."

Iris tried not to make a face. It was easy for him to say. He probably believed in stomping, too.

"Do you think your sister thinks you're bad for her?" he asked after a moment.

"I don't know."

"Alice . . . did not always appreciate me, I fear. She told herself stories. She kept secrets."

"Lark doesn't keep secrets from me."

"And you? Do you keep secrets from Lark?"

"I . . ."

"Sometimes you must keep secrets. To protect someone. You understand that, right?"

Iris nodded slowly.

"We must protect our sisters, you and I. There are many monsters in the world, Miss Maguire. And they are happy to prey on the vulnerable."

She did not want to talk about monsters. She wanted the *Child's Guide to Our World* and its bright illustrated pages. She wanted to draw wings on dinosaurs herself. She understood, suddenly, why someone would do that: you could make a world as strange as you want, as long as you had control of it.

"I should go home. Lark is home. I need to talk to her. Tell her I'm sorry. I don't want her to worry."

He eyed her. "Will she worry? Doesn't she know where you are?"

"Not . . . not really."

"Ah." He studied her for a moment. "I like you, Miss Maguire. You are a most unusual girl. Listen to me." He leaned in. "You do not need to feel powerless."

Mr. George Green seemed different now. Less silly, less ineffectual. Less mustardy and less like a mole man.

"Do you still have that encyclopedia? Alice's?"

"I do. It is upstairs."

"Could I look at it again sometime?"

He nodded slowly, studying her.

"Come back tomorrow," he said. "I have many things I would like to show you."

*　*　*

Iris biked home, the air biting at her cheeks, her thoughts biting at her mind.

Do you think your sister thinks you're bad for her?

Before today, Iris would have said no, of course not. Lark would never think that. But that was before Lark looked at her like Iris had personally forced her to dissect seventeen owl pellets.

Maybe Lark did think so now. But Iris could apologize. She could do that. She could explain how weird this year had been, and how she felt like she'd been unraveled and then put back together wrong. She could tell Lark she just didn't know how to be a good sister anymore. She could tell her she missed her during the day.

She could try.

But when Iris got home, her mom was in the kitchen, alone.

"Your sister's asleep," she said

"Okay," Iris said. "Maybe I should go up?"

"No. She needs sleep. I don't want you to wake her. She had a hard day."

"I know!" It came out a little more forcefully than Iris had intended. But she did know. If there was one thing in the world she knew to be true, it was that Lark had had a hard day. And it was her fault.

Her mom's eyebrows went up. "Yes, I know you know. And I know you know you are not to be rude to teachers. And yet, here we are."

"I'm sorry. I am. I was mad—"

"I know that. Iris, you need to get your anger under control. You're too emotional—"

"That's not true!" She was not the emotional one.

"Oh, I think it is. I know you're upset that we separated you guys, but if you want to be involved in these decisions, you need to start acting more mature." She shook her head. "Do you think that helps your sister? Yelling at teachers, calling students names, running into the principal's office? Hasn't it ever occurred to you that it's hard on Lark when you do things like that?"

No. It hadn't occurred to her. If it had occurred to her, she wouldn't have done it. But it was occurring to her now.

Had it occurred to Lark?

"Is that why you separated us?" she whispered.

"Part of the reason, yes. There are many reasons. But the only reason you need to know is that you two girls are our solemn responsibility and sometimes we need to make hard choices to help you."

How could she explain that that wasn't true? That she needed to know so much more than that?

"Listen," her mom continued, "we're going to take care

of your sister. I'm going to let her stay home for another couple of days while we put a plan in place; I'm scheduling a meeting with Principal Peter and Mr. Hunt and the school counselor. We're going to help her—we have this, okay?"

Iris nodded.

"Mr. Hunt has a lot of good ideas about helping Lark manage. He called me after school and we talked for a long time. And"—she peered over her glasses meaningfully—"he told me not to be too hard on you, that you were just worried about your sister."

"He did?" She looked at the floor. Maybe her mom should be harder on her. "I need to go check on Lark."

"I told you—"

"I won't wake her. I just want to see that she's okay."

Her mom gazed at her in that mom way she had, the way that felt like it was tugging at all her secrets.

"Okay."

Iris turned to go, and her mom stopped her.

"Wait. Iris."

"Yeah?"

"Are you okay?"

Iris swallowed.

No.

"I'm okay."

When she got upstairs she knocked softly on Lark's door,

waited a moment, and then went in.

Lark was there, fast asleep, sprawled under a pile of blankets and stuffed animals, hair spread over the pillows like a troll doll, feet sticking out from under the covers. Iris tiptoed over and clicked on the bedside lamp, though really she didn't have to tiptoe. Lark slept like she'd been cursed by a poisoned apple and pricked by a spindle at the same time. Not even a meddling prince could wake her up.

The dollhouse stood with the Lark doll in the bedroom and the wolf in the closet. And the rest of the family in a pile on the floor, including the Iris doll.

Separated.

Lark had made other changes today, and was now apparently remaking the other second floor room back into a baby's room. Slowly, Lark seemed to be changing the house back to the way it once was, a normal dollhouse. The dollhouse of a girl who wouldn't put a campfire on the moon.

But, Iris realized, the baby's room wasn't really normal, not anymore.

Because the baby was still missing.

She looked back at Lark. There was no sign of Esmeralda, who was usually tucked into Lark's arms somewhere, so Iris crept back to her own room and got Bunny, and then tucked him into bed with Lark.

In the morning, Iris woke to Lark sitting on the foot of

her bed, Bunny on her lap. This happened—often during the night one of them floated to the other's room due to general sister gravity and just hung out until the other one woke up.

"I'm sorry," Iris said. "I'm so sorry."

"Esmeralda's gone.

Iris sat up.

"Yes, I've looked everywhere," Lark added quickly.

"I wasn't—I . . . What happened?"

"I came home yesterday and she was gone. Why is someone taking all of my things? Is someone messing with me? I don't understand." Her voice broke. "Everything's disappearing."

What could Iris say? Lark was right. Everything was disappearing.

"Well, if someone's taking my stuff, at least I'll be home to see it now," she said after a while. "Mom says I can stay home today."

"Good," Iris said softly.

"She's going to meet with Principal Peter and Dr. Brockenbrough and the ogre and they're going to come up with *a plan*," Lark mumbled, eyes on the bunny. "Maybe one where I never have to show my face in school again."

"Lark."

Her head popped up, and her eyes met Iris's. "I can't go

back there! I can't ever go back. How could I? It was humiliating."

Iris looked down at the bed, her face hot.

It was all her fault.

CHAPTER THIRTY-ONE

The Well

When Iris got off the school bus that afternoon, she did not even glance at the library. Mr. Green had said he could help her and Lark, and she needed help. She needed something. And it seemed like there were even more crows around, like they'd been slowly invading and soon the people would just give up and leave the neighborhood to them.

So she darted into Treasure Hunters, crows chattering at her the whole way.

When she got inside the shop was empty, save for Duchess, who was perched on one of the tables, tall and regal. Her head swiveled at the sound of the chimes, and she regarded

Iris with her big green eyes.

"*Meow.*"

Now, cats make all sorts of noises—some trill, some chirp, some squawk, and some let out a sound that is rather like a bark. But Duchess definitely meowed, a high-pitched, bell-like *me-ow*, clear as anything, as if this cat was the one who spoke for all cats, past and future, and catkind definitively *meow*ed.

Are you paying attention?

"Yes?" Iris said, for it seemed the sort of meow that required a response.

You're not paying attention.

"Where's Mr. Green?" Iris asked.

The cat meowed again, then jumped off the spindly-legged table, stuck her tail straight up, and strolled right past Iris, assiduously brushing her legs on the way past.

And then she walked right up to the entrance to the back room, gave Iris one last meow, and disappeared behind the curtain.

Fine. I'll help. Follow me.

Iris paused for a moment. Everything was so confusing today. Everything was so confusing every day. She wished she were sensible. If she were sensible she would know what to do.

Maybe something was wrong with Mr. Green; maybe

he needed help. There were stories like this, of dogs who summoned nearby strangers when their owners were hurt. Though Iris had never actually heard of a cat doing this.

Still. Duchess was calling for her. So she went. Carefully, she made her way to the curtain, and stepped through.

Then, for once in her life, Iris was astonished.

There had been clues all along, if Iris had been paying attention to them. George's insistence on magic. Duchess's movements. The strange aura of the shop as a whole. But Iris hadn't been paying attention, and even if she had been, she longed so much for a rational world that she would have irrationally disregarded any evidence to the contrary. People are like that.

The Green manor was attached to the back of the shop (as it is, every time, though the house itself grows a little each time it moves). It was unquestionably the same house, though: opulent, ostentatious, grandiose—the house of a man who wants to show the world how extremely wealthy he is and expects the world to revere him for it.

The house was impossible.

And yet it was true.

Iris stood on a shiny marble-tiled floor in front of the thick red curtain. Above her, two stories of arch-lined balconies supported a vast ceiling painted with some kind of fresco of a bunch of half-dressed people having a banquet. Every piece of the building's structure was ornately detailed, from the carved columns to the reliefs on the walls to the gilt edging of the ceiling. Way across the hall a vast red-carpeted staircase spilled down from the second floor.

Iris took a step forward, gawking. The hall itself was the size of her entire school building, lined with a series of arches, behind which she could see more vast rooms. And the hall was packed with *stuff*: imposing marble statues, a massive grand piano, weird modern sculptures, a whole wall of clocks, a towering oak organ thing that seemed to have stringed instruments attached, a giant stuffed bear, lamps and shelves and chairs and ottomans, a dinosaur skeleton, and display case after display case filled with treasures—one of china figurines, another of tea sets, another of small animal figurines, another filled with sparkling jewelry.

It looked like a museum where no one had bothered to declutter in a century.

Duchess appeared in front of Iris and gazed at her, as if to say, *See?*

Iris was frozen there, a statue herself. But a kind of statue that was all wrong, broken. The kind of statue people looked at and felt that there must have been something very strange about the person who sculpted it, to make something that looked so confused, so disrupted.

"Miss Maguire!" exclaimed Mr. George Green, appearing on one of the balconies, book in hand. "Did Duchess invite you? That naughty cat."

Iris did not move.

"Well, that certainly saves us a difficult conversation, anyway. Though," he added, looking pointedly at the cat, "I do prefer making my own decisions, Duchess. Wait right there."

Mr. Green disappeared behind a doorway. He did not have to worry about Iris going anywhere—she was a statue, and the thing about statues is that they do not move.

Soon he was pattering down the big staircase toward Iris, arms wide and welcoming.

"The Green Château," he proclaimed. *"Bienvenue!"*

"How—" Iris squeaked.

He cocked his head. "Why, magic, of course!"

Iris took a step back.

"I told you I had magic. You kept saying it was *science*."

"But—"

"Don't play coy with me. A sensible girl like yourself knows how the world really works. I would expect other girls to be 'oh my goodness gracious magic oh my goodness gracious!'—you know how girls are—but you're not, are you?"

She was. Whatever he was saying, she was definitely that. And no, she did not know how girls were, not at all, but that was a secondary problem.

"I don't understand," she breathed. "What is all of this?"

His mouth slowly spread into a grin. "This," he said, voice hushed, "this is *treasure*. I have here the world's most priceless collection of the most prestigious antiques and collectibles. Rocks from the moon, Wedgwood china, Qianlong jade, Fabergé eggs, Stradivarius violins, Tiffany lamps, Ming dynasty vases, The tooth of a hundred-thousand-year-old elephant, Chippendale furniture. You will not find a finer collection anywhere."

"I don't—"

"And I have a number of, how would you say it, *unique* items," he said. "Items that on their own would be the pride and joy of any museum, really any city. And maybe they once were," he added with a showy wink.

Iris gaped at the glut of treasures around her, at the impossible mansion. Her whole body was buzzing with questions, so many she might buzz her way into bits. But first and most important was:

"How . . . ," she sputtered, throwing her arms up to indicate everything around her.

Mr. Green tapped his fingers on his mouth. "I told you there was power for you, if you wanted it. I told you I could help you. Allow me to show you something," he said. With a gesture to her, he strode toward the archway to her right.

Duchess glided over to Iris and brushed against her legs,

and then followed him, glancing at Iris to make sure she was coming.

So Iris followed, gaping at everything, awash in wonder and fear. Duchess suddenly darted to the left and through another doorway, and the door opened a little to reveal a whole room filled with glass-covered shelves of small porcelain dolls. There must have been hundreds, maybe thousands, standing side by side on the shelf gazing blankly off into the distance with their perpetually open eyes. They were all the same size—about eight inches high—but all different, as far as Iris could see: a world's array of skin tones and hair colors, and a jumble of hairstyles and hats and big floofy dresses with layers of crinoline, as though all the dolls in the whole kingdom had dressed themselves up for the ball.

"*Meow,*" said Duchess, standing in the doorway to the doll room. *You should pay attention to this.* But Mr. Green was motioning her forward.

"This," he said, holding his arms out, "is the gallery."

Gallery was certainly the appropriate word. The walls were covered with paintings in all kinds of styles, from somber Renaissance portraits to bright abstract splatterings, so many paintings you could barely see wall at all, or really notice any of the paintings for the fact of all the paintings.

"You will note some of the most prized paintings in the Western world, of course. I have a Vermeer," he said meaningfully. "You know which one. The Picasso. Modigliani. Degas sketches. Van Gogh. We're working on expanding our contemporary collection and have recently made an exciting acquisition. But we can discuss that later."

There were doorways on either side of the gallery. One had a large plaque that read Office. But Mr. Green had stopped in front of the other one, which had a sign on it that read Employees Only.

With great ceremony, he took the giant ring of keys from his belt and unlocked the door, then flung it open.

There was a glow coming from the room, or perhaps it was a sparkle, or a glimmer.

Mr. Green stepped back and motioned to the doorway. "Magic," he said.

Iris could not help it: she floated toward the room.

"Not too close!" Mr. Green exclaimed. "Be careful!"

From behind, Duchess yowled at her. *Stop!*

Iris stopped herself. And it was a good thing: the room at the other side of the doorway was not a room at all, but some kind of shaft. Inside was a bucket hanging on a large crank, and whatever was below emitted the strange shimmer.

"It's a . . . well?"

"Certainly. One needs a way to access the magic. Wells are very efficient, actually."

"That's—"

"The magic, yes."

The magic.

Iris shook her head slightly as if to clear it. It was a well of magic. Magic was a thing, something you could scoop up like water.

She took another step forward and crouched down, peering into the well. It was hard to make out the substance below: it wasn't like water; it wasn't like goo. Upon closer inspection, it seemed to be no *thing* at all—just a shimmer, like the light around a full moon. And—

Iris.

It was like a hand tugging at her chest, so gently she barely knew it was happening. But it was happening, and it was good, and it was warm and safe.

Iris.

Iris, it's all right. Iris, I can help you. Iris, everything is in order; everything makes sense. There are rules to the universe. Everything is under your control.

I can help you. I can help you keep your sister safe. I can make people listen to you. I can keep the nightmares away. I can help you know who you are. I can give you power.

Everything will be all right.

The hand tugged, and Iris exhaled, and if she just relaxed and let the hand pull her forward—

Then, the yowl of a cat, and hands on her back, pulling

her backward—not gently at all. "Stop! Stay back!"

Iris started. She was on the cool marble floor. The tugging had stopped, the connection broken, and she was cold and alone and powerless. Mr. Green was standing over her, his pale face looking slightly green. "I shouldn't have let you get so close," he sputtered. "I'm so sorry. I forgot what it's like at first."

Iris wrapped her arms around herself, trying to get warm. She could not stop shivering.

"Do you know what would happen to you if you fell in there?"

"No . . ." Her voice sounded thin and broken.

"Bad things." he said. "You would not survive a second. You should be more careful, young lady. You know what they say: 'Curiosity killed the girl.'"

Iris pushed herself backward. ". . . I think that's 'the cat'?" she said weakly. "'Curiosity killed the cat.'"

"Hmmmpf. Well. Let this be a lesson to you. Don't go opening strange doors, and when magic in a well starts calling to you, run in the other direction."

"All right."

"You should know better."

"All right."

Iris pressed her back against the wall, shivering. He was so loud all of a sudden. And everything was so strange.

"Well"—he clapped his hands together—"that is the answer to your question. That is a well of magic, and that is how I have built my palace."

Iris shifted so she was hugging her legs, and took a deep breath. And another. "How do you have a well of magic?" she asked carefully. "Do you make it?"

That's right. Breathe, Iris. Clear your head. Ask questions.

"*Make* magic? I wish we could. Magic is not something you can make; it is something you can use. You are aware that some locations are sources of underground water and oil, yes? Well, some places are sources of magic. All one needs to do is dig a well. This is my innovation."

"There's a source of magic in . . . Minneapolis?"

She could do this. She could gather herself in this impossible place. She could figure out what was going on. She could handle the impossible if she just asked the right questions.

"Cities tend to spring up around them. You'll find an undercurrent of magic in many a major metropolitan area. Or at least, you could, once. I have used up quite a few of them, of course."

"You've used it up?" Iris looked at the shimmering doorway. Magic did not seem like a thing you should be able to use up. "I don't understand. What do you use it for?"

He opened up his arms and indicated everything around

him. "Why, this, of course! I use it to make a home for myself commensurate with my status. I am a man with access to tremendous power; I must look the part."

"And . . . you just really like art?"

"Oh, you know. All the best people possess major works of art. And I, I have the most art. The best art. And not just art. I have the rarest and most valuable collectibles and artifacts—books, manuscripts, stamps, old coins, weapons, fossils, musical instruments, furniture, decorative silver, vases. So much creativity, so much artistry. So valuable! I am the envy of every collector in the world."

"But . . . why do you need a store if you have all of this?"

"Oh, I enjoy antiques and collectibles myself, and do so love conversing with my fellow aficionados. The store is a bit of a hobby of mine, a way of networking face-to-face, though it is in the online communities where I can trade in my more high-end goods."

"Magic has a cost."

He cocked his head. "What did you say?"

"Magic has a cost. What's the cost?"

"Perhaps magic has a cost for other people. But not for me."

Iris felt her face scrunch up. She did not understand. "What about Alice? Shouldn't you be using magic to find her? To help her?"

His eyes widened. "Of course, Miss Maguire. That is my primary objective. Alice is my greatest loss, my greatest prize. Alice is my treasure, you understand. That is why I am here. Our family must stay near magic. If she is alive, she is near a magic source, somewhere."

"But . . . you said she just disappeared. Couldn't that have been magic?"

He looked aghast.

"Alice was not allowed to touch the magic. She would not have known how to use it properly."

Something was wrong, something was strange—even stranger than everything that was happening right now.

And then it hit her.

"You're the thief. The museum thief. You took the cherry and the spoon."

He grinned, eyes alight. "*Spoonbridge and Cherry*, you mean to say. That is a special piece of art indeed. Beloved by a whole city. I daresay it is the most valuable thing in all of Minneapolis, wouldn't you? And now it's mine. No ordinary collector could do that."

"But no one can see it now."

"Exactly." He squatted down, looked her in the eye. "Miss Maguire, I told you power was out there for you. In fact, it's right here." He gestured around him.

"What?"

"This is my proposal for you. I have not been successful in finding my sister. The truth is, I fear her disappearance was her own doing. She did not always understand what was best for her. And she was so impulsive. I am afraid that she is not coming back because she thinks I will be angry at her for leaving. But . . . she always longed for a sister. A true companion, like you are for your sister. If I got her one, then maybe she'd come back. But it couldn't be just any girl. We need a sensible girl, one who would be a good influence on our Alice."

Iris closed her eyes as the world crumpled around her.

"Imagine, Miss Maguire," he continued. "You could travel the world with Alice and me. We could show you wondrous things. We would listen to you, value you. And"—he leaned in—"then they'd all be sorry."

Iris buried her head in her hands. This was not happening. None of it. She'd gone to Camp Awesome like she was supposed to, biked home afterward, made everything up to Lark, and they were sitting on her floor making magic out of ordinary things. An infinite supply.

"What do you say?" he asked, grinning as if her answer were obvious.

Iris looked up. "No," she whispered.

"Pardon me?"

"No. I don't want to go with you. I want to stay here."

"Here? What is here for you? Remember, I have *Spoonbridge and Cherry* now."

"No, that's not it."

"There's nothing for you here. You said no one listens to you. You feel powerless."

"That doesn't mean I want to leave! Lark is here!"

"But . . . you said yourself that you were bad for Lark. Everyone thinks so. Even Lark thinks so. Wouldn't you be doing her a favor? She'd be better off in the long run, don't you think?"

"I have to go home," Iris said, pushing herself up.

"But this can be your home now. And then Alice will come back, and you'll have another sister."

"No," Iris said, backing away.

He grabbed her arm. "Are you saying no to me?"

Iris froze.

A yowling sound—then Mr. Green yelled, "Ow!" Duchess was at his ankle, biting. Iris wrenched free from his grasp and ran forward, and then she heard another yowl, this time in pain. Mr. Green had kicked the cat. Then his hand wrapped around her shoulder again, and the next thing she knew, she was being thrown into the doorway marked Office.

"I am going to keep you," Mr. Green yelled as he pushed her inside. "One way or another."

Then he stalked away and the door closed behind Iris.

CHAPTER THIRTY-TWO

The Doll Maker

I ris dove for the door, only to find there was no doorknob on her side, just a small keyhole. She tried to wedge her fingers in between the door and the frame, but they didn't fit. Trying the crack under the door yielded the same results.

It didn't matter, though. The door had clearly locked behind her and was not going to budge unless someone opened it from the outside.

This was no office. It was a storage room of some kind— gray cinder-block walls and a hard gray floor, metal shelving, ugly flickering light, and one tiny window up near the ceiling. Across from her was a big worktable filled with all kinds of small tools, paintbrushes and paints, scraps of fabric and lace.

One wall of shelving was lined with wooden bins, and perched right in front of it was a big shiny black-and-gold sewing machine with a foot pedal. Another was filled with sealed jam jars of shimmering magic.

And next to that stood a huge industrial sink brimming over with doll parts.

They looked like pieces of the small dolls that Iris had seen earlier—same size, same faces. But those were finished dolls; these were just pieces, a great tangle of arms and torsos and bald heads. Hundreds of pieces.

She backed away, her whole body buzzing and maybe even shaking, and then she bumped into something hard. She whirled around to see a small wooden chair with clamps on the arms and legs.

And then Iris remembered what George had said about Alice. She'd been resting in his office when she disappeared.

Alice was here when she disappeared. And this was no office.

As horrifying as that was, Alice had gotten out somehow. There was a way out.

Iris looked frantically around. There was no escape that she could see. Just the small window, locked from the inside. Even if Iris could scale the bookshelf, it wasn't big enough for her to fit through. And Alice had been sixteen.

Before she could investigate more, the door opened again. Iris whirled around. Mr. George Green was back, standing tall. He looked bigger than he had before, or maybe that was just Iris's fear making him that way. But he didn't look like a mole man anymore. He looked like a monster.

"All right," he said, his voice booming. "I have decided that you would be a terrible sister for Alice. A terrible influence. You are not welcome in our family."

He took a step closer, and Iris took three steps back. She could not breathe; she could not think.

"But I am keeping you. I am keeping you because I want to. I am keeping you because I can. I am keeping you because I have the power to do so, do you understand, young lady? I am a great man. I have vision. I am a visionary."

That word. Ms. Messner had called Lark that.

And there, underneath all the terror, Iris found a thread of anger. She pulled on it as hard as she could.

"You're not a visionary!" she snapped. "*Visionary* means you have imagination. You don't have any imagination. All you do is steal stuff and copy stuff. This house looks just like you're some dead rich guy from a hundred years ago trying to cover everything in gold so you look like you're fancy. You stole everything else. You don't even care about it or know why this stuff is important; you just stole it because someone else thinks it's valuable. You're just a pathetic copycat thief. You make nothing."

A storm of anger was gathering over his face as she talked, but at these last words the storm broke. A slow smile spread across his face. Iris shuddered.

"I do make something," he said, gesturing behind her. "I make dolls."

Iris turned. The hideous sink with the doll limbs. She hadn't had time to realize what it was for, other than terrifying her.

"But," he said, taking a step closer to her, "I don't just make them out of plastic. Though I do love doing that. The magic is hard to work with, but it does excel at one thing in particular." His voice was low and soft now. "It excels at transformation. This is very useful when you need to walk out of a museum with a painting or take a sculpture the size of a semi-truck out of a public garden. It can also be useful in other ways. And I think, Miss Maguire, I know the best way to keep you. . . . Perhaps I can give you as a gift to Alice after all."

A doll.

He was going to turn her into a doll.

Unless she drowned in her own fear before he could.

"You're a monster," she spat.

His eyes narrowed. "There's no need to be rude."

Was this it? Had this been his plan all along? Forget Alice. Had Iris wandered into his shop full of collectibles one day and he'd just decided to collect her?

"Wait a minute. Did you take our stuff? Lark's bracelet? The ogre figurine? Baby Thing?"

His eyebrows went up. "A bracelet? A toy? What would I do with a girl's things?" he sneered.

"But . . ." No. There was a way to make this all make sense. There was a way to make everything fit. "This was the plan all along. You saw us, in August. The day the school letters came. You made all that happen. You took Lark away from me so I'd be all alone and I'd keep stuff from her and I'd be a mess and everything would fall apart. You did that."

His face twisted into a slow, horrible grin. And then he began to laugh.

"Why would I go to all that trouble for a worthless little girl?"

His laugh had sharp edges. It filled the room, and soon all the sharp parts were pointed right at Iris.

She blinked rapidly.

It is a horrible thing, to be laughed at.

She was not going to cower in front of this man anymore, even if panic was eating away at her internal organs. She pushed herself up and stood as tall as she could, chin out, arms at her hips.

Iris could barely breathe. There was no way out, no way around Mr. Green. He was a grown man and he knew how to use magic and he thought he was right and that she was nothing and that she could do nothing and he would go on traveling from magic well to magic well trapping girls and no one would ever be able to stop him.

She felt like she was being swallowed by a boa constrictor.

But she was not going down without a fight.

She dove over to the shelves with the jars of magic, grabbed one, and hurled it at Mr. Green. He yelled and ducked out of the way. The jar exploded on the wall, and the magic inside splattered and oozed and steamed and hissed, and Mr. Green slapped his hands over his face and screamed.

He screamed and screamed, and it was a terrible sound, like the sky ripping open. Iris threw her hands to her ears to stop the noise, but still it vibrated through her whole body.

"I will get you for this!" he yelled, and then opened up the door and lumbered out. The door slammed behind him.

With a choking gasp, Iris sank to the floor and watched the magic drip down the wall.

At least she had hurt him. At least there was that.

Maybe the magic would leave a scar.

A really bad one.

Maybe it would melt his face off.

Iris sat next to the jars of magic, shaking, holding herself, trying to catch her breath. She had to catch them while she could. Who knew how many breaths she would have left?

She was supposed to be the strong one.

"I'm sorry, Lark," she whispered. "I'm sorry."

CHAPTER THIRTY-THREE

The Pied Piper

I ris had no idea how long it took to recover from a magic injury to the face. How long did she have left? Five minutes? Five hours? Five days? How long before Mr. Green came back and did . . . whatever it was he did?

Was he really going to change her into a doll?

Was it going to hurt?

What had she done?

Why had she kept coming back?

Why had she ignored all the weirdness?

He had told her what she wanted to hear. He'd told her about his sister and the crows. He'd told her she was sensible. He'd told her he understood what it was like to feel powerless. He'd told her he could help her feel powerful.

He was a Pied Piper, playing a song just for her.

Yes, he was powerful. There was great power in knowing just what song to play to get people to follow you off a cliff.

And he'd done it.

Magic has a cost. Mr. George Green said it didn't for him, but it clearly did. The cost was his humanity. Which did not mean making yourself less human. It meant making yourself less humane.

But . . . how much humanity could you have had in the first place if you wanted to sacrifice your humanity for magic?

Yes. She'd wanted there to be magic. She would never have admitted it to anyone, even herself. But she'd wanted some kind of magic that would have made people listen to her, that would have made everything make sense, that would have just let her and Lark be. Be sisters, be twins, be best friends. Be themselves, without people poking at them all the time to be different. To be able to struggle and fail and pick each other up in the way they knew how without anyone thinking they understood the girls better than they'd understood each other.

And wanting it had had a cost.

But what they had, too, was magic. She'd always known that on some level, but now she really understood it. All the Awesome girls, none of them had twin sisters, so they all had to feel alone in their aloneness.

But she'd been wrong about one thing: the cost of the magic of having Lark wasn't that people would try to take it away. The cost was the desperate fear of losing Lark. And now she was here.

Why hadn't she told Lark where she had been going?

No one knew where she was. All they would know was that she had been on the bus, but she hadn't shown up at camp. No one would ever think to check the shop, because Iris hadn't told anyone she'd been going there.

She hadn't told Lark.

She hadn't told *Lark*.

She'd kept it from her sister. Because there was a crow flying around the house and a lie fell off her tongue. Because she was late coming home one day, and Lark was upset that she was late, and so another lie fell. And then she could not tell the truth because she didn't want Lark to know she'd lied. Because she didn't want Lark to think she'd betrayed her, even in some small way. She didn't want Lark to think she wasn't putting her first at every single minute. *She* didn't want to think it.

She wanted to be the perfect sister for Lark. And so she had failed her.

Iris wrapped her arms around her chest and squeezed as tightly as she could. Oh, she missed her sister.

She missed her for now, and for the future. She missed the rest of their lives, the way it was supposed to be. Iris and Lark.

She missed her sister so much that it filled her whole body, that it pulled at her skin, threatened to rip it apart.

She hugged herself even tighter, trying to contain that ache in her chest. She clenched her face, her hands, her legs, her whole body, and then with a gasping exhale let everything go.

Her hand drifted to the floor, where she tapped three times—their code that meant *I am here* and *I love you* and *Iris and Lark*, and something like all three of those things together.

There are differences between facts and truths. Facts are something you know in your brain; truths are things you know in your heart.

The facts were that Mr. George Green was bigger and more powerful and she had little hope.

The truth was that she was Lark's sister, and she was going to fight.

Lark had been training her for this for years. *And then the girl fought back. And then the girl rewrote the story and stopped the monsters and saved everyone.* She couldn't quite do that. She couldn't change the end of the story.

But she could make it more exciting.

Iris popped up and went over to take her place by the jars of magic.

She would keep throwing magic at him as long as she could. Maybe she could get through him. Maybe she could incapacitate him. Maybe all she would do was cause him pain and skin melting. But that was something.

She waited, a jar in her hand at the ready, aching and buzzing, feeling like a doll with jumbled-up parts.

She waited, and waited.

And then she heard the door opening.

Her hands clenched around the jar.

The door swung open.

And right behind it stood Lark.

And at her feet was Duchess.

The magic jar slipped from Iris's hand. Lark was frozen in the doorway, eyes like oceans. Then with a start she held her hand out. Iris grabbed it, and Lark pulled her sister into the hallway.

"We have to be careful," gasped Iris in what she hoped was a whisper. "There's a man, Mr. Green, he's a bad guy—"

Shhh, Lark tapped.

"How did you find me?"

Later, she tapped. She squeezed her sister's hand and crept forward, pulling Iris behind her. It seemed like Lark made no sound at all as she moved, or maybe Iris's whole brain was focused on listening for the sound of Mr. Green and she could hear nothing else. But her hand was in her sister's, her hand was in her sister's, it was going to be okay.

But where was Mr. Green?

Duchess seemed to want to know the same thing. She prowled around the gallery, weaving through the shadows, while Iris and Lark crept around the corner of the gallery into the entrance hall. Still, no noise. Nothing.

The curtains were just ahead now. All they had to do was get through them and get out and then they could run away and never ever come back. Iris held her breath as Lark pulled her forward. Ten more steps. Eight. Six, and then—

"*MEOW!*" yelled Duchess, as a hand clamped around Iris's mouth. A voice next to her growled, "You must be Lark." And Lark screamed.

The girls huddled under the table of the office while George paced around the room in front of them. The right side of his face was red and swollen.

"You escaped," he ranted. "I don't understand. How did you escape? How did you know she was here? Who is helping you?"

He didn't seem to want answers to these questions, and neither sister gave him any. Iris could barely think. She thought things had been as bad as they could possibly get, but Mr. Green had shown her that it could be far worse.

He had Lark. He was going to turn Lark into a doll. Then

he'd have a matching set. And it was all her fault.

Iris was looking wildly around for a way out. The door? No, you couldn't open the door without a key, so that wouldn't work. The small window? No, it was too high. The magic? Well, there was always the magic. Iris tried to scoot herself over closer to the shelf.

"I see you!" Mr. Green yelled, stomping toward her. "Go back over there! Do I need to tie you up? I had to tie Alice up. Always trying to escape. Me! She tried to escape from me! Her brother! All I wanted was what was best for her."

Lark grabbed Iris's arm and held it tight. Mr. Green saw, and his eyes suddenly brightened. He turned to her.

"So," he said, voice suddenly sweet, "you're little Lark. At long last we meet. I've heard so much about you!"

Iris turned to ice. Lark went straight and haughty. "Yes, I'm Lark," she spat back. "Don't you dare hurt my sister."

"Sooooooo, how's school going for you these days?"

Lark flinched. "How does he know about that?" she whispered.

"Don't whisper in here! *Acoustics!* I can hear everything! I know because your sister here has told me all about you."

Lark glanced to Iris. But her face was confused, not hurt. She still did not understand the extent of her sister's betrayal. Iris was dissolving in her own shame.

"Yes," he continued. "How you're not quite made for this

world. How you're just *too sensitive*."

Now Lark understood. Now the hurt splashed across her face. "You told him that?"

Iris opened her mouth helplessly.

"Oh, yes, she told me everything. How you can't even handle throwing up in school. How she needs to take care of you. How she's so worried you'll just walk off the face of the earth one day. What do you think, Lark? Do you think Iris needs to protect you?"

"Stop talking," Lark gasped.

"Did you know she was visiting here? Did she tell you about Alice?"

"The girl on the sign?"

"Oh, much more than that. She was my sister. And Iris knew all about it. We had extensive conversations about how similar you two are. She couldn't take care of herself either. She was broken, our Alice."

The look Lark was giving her, like Iris was hollowing her out.

"What?" Mr. Green said. "She didn't tell you any of this?"

Before Iris's eyes, Lark seemed to collapse into herself like a dying star.

What could Iris do? There was nothing she could do. What he'd said wasn't true, not really. But it wasn't not true either.

Satisfied, he turned to Iris. "And you," he said. "You think you're special? You're not practical at all! You're *impractical*! Don't know what's good for you, don't know what's best, think you can just say no to me. To *me*? I gave you the chance of a lifetime. All of this could be yours! But no. You're too foolish. You're just like your sister. Both of you, all wrong. Not made for this world."

He was railing at them now, and he seemed to take up the whole mansion.

"Both of you, weak. Too weak. Too needy. Can't live without each other. I can't believe I thought you could help Alice, Iris. You're just like the rest of them, useless. I'd never expose her to you. You're a terrible sister."

"Stop it," Lark hissed, grabbing hold of Iris's arm again. "She is not."

"Did you contradict me?" he spat.

"Yes. You're horrible. You're a monster. You're an ogre banging your silly club around." Lark straightened. "Think you're special because you have a fancy house and lots of stuff and a big club and a collection of people's hearts, but every-one knows you're nothing but a smelly ogre. The worst."

Iris might have been made of ice, but Lark was made of fire now, spitting words back at him.

"How dare you," he growled.

"You're an ogre. Everyone's laughing at you. No one's

impressed by your stuff. You're the weak one. You're pathetic and everybody knows it."

Just then, a large crashing sound came from the distance. Mr. Green's attention broke from the girls and he looked behind him. Lark stiffened, and her hand tightened around Iris's arm.

"I—" began Mr. Green.

Crash.

He exhaled. "I need to attend to something. Don't go anywhere."

And then he was gone.

Lark turned to Iris, cheeks red, breathless. Iris could barely look at her, but needed to look at her; she needed to look her in the eye. So she willed her eyes up to meet her sister's.

"I'm sorry," she gasped. "I'm so sorry."

"Not now." Lark had followed him to the door and was listening carefully.

"I didn't mean it. Any of it."

"I don't want to talk about this right now," Lark said, her teeth gritted. She'd stooped down and was examining the small keyhole.

"I do!" Iris exclaimed. "Something bad could happen and you'd think I thought all of that stuff about you."

Lark turned around with a sigh. "Iris. You kind of do."

"I don't!"

"You do. You wrote on my project. You talk about me with random ogres. You go running around the school yelling at everyone. Because you think I can't take care of myself."

A protest rose in Iris's mouth.

"Can you please not talk for once?" Lark snapped. "Your job is not to take care of me. Not any more than my job is to take care of you. We take care of each other. We're a team. Iris and Lark. That's it. What would I do if something happened to you? What? What if you go and get yourself killed trying to take care of me?"

"I—"

"No, you didn't think about that part, did you? You're going to leave me all alone? I don't have you, and it's my fault you're dead? And it's because you thought I needed you to *protect* me? If *you* of all people think I'm totally helpless . . ."

Lark could not finish her sentence, but Iris didn't need her to. She was supposed to be the one who saw Lark for all she was. It was just that everything had gotten so jumbled up.

"I'm sorry. I don't think you're helpless."

"If anyone needs protecting around here, it's you."

"That's obvious."

"You're the one getting locked in rooms by an evil art thief."

"Yeah."

"That's a lot of protection to need. I might have to clone myself. That would confuse people. No, this is my twin sister; this is my clone. I needed her because my twin sister is hopeless."

"Lark?"

"Yeah?"

"I'm sorry."

"Don't do it again. Now, come on. Let's get out of here."

"What? How?" Another huge crash came from the building somewhere. "What is that?"

Lark held out her hand to show a small key. "We are going to get out of here with this key. And that crash, I believe, is us being rescued."

CHAPTER THIRTY-FOUR

Lark

Here, come with me.

Let's go back in time a bit.

Lark was at home that afternoon while things were going missing around her, thinking of the person she used to be. She used to be a person with a bracelet the crows gave her; she used to be a person with a stuffed beanbag cat with magical healing powers; she used to be a person with a dollhouse baby that could have campfires on the moon. She used to be a person who went to school, and art camp. She used to be a person who could change the rules and make things and remake things, and now no one wanted her to be that anymore.

Not even Iris.

Even Iris thought she should be a girl with computer printouts of other people's constellation drawings from the internet.

She could have seen it coming. As soon as the school letters arrived, Iris had started getting more and more wound up inside, and this last week everything inside her had been so tight Lark herself felt the strain inside. She was wound up so tightly that she was bound to unwind.

If Lark had been able to keep it together, none of this would have happened. If she'd adjusted to Mr. Hunt, if she'd ignored Tommy, if she'd been able to get through the owl-pellet ordeal—which really was the most disgusting and sad thing she'd ever seen in her life, but if she'd been able to get through it anyway—she'd have been able to help Iris unwind. That was what she did. It was her job.

So she was going to need to show her sister that she was okay, and then she could help make Iris okay too.

And then tell her to never ever draw on any of her projects, ever again.

She was struck then with an overwhelming desire to see her sister—*right then, right now*. Like if she didn't go find her, Iris herself might disappear.

And so when her mother told her she was going to work for the afternoon, Lark asked if she could drop her off at the library. Her mom had no problem with that—she seemed to unwind a little, seeing Lark wanting to go out—and she even offered to pick them up and drive them home after Iris's camp was over, though she couldn't get there until a little before seven o'clock.

And that was fine. Lark wanted some time with her sister.

At the library, she got some books and parked herself in a chair near the community room so she could catch Iris as she went into Camp Awesome.

And then she would say—

What?

I miss you.

I am not weak.

We can both be the strong ones.

We can get through this.

I am mad at you.

I miss you.

Lark eyed Iris's camp mates as they went into the room; Iris had told her all about them. Perky Abigail with the bouncy ponytail. Hannah, the Ravenclaw with the sparkly glasses. Eerie Emily in the softball clothes. Amazing Amma, who fenced and did gymnastics. Maleficent Morgan with the freckles and range of Disney T-shirts. Preeti with the purple streaks in her hair. Tall sixth grader Gabrielle, who had four cats. Small Novalie with the curly blond hair. All these girls who were now in the regular cast of her sister's life, and Lark didn't know them at all.

She would like to know them. She would like to know the people that Iris knew.

And then the door to the community room closed. No Iris.

Something was wrong.

No, Lark told herself immediately. This was a perfectly normal thing and there was a perfectly normal explanation for it and even if it was perfectly normal for her to worry she also needed to understand that the truth was likely perfectly normal.

Obviously Iris must have gone home after school for some reason. And she'd figure Lark and her mom were at her mom's office, and maybe then she'd draw all over more of Lark's homework.

And even though Lark had a terrible feeling in her stomach, she should recognize that that was her worries making her feel that way and nothing real.

Right?

When the girls came out of the community room for their break, Lark popped up. Amma cocked her head and studied her for a second, and then grinned and waved her forward.

"You're Iris's sister!" she said.

These were strangers, and she did not feel comfortable talking to strangers—and for a moment her words caught in her throat like they always did. But that only lasted a moment, because Iris knew them and that made them okay.

"Yes, I'm Lark. I was looking for her?"

"I thought maybe she was sick?" Amma said.

"No," said another girl. Gabrielle. "I saw her get off the bus and go into that weird antique shop."

Lark gaped at her.

"Have you been in there?" the third girl breathed. Hannah. "I went in with my parents. That guy creeped me out."

"What do you mean?" Lark asked.

Gabrielle repeated herself—yes, she'd seen Iris get off the bus and go into Treasure Hunters. And not only had Iris gone in there today, but she often went there after Camp Awesome was over. Gabrielle had been in there once too and thought the guy was weird.

"My dad said it was mean to say that guy was weird," she added. "But—"

"He's super weird," Hannah finished.

Now there was no explaining away the feeling in Lark's stomach.

Soon the other girls had gathered around Lark, and Novalie said that Iris had never really talked before yesterday, and Lark could not believe that. And then Hannah said that Iris had gotten really sad about fairy-tale girls yesterday and actually cried in front of everyone—and Iris never did that, either; Lark was the one who cried.

Thoughts fluttered frantically around Lark's head, looking for somewhere to roost. Iris was keeping things from her. Iris was sad. Iris was crying in camp. Iris was skipping camp. Iris had been wound up so tightly, and now she was unwinding everywhere.

"Something's wrong," Lark said quietly. "Really wrong."

She almost swallowed the words. She did not need to hear right now that she was being silly, that she was imagining things, that it was probably all fine.

But no one said that. Instead they all looked at her as if her words were very serious, and then Morgan said, "Well, if she's in trouble, we have to rescue her."

All seven of the Awesome girls nodded, and the fluttering things in Lark's head found perches and settled there.

"I'm going to go over to the shop," she said.

"By yourself?" Preeti asked.

"We should come with you," said Amma.

"We'll all come," Gabrielle said.

"Like a girl gang," Morgan said. "Girl gangs are the best way to fight bad guys."

"But what do we tell Abigail?"

Lark needed to go. This second. "I'm going to see if I can

find Iris. Then we'll come back here. And if I don't come back—"

"Should we call the police?" Emily asked.

Preeti shook her head. "What if they don't listen to us? There's no time. We have to do this ourselves. If you're not back by the time camp is over, we're going over there too."

"What do we do?" Morgan asked.

Preeti lifted her chin in the air. "I have an idea."

And it was sealed. The girls went to call their parents and tell them they were staying at the library late, and Lark was going to go get her sister back.

"Are you okay?" Amma asked her.

Lark nodded.

"It must be nice to have a twin sister."

". . . It is."

Lark does not remember much of being in the hospital when she had meningitis. She does remember the emergency-room trips when she was little, though: that terrible feeling of her lungs trying so hard to get air, the feeling that no matter how hard they worked she would never get enough breath.

This is how she felt leaving the library.

And then, something very strange happened.

When she walked out of the library all the crows of the neighborhood started cawing to one another and fluttering

their wings and strutting around on their various perches—
a hundred birds calling attention to themselves at once.

And across the street, perched on top of the sign in front
of the antique store, was a giant crow. The biggest of them all.

Her crow.

It cocked its head, listening to the cawing around it. And
then it saw Lark.

Come here, the crow said.

And so Lark crossed the street. As Lark approached, the
bird took off from its perch on the sign and flew to a hole
in a nearby tree. It emerged a moment later with something
small and shiny in its mouth.

A key.

Lark held her hands out, and the bird dropped the key
in them and then alighted on the sign again, watching Lark.

"Is it dangerous?" Lark asked.

The bird blinked.

"Is Iris in there?"

Blink.

Lark gulped. "Can I save her?"

Blink.

Lark's body did not always do the things she wanted it to
do. Including breathe right. She spilled things, broke things,
knocked things over, bumped into things. She didn't have a
lot of strength. She flunked all the presidential fitness tests.

Something about having been born too early: nothing quite worked the way it should. She was not the girl anyone would send into a dangerous situation.

But she would be that girl for Iris.

If Iris was trapped in some nightmare, Lark would have to rewrite it for her. That was what she did, after all. And she was not alone. Lark had the Awesome girls behind her, and the crows on her side.

Her sister needed her. So, she took a deep, full breath and went into the shop, where she was greeted by a beautiful green-eyed cat who meowed insistently at her.

And that meow said, very clearly, *Follow me.*

CHAPTER THIRTY-FIVE

The Flock

Noise filled the gallery as Iris and Lark crept back through it. Chaos. From the shop came the sound of Mr. Green yelling and things breaking. Through the gap in the curtains Iris could see Hannah and Morgan standing on a counter grabbing plates off the wall and throwing them. Preeti had grabbed a fireplace poker and was smashing vases with it while Mr. Green tried to grab her. Amma was wielding what seemed to be a small sword and was swinging it wildly.

"They said they'd create a diversion," Lark whispered.

That they had.

They were all there—Emily, Novalie, Gabrielle, too—and

Mr. Green was in a corner holding a table clock menacingly, dodging the plates being hurled at his head.

"I don't understand," Iris whispered.

"Iris. They came to save you."

The words flew around Iris, unable to find a place to land.

They came to save her.

The Awesome girls.

Iris should do something, she knew she should do something. Grab a poker and start breaking things. Come up with a clever plan to lead Lark and the rest of the girls to safety. Stomp over to Mr. Green and dump magic on his head. But she could not seem to move, could barely seem to think.

He was an evil ogre, swinging his club around wildly to protect his mountain of treasure.

And Iris had caused every single one of these girls to come to his lair.

"Iris," Lark hissed. "Stop it."

"What?"

"It's not your fault."

"It's entirely my fault."

"It's not your fault. It's his fault. He's the monster, do you understand? And who are we?"

They were Iris and Lark. "A team."

"Right. And what else?"

Iris swallowed. "We're the girls who defeat the monsters."

"That's right. Come on." Lark started to pull her forward. And now, a scream from the room.

"Hannah!" yelled another girl. And then the sound of heavy feet pounding toward them.

Mr. Green came running back, holding a writhing Hannah in his arms. Hannah, who had seen Iris keeping track of all the girls in her journal. Hannah, who had forgiven her for it. He was leading all of the girls into his lair.

"No!" Iris shouted, but it was too late. All the girls came running back through the curtain. Preeti had her poker, Amma the sword; Gabrielle was holding a giant lamp high above her head. Preeti poised herself in front of a girl-sized vase, Amma by the dinosaur skeleton. Morgan and Emily grabbed a painting off the wall and held it high.

"Put her down or we'll break more stuff," yelled Amma.

"You will not touch anything," he said, his voice controlled again. "If you do, I will hurt your friend. Now, all of you, put down my things. Carefully. Any more damage to my property will be inflicted back upon you."

Silence, terrible silence. Iris could not move, would never move again. No one else moved either, but then Mr. Green squeezed Hannah hard and she yelped. Amma put down her sword. Everyone else followed suit.

Iris did not notice the motion next to her until it was too late, but Lark had grabbed a statue and was creeping toward him. Lark, the girl who lived in her head so much she could never seem to keep track of her own body. She wanted to yell at Lark to stop, but she couldn't speak.

He swore, then threw Hannah across the room and kicked Lark in the stomach.

She stumbled backward. Iris dove to her.

"We can do this in a way where each of you suffers, or a way in which you never have to suffer again," he growled. "That is entirely up to you. Now I am going to lock the front door, and then I have plans for—"

A huge crashing sound—then a blink later the room was filled with shrieking crows, dozens and dozens of them, a great and glorious murder of crows swarming the front hall. The girls all yelled and ducked, but the crows were not there for them. One dove at Mr. Green and pecked at his head and flew away, then another. He yelled and picked up Amma's sword and began swinging it wildly at the birds.

This was it. Their chance to get away. But Lark was holding her stomach and whimpering and Hannah was clutching at her leg. Mr. Green let out a yell loud enough to break the sky and was swooping up Iris in his arms.

"Get out! Get out, you filthy beasts," he yelled at the crows, using Iris as a shield.

He was so strong and he was squeezing her so hard and it hurt and she could barely breathe. She struggled to throw her hands over her face to protect it from the birds but Mr. Green had her too tightly.

But the crows just circled the room, and did not attack.

"Iris!" screamed Lark. She was sprawled on the floor holding her stomach, and her cry sounded like she was choking.

"You monsters. You scavengers. You vermin."

The crows slowly alighted around the vast hall, settling on sculptures and displays and the organ and the dinosaur skeleton. They fluttered their wings and squawked back and forth at one another.

Iris writhed but she could not get free. He just squeezed her harder.

"Just let them all go," Iris said. "Please. You can have me."

"Iris!" Lark shouted.

"And why would I want you?"

"I'll be Alice's sister. A real sister, not a doll. I'll do whatever you want. Just let them go."

She felt something shift in his body.

"I promise," she continued. *Keep talking, Iris.* "Once they're all safe! I'll even help you find Alice!"

She was lying about that last part. She would never do that. And if he did capture Alice, she would be her sister all right. And they would band together and destroy him. Because that is what sisters do.

"Fine," he said, voice icy. "The rest of you can go."

With Iris in his arms he stalked over to a cabinet and

grabbed a jar of magic, and then he threw her down on a hard wooden chair next to the gallery. "Do not move or I'll kill them all," he growled at her. And then he duct-taped one arm to the chair. Then the other. Then he bound her ankles. And then her mouth.

"Stop it!" Lark shouted.

Let them go, Iris thought as hard as she could, while the tape itched at her face and her wrists. *Let them go.* All of them. Please.

"Don't try anything," he snarled at Iris. She could not try anything; she could not move. He looked up at the crows, which murmured and fluttered their wings. "You too," he said to them, looking meaningfully at Iris.

"Now," he proclaimed. "You can all go. Out the back door." He motioned to the Employees Only door. "So no one sees you. Lark first. Then the rest of you."

The magic well.

He was not going to let any of them go. He wanted to punish Iris by letting her watch her sister fall into the well, where the magic would consume her.

"Get up!" he yelled at Lark. "Now or never. The fate of all these girls is up to you, Lark."

Slowly, Lark picked herself up off the floor, staring at Iris. The other girls gathered together behind her, watching carefully.

Iris could not breathe, she could not call out. She could

barely move in her chair. They did not have ESP and they needed to have ESP now so Iris could tell Lark what was behind that door.

A flutter of movement next to her. A crow perched on the back of her chair. Then another on one of the arms. It cocked its head at Mr. Green, who had his attention on Lark, and pulled at the duct tape with its beak.

But it would not be fast enough. Lark's eyes locked with Iris's. Iris knew she understood that this was a trap some-how—but there was no way she could understand that opening the door could so easily lead to her death.

But they were a team. *Iris and Lark*, forever, no matter what.

And then she knew what to do.

She met Lark's eyes and then glanced down at her fingers and tapped on the arm chair:

G-R-E-T-E-L.

"Go ahead," said Mr. Green. "Open the door. Be on your way."

"I think you broke my wrists," Lark said, voice sounding pained. "When I landed after you kicked me. I can't open the door." She clutched her arms to her chest.

Mr. Green cocked an eyebrow at her.

"I can't," Lark said, voice breaking. "I can't use my hands! You do it."

"Do I have to do everything around here?" he yelled. Pushing her forward, he stormed over to the door.

It wasn't going to work, Iris realized. He could still push her in.

Then several things happened at once. Mr. Green pushed the door open. As he did, Lark jumped backward. A crow let out a cry and dove toward him. He whirled around, and out of nowhere Duchess came barreling forward, right toward his ankles.

He bobbled.

Lark thrust out her hands and pushed.

And he slipped backward.

And he fell.

Into the hungry, waiting magic.

Lark slammed the door behind him. She stared at all the girls, jaw set, cheeks aflame, eyes on fire. They gazed back at her. The crows smacked their beaks.

Iris could not catch her breath. Everything rushed at her at once from all directions.

"Iris!" Lark yelled. A few moments later Amma had scissors and was cutting Iris free from her chair. Everything was still rushing and tumbling: even as Iris was being freed, inside she was raveling and unraveling. She burst up and kicked over the chair, but it was not enough.

So she snarled, and then grabbed the sword from the

floor and started smashing everything around her, all of it: she wanted to destroy every single last thing Mr. Green had ever cared about or touched. She would turn his world into smithereens, and then the smithereens into smithereens.

She smashed, and smashed, and smashed, and then Lark's hand rested on her shoulder, and Lark tapped three times. *Iris and Lark*. And Iris stopped.

They had defeated the monster.

CHAPTER THIRTY-SIX

The Crow Girl, Take Two

It was Amma who first stepped forward and hugged Iris and Lark, and then Gabrielle who joined in, and then Hannah, and then Morgan, and then one by one all the girls joined in, and slowly they all put the pieces of themselves together, and slowly they put Iris back together again, as much as they could.

Eventually Lark swept up Duchess in her arms and together they all headed back to the library, where they would try to pretend they were the same people they'd been two hours before.

As for me, I watched them as they moved out of the store and across the street, and they reminded me of a flock in the way they moved together—there was some consciousness in not just the individuals, but also the group, creating something startling and beautiful.

There'd been a moment, as they fought together in the shop, that it happened, that nine girls suddenly became a flock. I saw it. And I saw George fall down the shaft, arms flailing, and I saw the magic swallow him whole.

It was a poetic death.

When it was over, I flew back to my sign. I like my sign.

Alice, where are you?

I am in no danger anymore, and so I can say this:

Brother, I am here. And I can see everything. I am flying above you; I am perched on your sign; I am looking into your mind, into your history, into your twisted heart. I am swarming with the other crows; I am a piece of the murder; I am leaving shiny trinkets for the girls who will destroy you.

And now I am telling their story.

Brother, if you can hear me, I tell you this: The girls have destroyed everything you built, including the story you fancied yourself starring in. They have rewritten it, and turned you into the pathetic villain that they triumph over. That is how you will be remembered.

Iris was right—I did run from you. You locked me in a room, you said it was for my own good, and I pulled all the magic I could from the room and turned myself into a crow.

I made a tool to open the latch and flew out the window. Crows are very good with tools.

Magic has a cost. You gave your humanity willingly to it.

I gave mine, too, but in a different way. I like my way better.

It helps to be able to think creatively.

I like being a crow. I collect shiny things. I soar in the air. I move in a flock with my fellows and create something greater than myself. I pronounce my displeasure to passersby, and there's nothing they can do to stop me.

Still, I miss being a girl. He took that from me.

But he won't ever take that from anyone again.

I wish I had been the one to defeat him; I wish I had understood that that, too, was possible. Perhaps I would have done more if I had had a sister, if I had had friends—a camp, a pod. Perhaps I could have understood that you can remake a story and change the world.

I did not know what would happen when I first saw Iris and Lark, but maybe I sensed it. Maybe I saw, in the magic between them, their ability to rewrite the story. Maybe I saw my brother's end.

And yes, they do have magic, of a kind. Not a kind my brother would ever see or understand. Iris thought that magic was something that had to be protected. And that had a cost.

Now she understands that it can be made, shared, grown. And there is no cost to that.

I understand, too, that I must give them their precious things. The bracelet. The ogre. The house key. The pen. The baby. Esmeralda. I should not have taken them, but I wanted to keep some of the girls' story with me, lay the pieces out and tell it and retell it. I wanted to share in their magic. I could not help myself. I am a crow, after all. But that was the wrong way.

I know now that I can do that without their things.

(I did not take their mother's electric bill, however. It was not interesting to me.)

I have their story, and I will tell it again and again to all the birds who will listen. But I am just the teller. Or at least I began that way. Once, I thought the best any story could hold for a girl was escape. But you learn things, watching sisters. You learn that you have the power to warn a girl in danger, to steal a key, to gather your flock.

You learn you, too, can rewrite the story and save the girls.

Or help, anyway.

But this story does not belong to me.

This story belongs to the girls who had the courage to do what I did not.

Now they are back in their library community room, surrounded by posters of superheroes, weaving lies to tell their unsuspecting parents—playground injuries, an accident in gym, a fall down the stairs when trying to walk on quickly growing legs, the sort of thing that happens to kids. No big deal. Don't worry.

Iris and Lark's mom picks them up at the appointed time, and the girls are so glad, because Iris could not bike home today, or perhaps ever again. Besides, Lark has the cat, and while Duchess is an extraordinary cat, she would not take to biking.

The cat requires some explanation, and Lark spins a tragic story, and while the facts of the story are lies, the truth is the same. *This cat was in a bad situation and needs a home and we're going to give her that home.* And, she adds, just holding the cat makes her feel better about going back to school. Better about everything, really.

In the car, Lark holds Duchess and chats away to cover for Iris, who can't talk, who is still full of cracks.

Iris stares out of the window, still feeling those terrible arms squeezing her, still feeling the terror of watching Lark head toward the magic well, of watching Mr. Green kick her, of the hand against her own mouth, of being locked in that room, of staring at the doll parts and imagining becoming them. Still feeling the specter of the loss of Lark, of her life, of Lark's life, of all her friends' lives, all because one creepy man thought they were something to be collected.

Eventually their mom notices how quiet Iris is, and Iris says she is tired. Lark glances at her and offers her Duchess, and Iris takes the cat and holds her tight. Duchess dutifully purrs, because she has been planning George's murder for years, because now that it is done, she has a good home.

Iris can never tell her mom what happened, can never tell her the truth of the world. Her parents love her so so much and they do not want to know about the monsters in the closet and under the bed. Adults hold on to facts, desperately, as if they were truth. They tell you that stomping around is enough.

Sometimes it isn't. Sometimes the monsters come harder when you dare stomp. Sometimes you need to bring the whole house down.

That is true.

Also true is that sometimes when you think you are most alone, a group of girls risk their lives to rescue you.

This truth is the hardest for Iris to hold: the Awesome girls all wanted to save her.

She does not quite know how to hold it yet, so she simply stares at it, trying to figure out what to do with it. Eventually, though, she will learn to hold it and she will grab on to it fiercely.

It is something, to have a flock.

Their mother is talking now, telling them the good news that their dad will be home two months early, that he will be very surprised about the cat but he will learn to love it, that she is looking forward to having the whole family back. And she takes a deep breath and says:

"Your father and I have been talking, and we owe you an apology. We were not forthright with you girls. We kept putting off telling you we were splitting you up and then suddenly the letters were there and in the moment I just—I don't know. But it was wrong, and I am sorry."

Lark still does not know what her mother is talking about; Iris never told her. Iris never told her a lot of things, but she will tell her everything now, because she understands that they are a team. But Iris can barely talk right now and Lark just nods at her mother like she accepts her apology, because it seems like the thing to do.

And her mother tells Lark that they're having a meeting at school on Monday and they will find a way to keep school safe for her.

"Mom, I want to go," Lark says. "To the meeting."

Her mother blinks, like something has changed. "Oh. Well, yes. You should. Mr. Hunt will be there. Is that okay? I know you're frightened of him."

Both Iris and Lark make the same noise at that, something between a laugh and the sound you make when you've been punched in the stomach.

"What's so funny?" their mom says.

"It's just—I'm not scared of Mr. Hunt anymore."

No. He is not an ogre. The real monsters don't try to help you when you're scared and sad—the real monsters take that fear and sorrow and use it to try to tear you apart, to take your heart.

What will happen now? Iris doesn't know; she can't know.

The only thing she knows is she loves her sister, and she loves their new friends, and she will stay with them and not ever let anyone separate them. They all have better outcomes when they are together.

THE END

ACKNOWLEDGMENTS

Thank you to Megan Atwood, Kari Pearson, Kelly Barnhill, and Jessica Corra for reading a nascent draft of this, and to Linda Urban, Olugbemisola Rhuday-Perkovich, Laurel Snyder, Kate Messner, and Martha Brockenbrough for helping me get this last draft to the end zone. To Debbie Kovacs, the Good Witch of the Midwest. To my own Camp Awesomes—the fabulous women of Hamline University's Master of Fine Arts in Writing for Children and Young Adults; the Harpies; and the Ladies Sewing Guild. To Mom and Dad, whom I can never write about because they're too wonderful to be dramatically interesting. To Laura Ruby, my chosen twin sister. To Dash, my favorite storyteller. And to Jordan Brown, who keeps me from getting lost.